A

PERFECT

TENANT

STEVE RICHER

NICHOLAS GIFFORD

SteveRicherBooks.com
NickGifford.co.uk/Nicholas

SUMMARY

Some people you shouldn't let into your home...

Times are tough for suburban couple Alice and Tom Granger. She still hasn't gotten her promotion and they need money to fix up their income property. Desperate, they ultimately decide to rent out their basement apartment.

They couldn't be happier when Libbie Burchett signs the lease. She's fun and friendly, always eager to help. She's a perfect tenant. But Alice and Tom don't know that Libbie has secrets.

That she isn't who she says she is.

That she's just been released from a mental hospital.

That she's here to get revenge.

As Libbie puts her ruthless plan into motion, driving a wedge between the couple, painful memories are dredged up for Tom and Alice. They'll need to dig into their past if they hope to stay alive...

CHAPTER 1

Libbie couldn't stand the institutional green of the walls anymore.

She couldn't stand the institutional flooring or the institutional furniture which was uncomfortable and appalling to look at. She couldn't understand how not a single chair was even. How was that possible? Did the tender call for wobbly chairs exclusively? Most of all, Libbie couldn't take one more day of institutional food.

These grievances had started on day one. Today—at last!—it was over. When she woke up and pushed down the sheets, definitely not Egyptian cotton, she noticed the stack of clothes on the dresser by the door. It wasn't state-issued sweats, always gray, or pink, or blue to put the patient in a pleasant mood. No, these were her personal clothes.

This must mean that, even though she had one last meeting with Dr. Holt, the decision had been made to release her as scheduled. The session would only be a formality. She smiled for the first time in ninety days.

She got up, went to the institutional bathroom, and quickly inspected the clothes they had brought her during the night. There was the dark blue Michael Kors lace-up side jumpsuit she'd gotten from Bloomingdale's. The one she'd worn when she arrived at the hospital. A cashmere hooded shirt from Saks Fifth Avenue. Her favorite velvet sweatshirt by Graham & Spencer. Everything that had been in her bag when she'd arrived.

She opted for jeans, an Armani T-shirt, and Giuseppe Zanotti sneakers. The colors of her ensemble were bright, completely clashing with what the others wore. It was exactly what she wanted.

"Hey, Libbie," she heard as she came out of her room.

She found old Greta staring at her. Seventy years old and no sign of her getting better. She'd been told that she would never get out of here. Libbie smiled tightly at her, but didn't reply.

She walked down the hall toward the cafeteria, her head held high. She wanted people to see her, to see how she was dressed. She was different. She wasn't like them. Most of all, she was a free woman.

Almost.

Following a breakfast of institutional powdered eggs and institutional coffee, she was made to wait in the community room. The nurses pointedly didn't treat her differently than usual. Maybe putting on this outfit had been the wrong move, she thought. She was bringing too much attention to herself and it made people hate her.

Libbie was used to being hated. She could handle it. She had handled it all her life. She could do it a few more hours.

She watched a morning show on TV. She resisted the urge to bribe another patient for her Valium, just to be able to tolerate the vapid hosts. She flipped through magazines she had read a dozen times already. She played chess by herself, handling both sides, and the match ended in a draw.

It was almost lunch when the nurse with the bad perm came to fetch her. "Dr. Holt will see you now."

Libbie walked ahead of her, once again the center of attention. She didn't need to be escorted, yet she couldn't escape it. The only way to get dignity out of it was to walk as if it was her choice. Again, people openly gawked as if she didn't belong here. She didn't.

Nurse Bad Perm hurried past her to knock on the door and open it. "I have Libbie for you, Doctor."

"Thank you. Libbie, come in."

The nurse disappeared, closing the door behind her as Libbie entered the tiny institutional office with the green walls. She had asked about the unfortunate color choice and he had told her that it was supposed to be soothing. Personally, it made her want to murder someone.

"Have a seat," he said as he opened a file on his rickety institutional desk.

She sat in the plastic chair across the desk from him. "Good morning, Doctor."

He gave her a pleasant smile before making a show of reading the documents before him.

He was a handsome man, about thirty years old and still getting his feet wet in the world of psychiatry. He had to pay his dues before he could afford to open a private practice in the suburbs. He had dark curly hair and olive skin. His beard was carefully trimmed. Libbie had heard most of the nurses gushing over him at one time or another.

"I see you're already wearing your own clothes."

"Wasn't I supposed to, Doctor?"

"It's fine."

"Do you think I look pretty?" she asked, crossing her legs and cocking her head to the side.

He didn't take the bait. "You look well."

"I feel well. That was the point of me being here, wasn't it?"

"Of course, Libbie."

"It's a beautiful fall day, I'm happy, and I'm feeling great. I can't think of anything negative right now. I can't think of any reason why I have to stay here."

The psychiatrist squinted. "You don't?"

"That's why I'm here, isn't it? That's what this meeting is about? I've been here for the mandatory ninety days. You've evaluated me and now you can see that I don't belong here anymore."

"Is that the truth or what you think I want to hear, Libbie?"

She leaned forward slightly, her turn to squint. "I think you already made your decision. That's why my things were in my room when I woke up."

Dr. Holt scribbled something in Libbie's file. She couldn't see what it was.

"What are your plans after being released?"

"I have a life to get back to. I have plans."

"What plans?" he inquired.

"I want to visit old friends, maybe make new ones. Thanks to your thoughtful care and therapy, I'm a healthy woman now."

He studied her closely, letting the silence draw out. He wasn't buying it. Libbie's skin prickled. She was almost out of here. She could taste her freedom, but this man could still screw everything up.

She said, "Dr. Holt, I know I did something bad. I did something absolutely terrible to land in here. I realize that now. More than anything, I learned not to act out my frustrations with a baseball bat any longer. It won't happen again, I promise." She smiled so he knew she was joking. Humor was good, right?

Maybe not, going by the look on his face.

She smiled again. "I have a support network out there, Doctor. Family."

They both knew that was a stretch of the truth. She had no real friends, and the only family she had left was her brother Jonathan, who always seemed more concerned about protecting the family name, usually by throwing money at problems.

There are some things money can't buy, though.

Like revenge.

The psychiatrist looked at her for a long time, then at her file, and finally at the stack of documents on the corner of the desk. She was ten minutes in a fifty-patient day. He sighed and shook his head with resignation. He pulled a form from his drawer and wrote something down before scrawling his name at the bottom.

"I'm signing your release, Libbie. I really hope you told

me the truth because the next time you get frustrated, as you said, I'm afraid you're going to go back to your old ways. I'm afraid you might go even further. You need to promise me you won't."

"I won't, Doctor. I swear I feel better. I don't have a violent bone in my body. Not anymore."

She couldn't prove it though, and they both knew it.

CHAPTER 2

Tom walked around the kitchen island and took the wooden spoon away from Alice. She was mildly surprised but he winked, as always making everything all right with that small gesture.

"You're such a gentleman, taking over for me so the onions don't make me cry."

He shook his head. "I'm taking over so you don't *burn* the onions. Some of us want to eat dinner in this century."

She extended her tongue at the playful jab and he swatted her on the butt as she moved out of the way. Tom stirred the onions before they caramelized and added chopped celery.

"You know," Alice began, "a good stay-at-home husband would have done this in advance before his wife got home from work."

"Who ever said I'm a good husband?"

She laughed and he smiled in return, taking his attention away from the pan long enough to admire her. She looked smart in her charcoal pantsuit, her fair hair pinned on top of her head. She was the very picture of a high-powered executive which they both knew she was about to become.

"How's the house, Alice? Did you get a chance to drop by on your way back?"

"I did, just for a minute." Her attention wasn't on him now. She washed her hands and fetched the little black case on the counter which contained her glucose meter. "The guys were still working."

"And?"

"And what?"

"How does it look? Still on schedule?"

She shrugged as she stabbed her finger with the spring-loaded needle. She didn't even feel pain from this anymore. "They say they're on schedule, but who really knows, right? That's what they always say."

They had purchased a house on the other side of town four months ago. It was run down and the neighborhood wasn't ideal, but they'd had a good deal. They were now in the process of having it fixed up.

They weren't quite sure what to do with it yet, however. Tom was in favor of getting it to code, slapping a fresh coat of paint on it, and selling the place for a quick profit. For her part, Alice was thinking long-term. The neighborhood was bound for gentrification and she argued that the house would pay for itself if they rented it out.

Approaching things differently was one of the reasons their marriage worked so well, she thought. They saw things from a different perspective. He was more cautious while she was willing to take a risk. He was okay with small guaranteed victories while Alice angled for bigger long-term gains. Tom was the kid who ate the first marshmallow right away while she waited the fifteen minutes for a second one.

She dipped the strip in her blood and inserted it in the tiny machine.

"Everything okay, sweetie?"

She waited until the device beeped and flashed the results on the LCD screen before speaking. She winced. "It's a bit high."

Tom turned down the stove heat. "You want me to cook something different? It's no bother. I can have this for lunch tomorrow."

"No," Alice said, shaking her head. "I'll just adjust my dosage later. But thank you for offering."

"Well, I only offered because I knew you'd say no."

She rolled her eyes and they chuckled. She came close enough for him to lean down and kiss her. It was light and fast, but passionate nonetheless.

"Behave, Tom."

"Resorting to threats, are we?"

"Not a threat, a promise. If you keep this up, it will be nothing but canned tuna, brown rice, and oatmeal for you."

"Alice Granger, you are a cruel, cruel woman."

"I just know how to get what I want," she replied with a wink, her turn to swat him on the butt.

She went to the fridge and peered inside.

"Looking for something?"

"My insulin. I swear that thing moves around at

night."

She was still searching when her phone rang. She got the phone from her pocket. The caller ID read *Michael Tuckett*.

"Hey, boss. What's happening?"

"Sorry to spring this when you're at home, but I have some news."

"Good news or bad news?"

"Probably a bit of both," the older man said. "We had a meeting after you left and we made our decision. I want you on the Mapleview account."

Alice straightened up. She was agape and motionless for several seconds.

"Alice, are you there?"

"Yes, yes I'm here. Thank you!"

"You can probably guess why I say it's both good news and bad news. This project is going to take up a lot of your time and energy. It's going to be hard. On the other hand, you nail this and you can write your own ticket."

Alice had been dreaming about getting this assignment ever since it had been announced. She worked for Pierson Newport, a midsize real estate holding company. They had made a small fortune following the 2008 financial collapse, snatching up houses and commercial buildings when their values dropped. Now times were tougher again, which was why they were looking at expanding. Acquiring Mapleview would make them a national contender.

Controlling her breathing, Alice looked into the fridge again to keep herself occupied. She moved the mayonnaise and found her insulin.

"Thank you so much, Mr. Tuckett. Thank you for the vote of confidence."

"You deserve it. Now celebrate and we'll talk more in the morning at the office."

They said goodbye and Alice took a step back from the fridge as Tom added mushrooms to the pan.

"Everything okay?" he asked.

"I got the Mapleview account."

"Really? Congratulations! You've been talking about that like Molly Ringwald talks about Jake Ryan. So what happens next? They make you vice president?"

"Well, first I have to put the project together. I have to crunch numbers, put a figure on Mapleview, see how much we can afford. And then I have to prepare my pitch which is going to be like a college thesis. I'm putting a case together."

Tom nodded. "But after that you get a promotion, stock options, and we fly on private jets?"

"Maybe business-class. Maybe."

"Cool. I've never even *seen* business-class. Must be nice."

Before answering, Alice came closer, gauging his reaction. She put a hand on his elbow, delicate and nonintrusive.

"Are you sure you're okay with this, Tom?"

STEVE RICHER AND NICHOLAS GIFFORD

"Okay with what, my wife becoming a juggernaut of finance? What's not to like?"

"Me making more money than you. This whole thing was supposed to be temporary but…"

"Sweetie, it's fine. I'm a kept man. I'm the lucky one here."

He flashed her a broad smile and pecked her on the lips. She returned the smile but she couldn't help detect an edge in his voice. He was telling her this to make her happy. She couldn't help but wonder if he actually resented her success. Sooner or later, they'd need to address this. She dreaded that day.

She wondered if she shouldn't get it over with now and opened her mouth to speak. Right then, a shadow fell across the kitchen. The side door contained a window in the upper half and someone was standing outside. They both turned toward the visitor and recognized him.

Alice rounded the island and opened the door. "Hi, Rusty."

"Hey, Mrs. Granger!" He craned his neck further into the house. "Hi, Mr. Granger."

"What's up, big man!"

Alice invited him inside and he didn't have to be told twice. Rusty lived a few houses down the street. He was eighteen, a high school senior. He'd been mowing the lawn ever since they had moved into the neighborhood. He was tall and lanky, his face still peppered by acne.

"Smells good. I'm not disturbing your dinner, am I? I can come back later."

"It's okay," Alice answered. "Is something on your

mind?"

"Well, I'm doubling down on my efforts to get college money."

Tom snorted. "Given any thoughts to robbing a bank? That can get you halfway there."

Alice held back laughter, but Rusty didn't quite get the joke.

"I've been cutting your grass, working on your flowers and things. I was wondering if you guys need help preparing your yard for winter. I could trim the bushes, wrap the flowers, all that stuff. I've been reading up on it. It's October and the weather is still kind of nice, but I wanted to ask you before it's too late."

"Too late for what?"

The teenager fidgeted. "Before you hire someone else."

"Now now, you know you're our number one guy, don't you?"

"So are you hiring me? Same rate as last summer."

He looked between Tom and Alice. Tom shrugged and deferred to his wife.

"Sweetie?"

"Sure thing, Rusty. Nice presentation. You got the contract."

He beamed. "Awesome! Thanks!"

Alice extended her hand and they shook on it. The young man blushed.

"Welcome aboard. I'm sure you'll do great."

He nodded, thanked them both once more, and left. Tom rolled his eyes and laughed to himself.

"Poor kid," he sighed.

"What?"

"Oh, come on. You know the only reason he ever comes here is because he has a crush on you."

Alice was stunned. "He does not! That's ridiculous. I'm nearly twice his age."

"So? You're a hot MILF. You could be his first cougar."

Alice grabbed the dishtowel and threw it at her husband who dodged it while breaking down in laughter.

"You're just jealous."

"You bet your ass, I'm jealous. Who wouldn't want to be eighteen again with a face like a four-day-old pizza?"

Once they were done goofing around, Tom returned to cooking dinner, this time checking on the chicken in the oven. Alice crossed her arms, settling next to him.

"This brings up another problem," she began.

"You mean besides the possibility of a teenager stealing my wife?"

She ignored the joke. "He's nice, but he's not doing that work for free. The budget is getting tight, Tom."

It was his turn to become serious. "I thought we were fine."

"Borderline fine. Between this mortgage, the new house's mortgage, and the renovations, we're running out of wiggle room. If a pipe breaks on Whitetail Lane, we could go under."

"But with your new job…"

"A job I don't have yet. It's in the cards, but it could be in a year. Or more."

"Then I guess maybe I should start looking for a sugar mommy, uh? I mean, if I want to keep to the lifestyle I'm accustomed to."

"I'm serious, Tom."

"So am I. There has to be some old widow looking to get freaky with a vigorous young stud."

Alice groaned. "*Vigorous young stud*, right. Three words that *so* don't go together as far as you're concerned."

"Ouch, my feelings!" He tossed the dishtowel back to her.

"Honestly though, money is becoming an issue. We might have to do that thing we talked about."

"I know. I was hoping we wouldn't have to."

"We don't have a choice, Tom. Not anymore. We're going to have to rent the basement apartment."

It had been the feature that had convinced them to buy this house two years ago. It was a large one-bedroom apartment and they had furnished it with extra items they had. Until now, money had never been a problem so they had put it off. Things being as they were, though, they didn't have the luxury of waiting for their income property to become profitable.

Tom nodded reluctantly. "Yeah, you're right. We have to pull the trigger."

Alice put her arm around his waist and snuggled against him. "I'm sure it'll be great."

It would, in fact, be the opposite of great.

It was the beginning of their nightmare.

CHAPTER 3

It was with a happy smile that Libbie walked into her expansive Manhattan apartment.

It was a loft in the heart of SoHo. She loved the Lower Manhattan location and the decor suited her. The walls were made of decrepit brickwork painted stark white, exposed pipes ran along the ceiling, and the floor was highly polished granite. The furniture was colorful to contrast the surroundings. She was comfortable here and she had missed it for the last three months.

She set down her Louis Vuitton bag and walked further into the apartment. She would've expected the smell to remind her of how things used to be. It didn't. She couldn't smell the woodsy aroma of the candles she used in the living room. There was no trace of the cinnamon she usually smelled in the kitchen.

She rationalized that as she had been away for three months, it was natural that these fragrances weren't present. In fact, it would have been suspect if they were because it would have meant someone had used her favorite candles during her absence. What she would've been expected to detect, though, was a wide array of housecleaning products.

She didn't smell that either.

Libbie felt her blood pressure rising. This wasn't how it was supposed to be. She approached a console table and ran a finger on the glass top. There was quantifiable dust.

Maybe this was an oversight. She shouldn't jump to conclusions. She hadn't belonged in that wretched mental institution, but if there's one thing she'd learned it was that she should think before acting. She should go through a list of grievances before anything else.

She kept her cool and went to the kitchen. She touched the red marble counter. Her fingers came away filthy. She opened the refrigerator and found the usual condiments and nothing perishable. The door handle was dusty again.

"No…"

The reading room faced west and had floor-to-ceiling windows. It was a sunny day, perfect for what she wanted to test. She hurried to the area. Sunshine beams were visible, fighting their way through downtown skyscrapers before landing on the eighteenth-century Persian rug.

She saw these light beams because there was dust in the air.

Her hands clenched into fists and she practically ran to the master bedroom. At first glance, nothing was out of the ordinary, but there was one test she could perform to make sure.

She firmly grabbed the bedspread and shook it fast. A layer of dust rose above the bed, like morning mist in the Adirondacks.

This was absolutely unacceptable.

She stormed out of the room and went to her home office. She resisted the urge to run a finger against the desk because by now she knew what the result would be. Instead, she found her charger and plugged in her phone. It had been locked away in storage at the hospital for three months.

It came on at once and Libbie scrolled through her contacts. She found the one she needed and called.

"Rosie Manhattan Cleaning Service, how can I help you?"

"My account is twenty-one fifty-five seventy-six. I need to talk to a manager right away."

"Please hold."

The line clicked, the operator's voice replaced by the instrumental version of an Adele song. It was the equivalent of institutional music and did nothing to calm Libbie down. The song played in its entirety before someone picked up.

"Hello, Ms. Burchett. My name is Maria. How can I help you today?"

"You can help me by giving me an answer."

"Certainly," the woman with the slight Puerto Rican accent replied cheerfully. "What kind of answer are you looking for?"

"I want to know what you did with my money."

"Excuse me? I'm not sure I understand."

"You operate a cleaning service. Your employees go to people's homes and they clean. We pay you for that. I sure know that I pay a thousand a month. I have the receipts and everything. So I can prove that I paid you and now I want to know what you did with that money, because you certainly didn't send anyone to clean my place."

"Uh, I…"

"I'm sure you're aware that I was out of town for the past three months, but my payments still came in, didn't they? I never specified to stop coming, did I? Check your records to be sure."

"Ms. Burchett…"

"Go on, check your computer," Libbie said.

The keyboard clicked. "No, ma'am. There's no instruction to suspend your service in our system."

"Then can you explain to me why my apartment looks like a newly discovered Egyptian tomb? There's dust everywhere. Clearly, no one from your company has been here in weeks."

"I'm terribly sorry—"

"You're sorry? That's all you have to say for yourself? You're just *sorry*? I pay for a service and I don't receive said service. This is a breach of contract. This is a breach of goddamn trust!"

"Ma'am…"

"You wouldn't believe the amount of dust around me at the moment. It's dangerous. It's a health hazard. What if I had asthma? What if I had a child? What if my child had cystic fibrosis? Uh, can you answer me that, Maria? How would you live with yourself knowing that you put my child in danger? We're not talking bad Yelp reviews here. We're talking lawsuits. We're talking life-and-death situation."

"Ms. Burchett, I apologize. Something must have gone wrong in our scheduling."

Libbie's face was strawberry red and she realized that she had paced so much around the office as she talked that her charger had gone unplugged.

"It goes beyond scheduling, Maria. If management can't properly supervise, then we have a serious problem. So here's what you're going to do for me. First, I want a refund for the last three months. We can do this now or you can get your boss on the line. And if that isn't enough, I'll have my attorney get in touch."

"There's no need to get lawyers involved, Ms. Burchett. I can certainly issue you a refund."

"Good. Good, Maria. Now we're getting somewhere. The second thing I want is to have someone here today. I can't stand being around all this dust and grime."

"Absolutely," Maria replied, typing once more on her computer. "I'm dispatching a team as we speak."

"And finally we come to the important part. My last regular girl was Trinh. So I suppose she was the one scheduled to clean my place these last three months."

"Yes, but…"

"I want her fired, Maria. I want her out on the street. And don't think you can just tell me that she's been let go when you're in fact sending her to other clients, because tomorrow I'll be sending someone to check. Do you hear me? You'll have lawyers and private investigators checking up on you. I want Trinh to know what it feels like to be betrayed."

"I… I understand."

"Good. Have a nice day."

Libbie hung up and at long last her vision cleared up. During the call, she hadn't seen anything. Her mind had been occupied by the fury she harbored against the cleaning service. Now she returned to reality. She glimpsed her laptop on the desk and grinned.

It was thankfully already plugged in so she didn't waste time turning it on and sitting behind her desk. That's what she had missed the most about being in state custody. She hadn't been online in ninety days. *Talk about curtailing my freedom*, she thought.

She opened her browser and only glanced at her email inbox. There were hundreds of messages and she knew instantly most of them were scams or spam. Her social life wasn't active enough to receive personalized emails. There would be a few, sure, but they didn't matter.

What interested her most was her OneNote document. In it was a collection of pictures, drawings, addresses, biographical data, and web links, all related to two people.

Tom and Alice Granger.

She knew this entire document by heart. It soothed her to peruse it again. She'd gathered this information over a number of years. It was part of her now. It was like getting into a warm bath. It was borderline erotic, that's how much she had missed this.

She went to Tom's Facebook page. She had friended him a long time ago under a fake identity, just to be able to see his friends and pictures. It was astonishing how unsuspicious people were of friend requests.

She scrolled down slowly, wanting to take everything in, to savor it, even though there wasn't much personal stuff. It was mostly memes and dull news articles. But one thing made Libbie stop scrolling. It was a shared listing from Zillow, the real estate database.

She hurriedly followed the link and discovered something magical. Tom and Alice Granger had put their basement apartment up for rent.

Being away for three months had been worth the wait. There would never be another opportunity like this.

CHAPTER 4

Leasing an apartment wasn't as easy as Alice expected. It was almost enough to make her want to give up on the whole thing.

After the listing went live, inquiries cascaded in. It was a good thing Tom worked from home because he was able to handle the majority while Alice was at the office. More importantly, nobody could hear him cuss with frustration every time he hung up the phone.

Most of the calls—as well as texts and emails—were a waste of time. People asked questions they wouldn't need to bother with if they had simply read the listing from beginning to end.

Yes, it's a basement apartment. No, there's only one bedroom. What neighborhood? There's a freaking map on the website, buddy!

After weeding out the truly clueless, some applicants showed up in person. One man had said that the price was fine, but when he showed up he tried to negotiate it down fifty percent. When that didn't work, he offered to barter for the difference, claiming he handcrafted delicious organic pickles.

That same day, another applicant arrived on a motorcycle. It was so loud—clearly modified to be so—

that neighbors actually walked out to see what was happening. No sooner was the man off his Harley that he tossed his half-smoked cigarette into the backyard. Alice was of the firm opinion that first impressions mattered, and it didn't bode well for this guy.

The week was filled with one bad choice after another. One woman shamelessly said she intended to sublet the place right after signing the lease, maybe even posting it on Airbnb. The next man who visited reeked of marijuana even before he got out of his car.

Tom closed the door and joined Alice in the living room after they had dealt with an old woman who promised that owning seventeen ferrets shouldn't disqualify her. She swore the ferrets were housetrained. She swore the ferrets were a gift from British royalty.

"Do you think we're in over our heads?" Alice asked, leaning back into the couch and wanting nothing more than for it to swallow her whole.

"Of course we are."

"Thanks for reminding me."

Tom crashed next to her and put an arm around her shoulders.

"In hindsight, maybe the pyromaniac biker wasn't such a terrible candidate?"

"We could always call back the pickle guy. Seems less dangerous."

They laughed without much amusement. Alice snuggled against her husband, the one stable thing in her life.

"Are we really doing this, Tom?"

"You want to call the whole thing off?"

"Yes. No. We can't. We still have that whole needing-money-to-live thing going on."

Tom nodded gravely. "Oh yeah, that pesky little problem. I suppose we just need to keep doing what we're doing. If we're diligent, if we act like good landlords, things should work out."

"Promise?"

"Another solution would be to torch the place. Collect the insurance money."

"Where are the matches?" Alice asked.

This time they laughed for real. Tom kissed her and she felt happy for the first time in ages.

"We have one more applicant scheduled." He glanced at his watch. "She's supposed to be here in an hour."

Alice exhaled loudly. "Great. With our luck, she'll turn out to be an ax murderer."

"Still better than Pickle Man."

~ ~ ~ ~

At six o'clock on the dot, the doorbell rang. Tom answered and found a beautiful woman on the porch. She had chestnut hair that fell in waves on her shoulders. The hair color matched her eyes. She wore a touch of makeup which accentuated her features. Her clothes were on the conservative side, but casual.

"Hi, I'm Libbie Burchett."

Tom was taken aback after the horde of weirdos that

had come over during the last few days.

Alice appeared next to him and said, "Please come in, Ms. Burchett."

"Thank you. And it's Libbie. I never got used to being called miz or, God forbid, ma'am."

Alice smiled warmly, moving aside to let the guest in.

"I'm Tom Granger and this is my wife Alice."

They shook hands and relaxed. She was the first applicant who appeared normal and it was jarring.

"I hope I'm not disturbing your dinner," Libbie said. "I didn't think twice of it when we made the appointment."

"It's fine, really. It's still in the oven."

"It smells good anyway. Is that rosemary?"

Tom was impressed and grinned. "Good nose! I'm roasting a chicken. This lady over here wouldn't know rosemary from thyme if her life depended on it."

"It's a good thing my life doesn't depend on it then, uh?"

Libbie turned to a cabinet just outside the living room. It was filled with at least three dozen figurines of all shapes and sizes and materials, from tin to plastic, to crystal.

"And I see that you're into… action figures."

"You can say figurines," Tom conceded. "It's my thing. No, I'm not a *Star Wars* nerd."

"So he says," Alice stage-whispered.

"Boba Fett is a cultural touchstone, thank you very much. Seriously, I've been collecting small, offbeat figurines for years. It's fun."

Alice rolled her eyes. "It's fine until you have to dust them."

Libbie smiled. "The two of you look happy together. It's nice to see. That's getting rarer and rarer these days."

Alice was afraid her husband would make a glib comment just to be funny, something like "We pretend to be happy when we have people over," but he had the good sense to keep his mouth shut.

She was about to speak when a shrill alarm went off. It was her phone, except not the regular ringtone.

"Is everything all right?" Libbie asked.

"Yes," Alice replied, turning off the alarm and checking her watch at the same time. "Sorry about that. Just a reminder about my insulin."

"Oh, you're diabetic? Do you need to…"

Alice waved the comment away. "It can wait. I'm sure you're eager to see the apartment."

"I am."

"Follow me, ladies!" Tom said.

The three of them went outside and walked down the porch. The house was a two-story ranch, though it had been somewhat modified from the original style. It had been built high enough so that the basement had small windows. It was covered with blue gray clapboard.

"The entrance to your place is here on the side."

They rounded an arborvitae bush and walked into the rather spacious backyard. Concrete steps dug into the ground, leading to a basement door. Tom led the way and unlocked the door. He flipped on the light switch.

"This is it!"

Libbie looked around, spinning on her heels. "Very nice."

It was a bit of an exaggeration, Alice decided. But at least she was polite about it. The kitchen was utilitarian at best even though the appliances weren't too dated. It dissolved into a small dining area where an oblong wooden table could seat six.

This led to a den in which was an L-shaped couch, the longest section running along the eggshell wall. Next to it was a black leather La-Z-Boy. A forty-two-inch flatscreen was screwed into the wall in front.

"The bedroom is over here," Tom said. "And this is the bathroom."

They gave her the tour. The bathroom and bedroom would never be featured in *Architectural Digest*, but they were tastefully decorated.

"Am I crazy or is the apartment smaller than the house?" Libbie asked as they all returned to the den. "I mean, this is your basement, right?"

Tom nodded. "You're very observant. About half the basement is on our side. It's, you know, just a basement. The previous owners had the other half made into this apartment."

"Oh, I see."

Alice looked at her husband and then at the candidate

who was still looking around, walking through the space as if she was already decorating it. She opened drawers, tested the faucets.

"Are you looking at other places in the area or…"

Libbie turned back to the landlords and smiled. "I am. I'm just moving into town. For the time being, I'm staying at this efficiency unit near the airport. I'm originally from New York City."

"This town is just a bit smaller," Tom offered, making everybody laugh at the massive understatement.

"What do you do, if you don't mind my asking?" Alice asked.

"I'm a photographer. Mostly weddings, bar mitzvahs, and school pictures, if I can get the contracts, but I'm actually working on my portfolio. My dream is to be featured in a gallery, you know? I do landscapes, portraits, collages."

"How interesting!"

Libbie's face became horrified. "Oh my God! I hope you don't think I'm some sort of strange Bohemian artist-type, or anything."

"I, uh…"

"I don't smoke. I don't party. I don't have any pets. I know artists sometimes have a bad reputation. I assure you that I'm quiet as a church mouse."

"So are we," Alice confessed.

"Well, we're a match made in heaven then, aren't we?"

"Wait," Tom began. "So you're interested?"

"The price is right. I like the location, too."

"You don't mind being in the basement?"

"Honestly, I don't know if I'll be here all that much. I expect to be out taking pictures most of the time. Otherwise, I'll be down here editing my pictures and trying to contact gallery owners. This is perfect for me. If you two lovely people are happy to proceed, I'll take it."

~ ~ ~ ~

Libbie drove away in her Toyota a few minutes later while Alice and Tom waved goodbye from the curb.

"I like her," Alice said.

"You're thinking about leaving me? *For her?* How can you?!"

She elbowed her husband and he pretended to be mortally wounded. "Idiot."

"I like her, too. So what do we do? She's the jackpot winner?"

She shrugged. "Yeah. Unless you're really into homemade pickles."

"Ugh, tempting. Between Pickle Man, the Ferret Queen, and her, it's a real Sophie's Choice situation here, sweetie." She elbowed him again as they headed back inside the house. "Okay, okay! I'll check her references."

When Tom discovered that the chicken wasn't fully cooked yet, he went upstairs to his home office and called the numbers Libbie had provided them. The references checked out, the same went for her credit score. A quick online search didn't return any upsetting news about her.

"And?" Alice asked him from the doorframe, having just taken her insulin.

"I think we've found ourselves a perfect tenant."

CHAPTER 5

It was Friday afternoon when Libbie moved in. Alice had come home early from work for the event, arriving just in time to witness Libbie signing the lease.

"I'm so excited," she said shaking hands with both her new landlords.

"I hope you'll like it here."

"I'm sure I will. This is perfect. Thank you again, Tom and Alice, for this opportunity."

Tom craned his neck and looked through the window. "I see that you drove a rental truck?"

"Yes, I did! I had most of my stuff in storage near my motel. I'll drive it back to the rental place in the morning and get my car. I don't think I'll be finished unloading the truck before nighttime."

"Sure you will," Tom said. "If we help."

Libbie shook her head. "Oh please, you don't have to do that!"

"Nonsense," Alice protested. "It shouldn't take too long. I mean, what do you have, just a bunch of boxes and luggage? You don't have any couches and beds in that truck, do you?"

"No, I don't."

"Then we can probably do this in a few hours."

Tom and Alice rose from the kitchen table, ready to go out, and Libbie sighed heavily, smiling in the process.

"You guys are just too sweet."

"I know, right?" Tom said. "Probably explains why Alice is diabetic."

They went outside and it was thankfully overcast. It wouldn't be too hot to work. While Tom went down to the apartment to open the door and keep it open with a flower pot, Libbie opened the doors of the U-Haul panel van. Inside were suitcases and cardboard boxes.

The women started with the luggage, which had wheels and was easy to carry. Tom grabbed the first box. It was heavy and it felt like books. They fell into a routine, grabbing something, going down the stairs, dropping it off, and climbing back up. The walk was the worst part.

"Hey, what's happening?"

Alice and Libbie spun on their heels at the voice as they were getting ready for another trip downstairs. It was Rusty. He waved before he was halfway to them.

"Hi," he said again as he reached the van.

"Hey, Rusty. How are you?"

"I'm awesome, always awesome. Do you, uh…" he looked between the unfamiliar woman, the truck, and the house, not sure if he understood everything.

"Rusty, this is Libbie. She's going to be staying in the apartment downstairs. Libbie, this is Rusty. He lives up the street and he's the reason why we have such wonderful landscaping."

The kid blushed and avoided Alice's gaze. "Thanks."

"It's very nice to meet you, Rusty," Libbie said, her voice dripping with charm. "I hope we can become good friends as well."

"Uh, yeah. Do you need any help? To move in, I mean? No charge!"

"You're so sweet!" Libbie said again, putting a hand on his upper arm which made Rusty blush even though it was Alice he was looking at.

The deal struck, Alice pulled a box closer to her. This one couldn't close all the way and a large computer monitor was poking out. Rusty swiftly moved past her.

"Hold on, Mrs. Granger. Let me get this one. It seems heavy."

Before she could reply, Rusty grabbed it and headed to the house. Libbie grinned but didn't say anything.

The four of them got in gear and things went faster. Alice climbed into the van to push the boxes toward the edge. Tom and Rusty carried the boxes from the street all the way down the stairs. From there, Libbie brought them into the house. It was a good system.

Some people were faster than others and before long Libbie found herself alone with the teenager at the bottom of the steps while he caught his breath.

"Rusty? Hold on."

"What?"

Libbie disappeared into the apartment and returned

seconds later with a glass of water.

"Thanks."

He gulped it down instantly, his eyes focused on the street above as if he was looking for something. Libbie remained by his side, sipping her own water as she observed him.

"You like her, don't you?"

"Who?" Rusty asked.

"Alice. You like her."

"Of course, I do. Tom and Alice are my neighbors. They give me work. They're nice people. They're my friends."

"You're sure it isn't more than that?"

"What? Of course not!"

Libbie came a bit closer. "It's okay, you know. There's nothing wrong with it."

"With what?"

"You don't have to pretend, Rusty. Not with me. It's obvious you have a crush on Alice."

He tensed up. "No, I don't!"

"It's cute," Libbie said with a smirk. "And there's nothing wrong with it. When I was your age, I had a crush on my art teacher."

"For real?"

She nodded. "I bided my time and one afternoon, after school, I made my way into his office. I made sure we were alone." She came closer still. "What I'm saying is that you can get anything you want, if you're patient. And clever."

Rusty's face was beet red and at her words he slipped off a step. It made him drop his glass which shattered on the concrete floor.

"What the hell?!" Libbie yelled with shock.

"I'm sorry."

Libbie opened her mouth to scream obscenities, yet managed to stop herself just in time. The anger didn't dissipate, but she knew that she needed to control herself.

It's just a glass, she told herself. It's just a broken dollar store glass.

Her expression changed in a flash. She smiled genially at him and patted his hand. "Everything's fine, Rusty. It's nothing to worry about."

"I'll... I'll pay for it."

"Don't be stupid. I should be paying you. You're the one who's helping me move into my new apartment, aren't you? You're such a nice young man and I appreciate everything you're doing for me."

Rusty remained dubious after her outburst. "Are you sure?"

"Absolutely, Rusty. Absolutely."

It took less than an hour to finish moving in her stuff and Libbie refused help unpacking. Rusty remained flustered until he left and she was secretly thrilled by having him on shaky ground. It was good to keep this sort of people on their toes. Young guys could get cocky, so it was best to knock them off balance from the start.

She drove the truck back to the U-Haul place and returned with her Toyota. It wasn't the kind of vehicle she was used to, but it served a purpose. It made her one of them, which was her most immediate goal.

She parked on the curb and watched Tom and Alice through the window. They were setting up the table for dinner. Libbie remained in the car for nearly half an hour, simply staring at them. She worked on her plan, outlining the steps to reach the objective she'd dreamed about for so long.

The day of reckoning was coming.

CHAPTER 6

Libbie readjusted her purse on her shoulder and rang the doorbell. Night had fallen and it was cool here on the porch, but she didn't feel it. She was thinking about her plan.

It took several seconds for the door to open. Alice stood in front of her, surprised by who the visitor was.

"Libbie, hey! Everything all right down there?"

"Yes, yes, of course. It's great. I just wanted to come up to thank you again. I brought this."

She opened her purse and pulled out a bottle of champagne. Technically, Libbie was well aware that Korbel was *California champagne*, a legal loophole American wineries had somehow gotten away with. As far as she was concerned, it was just sweet sparkling wine and had nothing on the real French stuff.

But she couldn't tip her hand by bringing Dom Pérignon to her landlords. And anyway, she somehow doubted they'd know the difference.

"How thoughtful!" Alice exclaimed. "Please, come in."

"I hope I'm not intruding, or anything."

Alice shook her head and moved out of the way. "No, of course not! It's Friday night. We weren't doing anything special. Tom, come down!"

Alice nudged a briefcase aside, sliding it under the foyer's console table. On top of the table were key rings and loose spares. As they walked into the living room, Tom joined them. He brightened up at once.

"Hey, Libbie! Everything all right?"

"Now I actually feel like I'm interrupting."

"Don't be silly," Alice said. She lifted the bottle for Tom's benefit. "She brought us champagne."

"I'm just so grateful for you guys. You're allowing me to basically live in your home. You even helped me move in. This seems like the least I can do. But I don't want to overstep."

Tom became serious. "Libbie, haven't you read the city bylaws? It's clearly stated on page seventy-nine, section twelve, I believe: he or she who brings champagne shall be invited in forthwith."

Libbie burst into laughter, just like Tom, and Alice joined in after a groan.

"Go sit in the den," she said. "I'll get glasses."

As Alice departed, Tom motioned for Libbie to sit. He took position across from her as she did so.

"Are you settling in okay?"

"Yes, it's great. I have months of opening boxes to look forward to, but so far so good."

Alice returned with wineglasses. She apologized for not having flutes — she said they didn't usually drink champagne. Libbie once more bit her tongue. It wasn't champagne! Couldn't anyone see that?

Tom didn't waste time removing the foil and untwisting the wire. Then he did a surprisingly good job of rotating the cork until it popped gently. Nothing spilled out.

"Am I a pro, or what?!"

"Stop fishing for compliments, Tom."

"How else am I going to get compliments, sweetie?"

Libbie chuckled at their antics, waiting dutifully for Tom to pour three glasses. "You guys are great. I hope that when I do find someone who's husband material, we'll have what you have."

"I'm sure you will," Alice said. "In the meantime, here's to you. To our new tenant."

Tom raised his glass. "To our new neighbor."

"Thank you."

"Cheers!"

They launched into mindless chitchat and Libbie did her best to seem interested. Truthfully, she kind of was because part of her plan was to learn as much as possible about this couple. She already knew them extremely well, her research had been meticulous, but nothing beat personal interactions.

"We haven't been able to talk a lot today, but I gather you work for a real estate company?"

"I do," Alice confirmed.

"Is that as glamorous as it sounds?"

"Of course," Tom answered for his wife. "We're in the presence of a future vice president."

Libbie tried to sound impressed. "Really?"

"No, not really. Not yet, anyway. It all depends on the Mapleview account."

Alice offered a quick rundown of the project, about how she was involved in the acquisition. Libbie asked pointed questions but was only mildly curious. It did appear important to Alice, though, and that in itself was valuable.

Before the conversation turned into an interrogation, Libbie volunteered information about her work as a photographer. She was an amateur at best and had memorized trivia about the business, anything to come off legitimate.

"But enough about work," she said dismissively while Tom refilled their glasses. "What I want to know is how it feels to be a teenager's object of lust."

"What?!"

Tom laughed. "See? I'm not the only one who noticed."

"I don't know what you're talking about."

"Rusty," Libbie clarified with a grin. "He totally has a thing for you."

"Stop it, both of you. He's just nice. Can't people be nice without having ulterior motives?"

"Teenage boys?" Libbie asked. "Not a chance."

Tom nodded and shrugged. "I can confirm. Especially at that age, you're always thinking of an angle. And that angle usually has something to do with getting a girl horizontal."

"Rusty isn't going to get me horizontal."

"Won't keep him from trying. He's in love."

Alice shook her head. "He'll get over it."

"Alice and Rusty, sitting in a tree," Tom sang.

"Shut up!"

Tom dodged a thrown cushion. "K-I-S-S-I-N-G…"

Alice hurled another cushion his way, which was difficult to do since they sat side by side. "You're impossible!"

"It doesn't matter, sweetie. I won. You're all mine."

"Not if you keep this crap up."

It was Tom's turn to throw a pillow at her. They broke down in laughter and finished their glasses.

"You guys are too cute," Libbie said, sipping her drink. "But you should be careful."

"Careful? Careful about what?"

Tom topped off everybody's drink.

"Teenagers, crushes, it's not always harmless."

Alice said, "Rusty is absolutely harmless. He'll find a girl his age soon enough and he will completely forget about me."

"That may be the case," Libbie conceded. "But at that age, there's a fine line between desire and obsession. Boys can be so fixated on someone that they start feeling entitled. They figure they love a woman so much that it's only normal for her to love him back, you know? And when she doesn't, well, things get dangerous."

"Dangerous?"

"In the news, it was a year or two ago, there was this boy. He was fifteen, sixteen. It was somewhere down south, Alabama, Louisiana, I can't remember. Anyway, he had this crush on his math teacher. It was innocent at first, or so she thought. She stayed with him after class to tutor him. In her mind, this was part of the job. But in *his* mind, she was showing him affection."

"What happened?" Tom asked as Alice silently drank next to him.

"He made his big declaration of love and, naturally, she told him she didn't feel the same. He continued to pursue her even though she had him reassigned to another class. He would show up at her house unannounced, bringing flowers and chocolate. She had to take out a restraining order against him."

"Geez..."

"And that wasn't enough. One night, the kid snapped. He broke into her house and shot her six times in the head. The cops found him draped over the corpse the next morning. He kept mumbling that now she was his forever."

"Holy shit," Tom whispered.

Alice swallowed with difficulty before speaking. "Rusty isn't like that."

"I'm sure," Libbie replied. "Does he ever bring you flowers or chocolate?"

"No!"

"Well, sweetie..." Tom began. "Remember your birthday?"

"That doesn't count! It was *my birthday*. I swear, Rusty isn't like that. He's not obsessive."

"I'm sorry I brought this up, Alice. I'm sure he's a nice young man. He appeared to be, anyway."

"He is. But you know what? I'm not the only one who's having to fight off someone's advances." Alice indicated her husband with her thumb. "This guy has a bit of a stalker."

"Really?!"

Tom shook his head. "It's nothing."

"Ha! Not so funny when we're talking about you, uh?"

"Who is it? One of the checkout girls at the supermarket?"

"Worse. It's Marissa Sigley. She lives the next block over. She's sixteen."

"Oh my God!"

"You're making this up, Alice."

"She first came over selling Girl Scouts cookies two years ago and she's been making excuses to come by ever since. She practically bats her eyes every time she sees Tom."

"She's not that bad. She's just fooling around, likes to make herself the center of attention."

"Maybe we should play matchmaker, get Marissa and Rusty together and get them off our backs."

Husband and wife continued to banter and Libbie took everything in. She made mental notes. *Rusty. Marissa Sigley.* This was extremely useful information.

"Oh," Libbie exclaimed. "Before I forget!"

"What?"

She grabbed her purse and rummaged through it. She pulled out a small bag the size of a can of soda. It was heavy and stuffed.

"I went shopping for groceries earlier, explored some of the stores, and I found this. Here."

She handed the bag to Tom. He was flustered and had no choice but to unwrap his present. It was a small porcelain figurine. It was a smiling brown bear in a white shirt.

"Oh Libbie…"

"I thought you could use it for your collection. And it's small gesture of gratitude for you guys being so kind to me."

"You didn't have to, but thanks. I love it!"

"I'm happy you do."

Tom was beaming. He examined the figurine, twisting it in his hands. "You know what? It reminds me of something."

"Really? What?"

"I'm not sure… Oh, wait! It reminds me of the mascot we had at this summer camp I went to as a kid. I mean, the colors are wrong, but it reminds me of it. I like the white shirt, though. It looks like the strip of my Little League team, the Brewers. I have a shirt just like that myself. It's great, thanks."

"No, thank *you*." Libbie was about to say something else when she noticed Alice's gaze was off. She was slumped against the couch. "Alice, is everything all right?"

"Yeah, I'm just dizzy. Nauseous."

"Too much champagne?" Libbie joked and chuckled.

"That's it, the champagne. It's too sweet."

Tom was all business because he understood his wife was genuinely ill. "Come on, let's go lie down. We'll check your ketones."

He helped her to her feet and they headed toward the stairs. Libbie stood up.

"Is there anything I can do?"

"No, thank you," Tom said. "I'll be back in a moment."

"Sure. Let me know if you want me to call a doctor, or something."

Tom and Alice nodded, yet they had already all but forgotten about her. They went upstairs. It suited Libbie just fine. This was better than anything in her wildest dreams.

Because the moment she was alone, Libbie went to the console table in the foyer and stole a house key.

CHAPTER 7

To Libbie, the worst feature of the apartment was the air vent just outside the bedroom.

It was an unsightly metal grate in the wall next to the bedroom door. She felt the architects and engineers could have placed it lower, by the floor, and it wouldn't have been such an obvious eyesore. Even better if they could have recessed it into the ceiling. This item alone seemed to sum up all the compromises she'd had to make to be here.

She changed her mind only a few hours after moving in.

As it happened, the duct went straight up to the house above. She wasn't well versed in physics and acoustics, but she understood enough how frequencies traveled. If she stood close enough to the vent, she was able to hear when Tom and Alice talked.

Now, it wasn't crystal clear and it wasn't every conversation. She figured there was a place in the house where the other end of the duct picked up sounds. The kitchen, maybe? The living room? The voices came out low and muffled. But with enough concentration, Libbie could get the gist of what they were saying.

It was almost three in the morning. She was conscious

that her body was tired, especially after an afternoon of moving boxes, but that was trivial. It was physical. Her mind was alert and that was what mattered. She was sitting by the vent on one of her new uncomfortable kitchen chairs.

She hadn't heard a single sound in over two hours. After the champagne incident, no ambulance had been called. Tom hadn't taken his wife to the emergency room. Libbie figured this was a common problem for them and they knew how to handle it. In any case, it was good to know that Alice's diabetes made her very sensitive to variations in her blood sugar levels.

Libbie closed her eyes and took deep breaths, sitting straight as she ran her hands up and down her thighs. She was so close to her goal. The anticipation was killing her.

She glanced at the wall-mounted clock and listened again. There was no TV coming from the house above. No music or chitchat. Was this a sign?

Slowly, not willing to make noise herself, Libbie stood up. She went to the bedroom, sidestepped the boxes and suitcases, and went to the closet. She reached for the top shelf and pulled down a black metal case. It was a gun locker.

She punched in the code and it clicked open. She lifted the lid, paying no attention to the pistol. Instead, she picked up the silver key next to it.

The key she had stolen.

With the same pace and calmness, she carefully opened the front door, not yet used to the creaking and sounds of her new place. She didn't want any surprises tonight. Once outside, she closed the door without locking it and gingerly climbed up. It was colder than before and her discount sweatshirt was wholly inadequate.

She rounded the bushes, went to the front of the house. The street was dim. Not one house in the area had their lights on. This was a blessing, although Libbie needed to let her eyes adjust to the darkness. Her one ally was the full moon, even if it was mostly hidden behind clouds.

She went up the porch and held her breath as she approached with the key. What if it had been mislabeled? What if it was for a different door? She hadn't seen an alarm system, but that didn't mean there wasn't one. Nevertheless, she had to take a chance.

She needed it more than anything.

She inserted the key and felt no resistance. It turned on the first try. The door was unlocked.

Libbie entered the pitch black house. She delicately shut the door behind her, before sounds from the suburbs could waft in and alert the owners to her presence. Once inside, she stood still as her eyes adjusted. After almost a minute, she was comfortable enough to walk around.

She went to the den first. The cushions were back in place. The wine glasses had been picked up in spite of the medical situation. These people were organized. They didn't suffer a house that wasn't in order. They didn't like chaos, Libbie realized.

She grinned devilishly at the thought.

She turned to the cabinet of figurines. She couldn't quite understand the fascination with these, but she knew that for some people collecting was both an obsession and a way to cope with solitude. She leaned closer to look at the dolls. The bear she had given Tom was prominently displayed on top.

Libbie wondered if he would realize she was taunting them.

She padded out of the living room and went to the kitchen. Because of the large window, moonlight came in directly here. On the refrigerator door were a number of pictures held up by takeout restaurant menus which acted as magnets.

On one picture, Alice was on a beach with palm trees behind her. She smiled demurely as if she was embarrassed to have her picture taken. On another, Tom was taking a break from mountain biking. He was sweaty but happy.

A third picture—this one the best and clearly a Granger favorite—featured both Alice and Tom dressed to the nines. It could've been a corporate event or a wedding. They were in each other's arms, beaming.

Their happiness made Libbie want to scream.

Without realizing she was doing it, she slid to the right. On the counter was a thick oak knife block. In one fluid movement, she grabbed a stainless steel handle and yanked out the carving knife.

Picking up speed, Libbie left the kitchen and found the stairs. She stopped herself before flat out running. She had to be smart about this. She tiptoed up the steps, her heart jumping a beat every time the hardwood complained under her feet.

Just before reaching the top, she paused. She could easily turn back now, before she did anything.

It was even darker upstairs, the carpeted hallway claustrophobic. She hadn't been here yet, but the layout left little to the imagination. There were open doors along the corridor and it was evident that the master bedroom was at the end.

Libbie gripped the knife tighter and crept forward. She heard snoring. It had to be Tom. She could handle him.

She could handle both of them.

The door was half open in front of her and she pushed it in further. Tom and Alice were in bed, asleep. A measly eight feet separated Libbie from the bed. She flexed her fingers. She changed her grip on the knife.

She could do this.

~ ~ ~ ~

Alice awoke with a start, sitting straight up in bed.

She blinked, breathing hard. She felt as if she'd had a nightmare, but was certain that she hadn't. Tom was sound asleep next to her, snoring as he always did even though he swore he didn't.

She wiped spittle off her chin and rubbed her eyes. The room was empty, but something felt off. Alice was a rational person. She didn't believe in the supernatural. She didn't believe in ghosts, spirits, or even New Age mumbo-jumbo like auras.

But as a businessperson, she did believe in instincts. There were times when her decisions were guided by something primeval, something within her which she couldn't explain. She doubted scientists had ever been able to define that sensation, and yet it couldn't be denied.

That's what she was feeling right now, something strong and compelling, albeit inexplicable.

Like she was being watched.

She had taken a self-defense class once, in college. There had been a rash of assaults on campus and self-defense instructors—either real accredited ones or scam artists—had seen their business boom. She recalled one sales pitch in particular. *I may not be a black belt but I can teach you to defend yourself. Isn't that worth taking a chance?*

Everyone had been so scared of being the next victim that cheesy sales tactics hadn't mattered. Every single instructor in town had been booked for months. In hindsight, Alice wasn't sure if her hundred dollars had been well invested, but there was one thing she remembered: instincts were real. Instincts should be trusted.

That's what she did tonight.

There wasn't much of value in the house. The neighborhood wasn't affluent or a destination for junkies in need. So why would anyone break in? To rape her?

She didn't completely dismiss the idea but, realistically, the odds of that were low. Statistically, she was more liable to be attacked when alone. But there was something Libbie—and Tom—had said earlier. Rusty.

Rusty had a crush on her.

Alice still believed that he was harmless, that it was nothing but an innocent crush. And yet Libbie's story echoed through her mind. That boy down south. He broke into his teacher's house and murdered her. Would Rusty go to these lengths? Was he that obsessed with her?

Even though she didn't want to put stock in this theory, she found herself unable to ignore it.

Isn't that worth taking a chance?

She swung her legs out of bed and slowly stood. She looked around her. Nothing was out of the ordinary. Her robe was on the easy chair in the corner. Her clothes were on the floor. Nothing had been disturbed.

Not bothering to cover herself up—she was wearing fuchsia pajama bottoms and a white tank top—she walked down the hallway. She peeked inside Tom's office, into the bathroom. Nothing. She went downstairs.

The lights were still off. She paused to listen. An intruder would be breathing hard, wouldn't he? She didn't hear anything aside from the ticking of the clock.

She dipped into the living room. It was as she'd left it after her embarrassing diabetic episode. She should know her body better by now. Why did she insist on taking chances? Drinking the champagne, so much of it, it had been a bad idea. She'd let herself forget the usual precautions during Libbie's visit.

She checked the front door. There was no sign of a break-in. The door was locked. She went to the kitchen and made sure that the side door was locked as well. It was and no window had been broken.

She relaxed for the first time. Her mind was playing tricks on her. It had to be the medication, not to mention the alcohol. She just couldn't trust her instincts anymore.

Fully awake after drinking a glass of water, she decided

to get her computer and start working on the project. She didn't give a second thought about the carving knife which was on the counter instead of sheathed in the block as usual.

~ ~ ~ ~

Libbie was back sitting squarely on her chair by the vent.

She was breathing heavily. The trip upstairs had been exhilarating. It had been sensual. She couldn't remember the last time she had been thrilled this way. No man had ever made her feel this level of excitement.

She heard the kitchen faucet through the vent. The lightness of the footfall meant it was Alice. She had unnerved her.

"Yes…" Libbie whispered to herself, closing her eyes and letting her fingertips run up and down her chest.

She could have ended it all tonight. It would've been easy. It would've been clean. Hell, it would've been amazing!

Only there was potential for so, so much more. She'd almost given in to her impulses. It was a good thing she'd stopped herself just in time. She had a plan and she needed to follow it.

Her revenge would be so much more rewarding if she drew it out. Cats played with their prey before killing them, didn't they? Yes, cats understood.

CHAPTER 8

"It's not working," Alice barked at herself, dropping her pencil.

She was at the kitchen table, her books and notes and laptop laid out in front of her on the table. Tom was at the sink washing vegetables for tonight's dinner. He turned toward his wife.

"I'm going to wager a shiny nickel things are not going well?"

Alice wasn't in the mood to banter with him but his smile was disarming. She mellowed and shrugged. She leaned back in her chair, opting to take a breather. Meanwhile, Tom returned to the vegetables and stared out the window.

"Landing the Mapleview account is going to be harder than I thought, Tom."

"Anything worth having is worth struggling to get."

She frowned and gave him the side eye. "Did you read that in a fortune cookie?"

"Fortune cookie or business school, can't remember. But it's not wrong, you know."

"I know," Alice replied with a sigh. "It's stressing me out."

"You're being too hard on yourself, sweetie. You got this. You're ready."

"I'm ready to put a proposal together, sure. I can crunch numbers, make offers, assemble this deal like nobody's business, but I'm stumbling on the basic stuff."

"Basic stuff?" Tom asked, drying a zucchini and getting started on some carrots.

"I want my presentation to be gorgeous, okay? That means graphics and tables and flashy animations."

"Aren't you putting the hobby horse before the apple cart?"

Alice groaned. "That's not how the saying goes."

"Sue me. Seriously though, don't sweat the little things. Do the financial work first and deal with the aesthetics after. Maybe you can get an intern for that or hire somebody once you get there. The point is, just relax. And take a break, for God sakes. It's Saturday."

"I thought you said I was going to be a VP. Weekends don't exist anymore when you're a VP."

"I thought you said you *weren't* a VP yet."

He winked at her as he said that and she had to concede the point. He had nothing left to rinse off and still he stared out the window.

"Tom, what are you looking at?"

"What?" he asked innocently.

"You've been stealing glances outside for half an hour as if you're expecting the Prize Patrol."

"No, it's nothing."

STEVE RICHER AND NICHOLAS GIFFORD

Suspicious yet getting in a better mood, Alice stood up and joined him at the sink. She followed his gaze and her jaw dropped.

"Well, I'll be…"

Libbie was in the backyard. She had dragged a lawn chair away from the garden table, making sure to land in a sunlit area. She reclined in her chair, wearing only shorts and a yellow bikini top.

"So that's why you've been so intent on making ratatouille tonight? You like the view?"

"I might also wash the windows later. You know, because I'm a perfect husband."

Alice elbowed him playfully in the stomach. "Tom Granger, are you looking to replace me?"

"Never."

"You just decided to be a pervy voyeur then?"

"Who wouldn't?"

She gave him another jab in the side and Tom pretended she had perforated his pancreas.

"She is quite beautiful, isn't she?" Alice mused.

"I'm afraid I'll have to take the fifth on that one, sweetie."

"Too late for that, buster. And I think you're right."

Tom's eyebrows flew up. "I am? And you admit it? Quick, get me a piece of paper so we can record this momentous occasion."

"I'll take a break for a few minutes, clear my head."

"Outstanding decision, sweetie. I'll finish working on dinner."

"Don't sprain your neck spying on her," Alice said as she headed to the door, comforted by Tom's laughter.

She went outside and found the air was rather cool. However, as soon as she stepped down the deck and got into the sun, she had to concede that the sunshine was nice.

"Hi!" Libbie called with a wave. "Come join me."

Alice fetched a second lawn chair and brought it closer. She sat next to her tenant and couldn't help glancing at her.

The bikini top left little to the imagination, Alice caught herself thinking. It had to be two sizes too small and she was spilling out of it. No wonder her husband had been gawking before. Libbie was drop-dead gorgeous.

"I wouldn't have figured this a day for sunbathing," Alice said.

She was herself wearing jeans and a long-sleeved blouse.

"The sun is strong. Most of the time there's no wind and it gets really warm. Wait a moment, you'll see."

Alice gave her the benefit of the doubt and leaned back. Sure enough, the breeze died and it was perfect. After a few minutes, she rolled up her sleeves.

"See?" Libbie asked with self-satisfaction.

"Yeah, but I'm dressed. You're… not."

At that, Libbie straightened up. "You don't think I'm

being inappropriate, do you? You said I could use the backyard and..."

"Oh no, it's fine. Don't worry about it."

"You sure?"

"Yes," Alice confirmed. "I'm just surprised. You don't expect beach behavior at this time of year, you know? But at least Tom enjoyed the view."

Libbie grinned. "Nice to know I still got it."

Alice didn't reply. Instead, she glanced sideways at her and inspected her body again. She definitely still had it, all right.

For a few minutes, they talked about mindless things such as TV shows, movies, and neighbors. People would start decorating for Halloween soon and Alice promised that it would be spectacular. Well, not so much the displays as the sheer number of people who fell off ladders or accidentally set themselves on fire.

"It's not funny," Alice began with a wince. "But it's kind of funny."

Libbie winked. "Totally understand. Hey, we could make a night of it, driving around the neighborhood while scanning for the Darwin Awards."

Tom came out of the kitchen with a garbage bag. He waved at them on his way to the trashcans.

"Alice?" the tenant asked.

"Yes?"

"You don't think I went overboard dressing this way, do you? I didn't mean to be too underdressed, especially in front of your husband and..."

"Oh no, Libbie. It's okay. I trust Tom completely."

"Great. That's good to know."

Just as Tom was heading back toward the side door, a visitor appeared on the street. Alice straightened up in her chair and she couldn't help but snort back a laugh.

"What is it?"

"You see that girl?" Alice pointed to the visitor with her chin to be inconspicuous because they could be seen from around the house where Tom met the young person.

"Yeah?"

It was a teenage girl. She was almost as tall as Tom, her figure slender and flawless. She wore a plaid skirt which stopped above her knees and a tight T-shirt that was almost sheer. From her position, Alice could see the outline of her bra. Her blond hair was in a high ponytail.

"That's Marissa Sigley. You know, the girl who has a thing for my husband?"

"That's her?! She's gorgeous."

"And she knows it, too."

In the distance, they could hear her talk to Tom. There was a clipboard in her hand and they heard something about her collecting funds for one school project or another.

"You're sure she's only sixteen?"

"Her Sweet Sixteen was a month ago. Her parents invited us just to be polite, but we didn't go."

"You think she wanted Tom to be there?"

Alice was taken aback. "No. It strangely makes sense now though…"

"Yesterday when I mentioned that teenagers have strong hormonal urges, I mentioned that boy. But I suppose it also applies to girls."

Libbie reached for her phone, tapped the camera icon, and took pictures of Marissa.

"So, first you say that Rusty is a stalker and now you think Marissa is planning to murder my husband?"

"No," Libbie answered with a laugh. "It's just that at that age their impulses are stronger than their self-control. Don't you remember being a teenage girl?"

"I never stole anyone's husband."

"But have you ever *thought* about it?" Alice kept her mouth shut. "Because that's what's really important. Intent. After that, it's only a question of opportunity. I'm sorry, here I go being serious again."

"It's okay."

"You have nothing to be jealous of, Alice."

"I'm not jealous!"

"And you have no reason to be," Libbie says, reassuring her with a gentle stroke on the hand. "Marissa might be young and beautiful, but you have her beaten, hands down."

"Tom would never do anything improper."

"Of course, Alice. If I were you, though, I'd still keep an eye out. For her, I mean. Not Tom. He's a gentleman, there's no doubt about that. But Marissa? Teenage girls? Sometimes they act without thinking about consequences."

"Right," Alice said. "Right…"

She trusted Tom implicitly. Of course she did. And she knew all too well what a slippery and treacherous slope jealousy could be. But still, for the first time in her life, she found herself doubting her husband and his ability to resist a woman's charms.

CHAPTER 9

The dubstep music was so loud that Libbie could feel her insides trembling. She ordinarily didn't like this sort of music, but the DJ was mixing it with a Rihanna hit. It was a strange combination, but it worked.

She walked through the club, which had been built in the belly of an abandoned textile factory. She felt people all around her. She could smell them, feel their heat closing in on her. It reminded her of the hospital. That was the last time she had been in a crowd like this.

Here, however, no one paid attention to her. Not yet, at least. The colorful lights flashed quickly, the strobes harmonizing with the music. It was euphoric.

She was wearing a black satin halterneck wrap dress that hugged her figure. The neckline plunged dangerously low and the hem stopped well above her knees. It was only when the lighting pattern changed that she began to get attention. Men who were dancing with their dates turned her way. Libbie saw more than one woman glare at her angrily.

It was perfect.

She reached the bar and ordered a negroni. It wasn't long before the first slimeball hit on her.

"Hey," he said, displaying sheer volumes of eloquence.

He was tall and his hair had more chemical products than hers. His silk shirt had three buttons undone. His cocky smirk did nothing to rehabilitate his image. He was downright smarmy.

"I'm waiting for someone," she said, sipping her Campari-sweet vermouth-gin cocktail.

"Let me wait with you."

About to reply, Libbie changed her mind. She smiled, came closer to him while holding her glass between them, and craned her neck as if she wanted to whisper. He reeked of CK One.

"I'd rather swallow a glass of flaming bleach than spend another minute with you. Okay? Thanks for playing."

Flustered, the man didn't know how to respond and retreated. Libbie grinned to herself, turning away.

The bartender gave her an appreciative smile, having witnessed the scene. She was proud of herself. Where was the fun in scoring a point if no one saw you?

"Another," she said, slamming her empty glass down before her. She should pace herself. She was out of practice.

Waiting for her second drink, she turned and studied the crowd. Why were people so depressing? So... *one-dimensional?* Everyone was just as dull as perfect Tom and his perfect wife Alice.

She took a long sip of her new drink, waving some money in the bartender's direction.

In the time it took for him to take a couple of bills and give her change, another guy had moved in beside her.

Head shaved, hipster beard, puppy-dog eyes.

She took her drink, paused to give him a look so withering he visibly shrank away from her, and then turned her back on him. She didn't know why she'd even come here. Seeking something.

Distraction, perhaps. Action, yes.

Not some carpet-chinned lightweight who no doubt wanted to have actual conversation and share his feelings and maybe even call her the next day.

She moved onto the dancefloor and started to twist and sway in time to the beat. Closing her eyes, she let the lights play on her lids, trying to lose herself.

Maybe that was why she'd come here. To lose herself, if only for a few minutes.

A sharp bump on her arm jolted her back to awareness, a cold splash on the back of her hand as her drink jerked and nearly spilled. *What the...?* She felt a flush of anger, a surge of rage.

A guy. Black hair, dark eyes and a *Who cares?* look plastered all over his face.

He'd bumped into her, but he wasn't going to apologize. He was too busy eyeing the low-cut front of her dress, weighing up his chances.

Libbie fought to control her anger. She took a step toward him, took a hold of his shirt with her free hand, and hissed, "You owe me a drink, dude."

For a moment, he looked like he wanted to argue. Then his expression faltered. She was sure he'd just seen how close she was to losing it. That rage that was always bubbling so close to the surface inside her.

"I…" he said, finally finding words and then seeming to lose them immediately. "Sorry." That shrug again. He nodded toward the bar and gave a smile that was somewhere between conciliatory and scared.

She liked that. Within seconds of meeting this guy he had no idea where he stood. But he didn't flee. He was clearly drawn, clearly interested.

Maybe this one would do.

For now.

~ ~ ~ ~

Saturday evening and here Alice was, pressing the car's LOCK button on her key fob and heading across the parking lot to the big glass doors of Pierson Newport's head office.

She'd felt bad leaving Tom home alone, but he'd assured her it was fine. "How else are you going to make vice president and keep me in the style to which I hope to become accustomed, sweetie?" he'd joked, ushering her out of the door.

"No parties, you hear me?" she'd told him. "And no inviting Marissa Sigley over while I'm out." She'd tried to ignore the slightly sour taste the quip had left in her mouth, triggering memories of Libbie's warnings about the dangers of obsessive, lust-filled teens.

Jokes. Banter. That was the basis of their marriage. But was it hiding something? Were they trying to mask something terrible from their past? It was best not to wonder, Alice decided.

Some things were best left alone.

She paused before swiping her ID and waiting for the glass doors to swing smoothly open. The place was in darkness, at least. That was good. She'd come here to work on her pitch.

Tom had been right about not sweating the presentation until she had the content fixed, but sometimes it helped to visualize things with a few graphics. It was far easier to juggle Photoshop and the sprawling Excel spreadsheets on her big office screens than on her laptop at home.

And coming here gave her space to think without distraction. To clear her head.

She hated to admit that Libbie's innocent warnings had been playing on her mind.

Seeing Marissa Sigley out front this morning, chatting and laughing with Tom. The kid was breathtakingly beautiful and she sure as hell knew it.

And Tom did, too.

He wasn't that kind of a guy, though. Alice knew that. He would never stray, and certainly not with a kid.

She sure doesn't look like a kid, though, and she's past sixteen.

She heard the words in Libbie's voice, that gentle, warning tone.

Maybe all guys were *that kind of a guy* in the right—or wrong—circumstances.

There was a light on in one of the back offices that led off the open-plan space. The dim light of computer screens. Had a machine been left running, or was someone working here late on a Saturday in the dark?

She approached warily.

"Hey, Walter," she called, letting go the breath she'd been holding. "Or should I say SwelterificJones?"

He looked up with a start, a guilty expression on his face. Not working late: *playing*. Every time she used the name of his gaming avatar he told her how much he regretted having divulged his online identity to her.

He'd told her the name came from an old joke, long buried in his childhood. She'd never worked out if the name was a fond memory or if it had been a name used by school bullies to taunt him that he'd now reclaimed as his own.

Walter was tall and skinny, with an easygoing smile and mid-brown hair that always seemed to have recently outgrown its cut. She'd known him since she'd joined Pierson Newport five years before.

"Ali." He was the only person to call her that. "You working on a Saturday?"

She moved into the dark office. "Mapleview," she said, the one word enough for him to nod knowingly. He got how much was at stake. Since Tom had quit last year and gone freelance, things had been tight. "I came in to work on the big screens. Just like you, Swel'."

She nodded toward his twin screens, a shoot 'em up game frozen on one, while the other showed the same scene from a different angle along with columns of figures and graphs. The game looked a lot more complicated even than the spreadsheets Alice had been juggling all day.

"You can't do all this at home?" she asked.

"What can I say? I like the office ambience. That, and the network here is so much faster than anything I have at home." It was a running joke that he was saving up to buy a really good gaming system for home but somehow he never quite got there.

He picked up the headphones he'd removed when she arrived and waggled them at her. "Promise I won't disturb you."

"It's fine."

Alice's office was two along from Walter's. In truth, she didn't much mind. She'd come here for the peace, but Walter's easy presence didn't really change that.

"You want coffee?" she asked, knowing he'd always say yes. Gaming and caffeine, the two real loves of his life.

He followed her through to the small kitchen area and then stepped in to make the coffees himself.

"Everything okay?" Had he sensed her mood?

She shrugged. "I guess. Yes, it is. Just things are a bit difficult right now. Money, you know."

"Don't I?"

He handed her a latte. He hadn't even had to ask what she wanted.

"Tom still working at home?"

"He's doing his best. Finding his feet again." Tom had been a middle executive at Pierson Newport until the pressures had all gotten too much for him a year ago. If he'd still been here, *he'd* have been the one trying to land the Mapleview account. *He'd* be the one gunning for vice president.

"He's getting transcription work online. And we have the investment property undergoing renovation, over on Whitetail Lane."

"You decided what you're going to do with that?" Walter sipped on his double espresso, wincing at the bitter caffeine kick.

"Tom wants to sell for a fast buck."

"And you want to rent." The two laughed. They'd had this conversation before and Alice knew Walter was on the side of a quick sale for profit.

"I know," she said. "You're always telling me rental's a trap. Too many complications and you can never find—"

"The perfect tenant." They both finished the sentence in unison.

"Well, that's where you're wrong," Alice went on, playing her trump card. "You remember that basement apartment we have?"

"Plan B?" That's what they'd called it: if all else fails, we'll rent out the basement apartment.

"Our tenant moved in this week. Professional, polite, friendly. She's the quietest thing. She really is the perfect tenant you say is an impossibility."

Walter just looked at her, eyebrows raised to indicate his disbelief.

"She's hiding something," he said at last. "She's a psychopath or a war criminal, or she has really bad taste in interior decoration that you'll only discover when she's

STEVE RICHER AND NICHOLAS GIFFORD

fled without paying rent. Really, Ali, you know there's no such thing—"

"As the perfect tenant!"

They laughed again, before Alice said, believing every word, "Honestly, though, Walter. I think we've struck gold with this one. She really is the quietest thing."

~ ~ ~ ~

The guy had zero interest in conversation, which suited Libbie just fine.

He bought her another negroni to replace the one he'd jogged when he'd been so distracted by her dancing he'd bumped into her drink arm. After that, they did shots.

She knew she'd drunk too much. Three months behind locked doors with only coffee and palmed sedatives to alter her mind had seriously reduced her alcohol tolerance levels.

She shook her head when the guy nudged their empty shot glasses toward the bartender. Grabbed him by the arm and led him back onto the dancefloor.

She had so much catching up to do.

She had to laugh when she recalled telling perfect Tom and perfect Alice how quiet and reclusive a life she led.

And that was when she realized where all this was leading.

The guy—did he even *have* a name?—was staring. She could tell he was unnerved by her directness and by the way she had just laughed at nothing, but he couldn't just turn away. He knew he had a chance with her, and no guy would turn away from that.

They were all the same. Every last one of them, whatever they claimed.

Not long later, they were out in the street. Fast food places, bars, and locked-up shops crowded the street. This wasn't an attractive part of town to be out in after dark.

As soon as they were outside and the cold air hit, Libbie grabbed the guy and drew him into a deep kiss. Long and intense, right up against the metal grille of a locked sportswear store.

There was a dark cross-street here and the guy tried to steer her down there, but that wasn't the plan.

She took his hand and led him to where she'd parked the Toyota.

As soon as they were seated he was all over her again, his mouth on hers, his hands taking all they could grab. After a couple of minutes, she broke free and gunned the engine. Soon they were cruising through the leafy streets on the nicer side of town.

"So…"

She silenced him with a glare. He was fit, he danced and kissed well, and he bought her drinks. She didn't need him spoiling any of that with conversation right now. Every guy she'd ever known had been a downhill route to disappointment.

"I—"

She slammed on the brakes, twisted in her seat and took his face in the tight grip of one hand, his stubble scraping on her skin. She thought he might run and felt his body tensing as he weighed his options.

Kissing him killed that thought.

Guys. Always the same.

A short time later, they pulled up at the curb outside the Granger residence. The lights were on, but Alice's Ford Focus was still gone. Libbie had bumped into her as she was leaving earlier, some feeble excuse about pressure of work.

She gunned the engine again before killing it and, sure enough, like any good neighbor, within seconds Tom was at the window of the den looking out.

Would he recognize it as her car by now, parked out in the street? Maybe. She didn't care.

She turned to nameless dude, who was studying her, judging his move.

"We going in or what?" he drawled.

"What."

This time when she kissed him, she swung herself over to straddle him. The extra space in this model of Toyota had to be good for something, she figured.

"Oh, baby," she purred into the guy's ear. "You like a gal who knows just what she wants?"

He reached up for her face, trying to take control, but she slapped his hands away, pinning him against the car seat.

When she glanced off to the side, she saw that the house window was empty. *What the...?* Why wasn't he even watching? Was he that uninterested?

She swung back, her butt coming to rest against the dash. Stretching back like this the streetlights fell on her like a spotlight and for an instant the guy paused. Then he reached again and started to paw at her, pulling at her clothing, until with a roll of the shoulders she reached up and pulled the halterneck top of her dress free and let it fall.

And with one free arm she swung, bumping a fist against the horn.

The guy below her flinched at the sound, but Libbie didn't care. She stretched back again, arching her spine, letting that street spotlight fall on her exposed body.

And when she looked, Tom was silhouetted in the window once again.

She smiled.

Let him look.

Let him dream.

Let him see her naked form every time he closed his eyes, every time he looked at his wife and felt guilty, every time he looked at that sixteen-year-old neighbor he had the hots for.

The mind games were only just getting started.

CHAPTER 10

Tom sat alone in the den, a half-consumed bottle of beer on a coffee table before him. His face was lit by the glow of his open laptop.

Libbie couldn't tell what was holding his interest so intently. She couldn't see the screen from this angle, peering through the window as she was. Facebook? Games? Porn? Was that what he did when he was all alone at home? When his perfect wife was out working all hours to earn their joint living?

She couldn't even remember how long she'd been standing here, but she was cold now. Didn't know how long it was since she'd sent that guy striding off down the road, cursing her for using him and abandoning him like that. As if he'd ever think twice about doing that to a woman!

She still didn't know his name.

She'd had fun. Surprisingly so. It had been a while. But she was done with the guy. She had been as soon as he'd opened his mouth to speak afterward, as if *that* was suddenly the time for conversation. So she'd sent him on his way. She'd scratched that itch tonight.

Now was time to return to a longer standing one.

She moved away from the window and paused,

gathering herself. And then she went up onto the porch, reached out and knocked on the door.

"I… Hi," she said, giving her best attempt at a clumsy, shy smile when he opened the door.

Tom's mouth fell open as soon as he saw her. He looked slightly alarmed, as if he assumed the only reason she might knock was that something was wrong. And awkward, too, his eyes flitting, not knowing where to rest. Libbie didn't help him by the way she stood there, her arms folded under her breasts, knowing how that both framed them and pushed them up, emphasizing her exposed cleavage.

Such a contrast with the last guy, who'd known *exactly* where to look!

"I just came to apologize," she said, letting him out of his misery. "For earlier. In case you saw anything… *inappropriate*. That's not like me. I don't quite know what came over me."

He didn't want to be having this conversation. He clearly didn't know what to say, or what to think.

Or, rather, he knew exactly what to think. Libbie thoroughly understood that simply by standing here like this, apologizing and telling him to forget all about it, his mind was drawn inevitably back to what he had seen, what she had been doing.

Sometimes this was such an easy game to play.

"I hope I haven't caused any problems by this little lapse," she said. "I'd hate to make things hard for you."

She smiled. Waited. His turn. She wasn't going to cut him any slack now.

"I… No. I mean. It's none of my business, is it?" He clearly believed it was, judging by how long he'd spent looking earlier.

"I don't mean to lower the tone of the neighborhood," she assured him. "Oh dear. I've gotten off to such a bad start, haven't I? Can we maybe just draw a line under this? Start over again?"

"Of course. Of course." So suburban of him. Politeness always triumphed.

"I'm sure Alice doesn't even need to know, does she?" Libbie said. "I'd hate her to think badly of me, just when we'd gotten off to such a great start."

"I…"

He must know this was a trap. One whose doors had already closed on him.

"Our little secret," she added. A smile. A shrug of the shoulders that drew her folded arms up, and drew his eyes down again.

"I…" He couldn't wriggle out of it. He smiled, then, as if conceding defeat. "What goes on tour stays on tour, right?" he said.

"Or out in the street." Make it into a bad joke, one he had to respond to with at least another smile, and she was reeling him in.

So easy!

"I hope I didn't disturb you?"

She peered past him into the house, and saw that he'd put his laptop down on the console table inside the door, the screen still frustratingly turned away from her scrutiny.

Tom followed her gaze and instinctively reached across to flip the lid closed.

"It's fine," she said. "Everyone has a secret, don't they?"

"Oh no," he said hurriedly. "No secrets. Just an automatic thing, you know."

"Yes, I know," she told him, twisting the knife deeper with another innocent smile. "Really, though, it's fine. Whatever you were doing. Whatever your little secret is. You do have one, don't you?"

He opened his mouth to answer, then stopped himself. That was answer enough for Libbie. He *was* hiding something! Maybe she'd been right about the porn, or maybe there was something else.

How interesting.

"I'll leave you in peace," she said, taking a step back but still facing him, encouraging his eyes to roam again. "And that thing you saw earlier... Just put it from your mind, okay?"

And then she turned, and with a sway of the hips walked around the corner of the house to her apartment.

~ ~ ~ ~

Sunday morning, Libbie was downstairs on the L-shaped couch in her den. Alice and Tom were out—Alice at the office again and Tom visiting their investment property on the other side of town. Libbie liked to know these things, and the half-conversations drifting down that ugly air vent were a godsend when it came to snooping.

Knowing she was safe from any intrusion, she got the scrapbook out.

It was such a safe, suburban hobby, scrapbooking. One they'd encouraged at the secure hospital. Self-expression. Handicraft skills. Design and creativity. Research. So many skills that could be developed through such a simple activity. Dr. Holt had been delighted when she'd taken to it with enthusiasm.

And like any man, the good doctor had been easily fooled.

Back then, her scrapbooks had been filled with images cut from magazines of the lifestyle Libbie had once had, and missed so sorely in the institutional grayness of the hospital. A delightful Luis Vuitton purse on one page, a pair of Christian Louboutin stilettos on another, one shoe tipped on its side to reveal the red-lacquered sole. A pair of Jimmy Choo patent leather slingbacks on another page, and on the next a Michael Kors lace-up jumpsuit almost identical to the one she'd worn on the day they'd brought her to the hospital.

Dr. Holt had been so impressed with her industry and creativity.

He might not have been quite so impressed with the direction her hobby had taken since getting out of that pointless place.

Libbie looked down at the open spread before her and smiled. A different one to the innocent smile she'd used to tantalize and confuse Tom Granger last night. This smile had a hard, cruel edge to it.

Unknown to Dr. Holt, Libbie had been into scrapbooking long before her unwanted stay in his establishment, and this particular scrapbook was nearly complete. Only a few more pages to go.

She'd started it years ago, with pictures she'd found in a variety of places. A school yearbook stolen from an old friend of Alice's. Photocopies from a couple of newspaper stories—a charity fundraiser Alice had organized, a big real estate deal that had promised to rejuvenate an entire district from when Tom had worked at Pierson Newport.

Wedding photos taken from Tom's Facebook page. Such a happy, well-loved couple!

Vacation snaps, taken from the same source. Alice looked good in a bikini. She should tell her that sometime. And Tom in his swim trunks. They really were a well-matched couple.

They looked so good together.

Even with their faces scratched out. Even with the distracting way someone had scrawled words like *bitch* and *dirty secrets* and *revenge* all over the scrapbook, so that the words covered both the pages and the photographs themselves.

Looking at the artful arrangements on the pages, somewhere between graffiti and collage, she had to acknowledge the creativity that had gone into this project. An aesthetic underscored by hatred and violence. It really was quite beautiful.

She reached for the picture she'd just retrieved from the printer.

Like many of the photographs in the scrapbook, it was

one she'd taken herself. She may not be the professional photographer she'd claimed she was to Alice and Tom, but what she lacked in professional skills she made up for in dogged dedication.

The picture showed Tom sitting in his den, the bottle of beer held close to his mouth, tipped at a jaunty forty-five degree angle. Face and beer were both lit only by the glow from the laptop's screen.

If you ignored the fuzzy pixelation of the image, it really was quite artistic.

Maybe when this was all done she'd have to find another creative outlet, perhaps even photography.

She glued the back of the photograph and positioned it on the page. She reached for a sharpened piece of wood and stabbed the point down sharply into Tom's eye.

The picture twisted on the page under the impact and she repositioned it carefully, lining it up with the edges of the page.

This time, when she scraped the point to gouge a line across Tom's face, she held the photograph in place, mindful of the glue not yet set.

She really was good at this.

Dr. Holt would be *so* proud.

~ ~ ~ ~

The sound of a doorbell took her by surprise. She instantly reached for the scrapbook and flipped it shut, before sweeping up her paraphernalia of scissors, glue, pens, ribbons, and a sharpened sliver of wood into a canvas bag.

It was a second or two before her mind caught up and she realized that the sound came from upstairs, perhaps made louder by carrying down the air vent. Was the doorbell's speaker positioned close to that vent upstairs in the house?

She hadn't had visitors here yet and so didn't know the sound of her own bell, or even if she had one. Now that she thought about it, wasn't there just a knocker on the apartment door? All this was new to her. It was natural to get confused.

She went to the door now and peered through the window next to it, but the corner of the house hid the callers from her view.

Probably a salesman, or snotty kids selling cookies or something, she thought. But she was curious. No aspect of Tom and Alice's lives should escape her scrutiny. There was gold to be found everywhere.

She went to her room to retrieve the house key and then went outside.

"Hey there." She gave her best suburban smile. Tried to do that thing Alice did so well—the being *nice* to strangers thing. "Can I help you guys?"

A kid in a suit, his hair slicked down. A girl in a prim little dress. Each of them carrying clipboards. A school project, Libbie guessed. *Dull*.

"Ma'am," said the guy, taking the lead. So predictable. "Would you be the homeowner? We're here on behalf of the Jackson campaign for the city council and we'd like to share with you what Mr. Jackson has to offer—"

"I'm not the homeowner," she said, trying hard not to snap at the kid. How old were they? It made *her* feel old that she'd thought them kids.

She forced another of those mindless suburban smiles onto her face. "That is to say, I'm not quite moved in yet. I'm just in the process of buying the place." She shrugged apologetically. "It's a bit of a fixer-upper, I know. Needs lots of work. But hey, what's a girl to do with her time?" She waved the key at them. "I just borrowed this so I can measure up."

"Well, in that case—"

"I'm afraid I'll have to stop you there. Things to do, you know. Must rush out."

She stepped past them onto the porch, and before she had time to think she'd slipped the key easily into the lock, twisted, and pushed her way inside.

Seconds later, she stood with her back pressed hard against the closed door, trying to calm her racing heart.

She was inside again! She couldn't keep away, now she was so close.

She looked around the gloomy interior as her eyes adjusted. She was right. A definite fixer-upper.

The place was almost institutionally dull. Too suburban. It wasn't that it lacked character, but that the character was *theirs*. The figurines Tom collected. The photos of the two of them on the walls. The color scheme of autumn browns and bronzes and all things beige.

You could do so much with a space like this.

When they were gone.

Libbie had never seen herself as anything but a big city girl, but for a moment she allowed herself the fantasy, rearranging and replacing the furniture in her head, changing the colors, the carpets.

Indulging herself, she strolled from room to room, trailing her hand over the surfaces, pausing every so often to redesign the place in her head. In the den she found a laptop, and for a moment thought it was Tom's. She flipped it open. Maybe there would be something interesting in his internet history.

It was Alice's. *Oh well…*

A short time later, she went upstairs. She knew the layout by heart. Had done so even before that night she'd let herself in and come to stand in the bedroom doorway to watch them sleeping.

She went to the bedroom now, stood where she'd stood that night. The bed was neatly made, the surfaces uncluttered. Another nauseating picture of the two of them up on the wall. Who would ever want to stare at themselves in every room of a house?

She sat on the edge of the bed, bounced a little. She swung her legs around and lay back. She was on Alice's side. She imagined rolling onto her side to face him, their faces up close.

So sweet an image!

She hadn't yet decided which of them should be the first to die. Alice or Tom? She'd want them to suffer first. She'd want them to know what they'd lost.

To understand.

She got up and went back downstairs, careful to leave

everything as it had been.

At the door, she paused for a final look around.

She'd keep Tom's figurines, if this place were ever hers. Something to remember them by. That and their mummified bodies preserved in that miserable basement apartment.

And when she finally stepped back out into the sunlight, you'd never have been able to tell she'd been there at all.

CHAPTER 11

Alice hadn't meant to work most of the weekend, but she'd gotten caught up in developing her pitch for the Mapleview account. She'd been right not to leave the graphics elements until later, too, despite the logic of Tom's argument. Visualizing all those figures gave her a whole new perspective on trends—and possible crunch-points—through the life of the project.

Tom didn't seem to mind, either. This was how it was going to be, after all, if this went well. Weekends and evenings lost their conventional meaning in a life shaped by work.

But now... Sunday evening... This was good. A temporary reprieve. A retreat into domesticity. Time to just kick back and simply *stop* for a time.

It felt good to be in baggy sweatpants, a string-strapped top and big fluffy carpet socks. Good to have scrubbed away the layers of make-up she felt the need to wear in the office, even on a Sunday when not even Walter was there. Good to settle back on the couch, her legs stretched out across Tom's lap as he massaged her feet through those ridiculous socks. They'd had dinner, they had wine, they had a cheesy old film on the flatscreen they'd seen a hundred times before.

Right now, life didn't get much better than this.

"What is it, sweetie?" Tom had noticed her mood, maybe seen that she was studying the lines of his face and smiling.

"I love you, Tom Granger."

"Well *that* sure is a convenient thing," he said, and then he gave that big wink of his and she pressed the backs of her legs just a little harder down against him, and—

Someone at the door.

Alice bit down on her frustration. She wanted to be selfish for once, to cling onto this moment. To make it last a while longer.

She pressed her calves down against Tom again and for a moment thought maybe he was going to let himself ignore the door. But no. Tom was a completer-finisher, steady and reliable, and it wasn't in his nature to leave anything incomplete or ignored.

He smiled apologetically, as if he could read her thoughts, then extricated himself to go get the door.

From the tone of his voice it must be an old friend, but she couldn't work out who that might be. She climbed to her feet, still resenting the intrusion.

When she joined Tom she saw that it was Libbie.

For an instant, that resentment blossomed. Was this how it was going to be? Having a neighbor so close? It almost felt like having someone in the actual house itself.

Then she saw the nervous smile on the girl's face— that eagerness to please and to impress. And the giant, cream-topped cheesecake she held out before her. Now she felt guilty for reacting in that way.

"I was just saying," Tom said, turning to his wife, "how kind, but totally unnecessary this is."

"And *I* was saying I just wanted to be sure you two sweet people understand just how appreciative I am of you letting me into your home like this. Well, the basement, at any rate." She thrust the cheesecake at Tom and he took it automatically. "And I saw the look on your face when you opened the door and saw this cheesecake: you're not going to say no, are you?"

He laughed, stepped back from the door, and said, "But only if you'll join us."

"I really don't want to intrude."

"We insist!"

"We really do," confirmed Alice. "This is so kind of you. And correct me if I'm wrong but that looks home-baked. Is there no end to your talents?"

"Oh, you'd be surprised." Libbie stepped inside, and added, "I always wanted to bake. And I had some free time recently to learn. I'm glad you think it looks okay."

"More than okay!" said Tom. He loved desserts, and baked chocolate cheesecake was his favorite—Alice was sure he couldn't believe his luck at Libbie's choice.

And they didn't often have desserts when it was just them, for obvious reasons.

It was as if Libbie had the exact same thought at that moment. Her jaw dropped and her eyes opened wide and she put a hand to her mouth and then, melodramatically, slapped the palm of her hand against her forehead.

"Oh, how embarrassing!" she said. "How very, very dumb of me! Can you even have any of this? You know, if you have an injection or something? Sorry, I don't really know how it works. Can you do that? Dose yourself up so you can eat cake?"

"It's fine, really."

"Oh, I feel such a fool. I should have thought."

"We have a deal," Tom said, with that winning smile of his. "In this type of predicament, I just eat for both of us. Win-win."

Alice smiled, and after a moment Libbie did too. Tom had a way of rescuing situations like this with a wisecrack.

"Come on through while Tom gets plates," she said. "Tell me all about how you're settling into the neighborhood."

In short order they were seated in the den. Tom and Libbie had the couch, Tom sitting with one leg drawn up so he could twist to face their guest. Alice sat across from them in the big easy chair.

"You had some callers earlier," Libbie told them. "Just political canvassers. They seemed very pleasant. I told them you were out."

"Thank you," said Tom. "But you really don't have to get our door."

"Oh, it was nothing. Really. Unless I'm being too much? I really don't want to be *that* kind of neighbor. You know, the ones you wish you never had in the first place."

"Oh no," Tom assured her around another mouthful of cheesecake. "We really appreciate it. We were just saying how happy we are to have you here, weren't we, sweetie?"

"Oh, you two! You really are too kind."

"It's true, though," Alice assured her. "You should have seen some of the other applicants! You're a real find. We like having you here, and we like that you're so friendly. We don't exactly socialize much these days—it's nice to have a friend nearby who feels free to call by."

"So tell us," Tom began, "is everything okay down there? Do you need anything?"

"It's perfect," said Libbie. "Really it is. I simply love the décor. You guys have done such a tasteful job—down there and up here, too. I was thinking that only earlier, I truly was."

"Oh, it's hardly planned. Just colors and furniture we like, you know."

"It's beautiful."

Alice smiled. Despite her claims, she really had put a lot of effort into getting this place how she and Tom liked.

Just then, she heard the familiar two-tone ringtone of her cellphone. "Sorry," she said, standing. "I should get that."

She took the call out in the kitchen and came back through a minute later. "Work," she said. "Sorry. That was Michael Tuckett. He's asking for the interim report from last week. I have a copy here I can mail him. It shouldn't take me a minute." Already she was reaching for her laptop.

"On a Sunday evening?" asked Libbie. "They sure do work you hard at that place."

"It's nothing," said Alice.

And it shouldn't have been, if she could only find the file.

She'd been looking at it on this laptop only yesterday—it was right there, listed in her recent files. But when she clicked on it she got an error message saying *Resource unavailable.* She checked all her usual folders, but nothing. In fact, even some of *those* folders appeared to be missing…

In theory, she should be able to log onto the Pierson Newport extranet from here and find a copy of the report there, but in practice the connection was never reliable enough from off-site. That was why Michael hadn't simply done so himself!

"Everything okay, sweetie?"

"Yes," she grunted. Then: "No. I'm not sure. I can't seem to find anything, that's all."

"Have you checked your recent files?"

She bit back a response. Telling her to do exactly what she'd done first of all wasn't exactly helping right now.

She was aware of a look exchanged between Tom and Libbie and tried to dismiss it. They could clearly tell she was frustrated and were silently agreeing to humor her.

"I'll get it in a minute." She tried not to hit the keys any harder than normal. What she needed right now was a Walter: in the office he was far quicker and friendlier than the company's official IT support. And better.

Still nothing.

"At the risk of being a pain," said Libbie, "I was in the Interactive Media and Technology program at NYU before I moved into photography. I even worked on the

IT Help Desk to help me stay afloat. I couldn't make any promises, but...?"

Alice glanced across at her eager expression. Perhaps if not a Walter, then a Libbie might be worth a shot.

Hell, *anything* right now had to be worth a try. Michael Tuckett was one of the big guys at Pierson Newport, one level down from the top. If Alice couldn't even mail him a lousy file on a Sunday evening, that was sure to go down as a black mark in her record.

Grateful, she passed the laptop across to Libbie. "The file's called *interim-dash-september dot xlsx*, all lower-case. I keep it in a folder called *Pierson Newport home files* in the documents area, and it should be in my recents because I was looking at it only last night. Thank you so much."

"I'm impressed you even knew that much," said Libbie. "I don't mean to be patronizing, but some of the things we came across on the IT help desk... Geez!"

Alice watched as Libbie ran her slender fingers over the laptop's touchpad and then tapped at the keys.

Every second was like watching a TV drama. Every narrowing of the eyes or sucking in of that lower lip a hint that disaster had struck the temperamental machine. Every glimmer of a smile offered release.

"Just one file, or a whole folder?"

"I think the entire folder it was in has vanished. Is it bad?"

A long pause, and then, finally, Libbie grinned. "Not bad, just a little embarrassing for you: you must have accidentally dragged that folder into the Trash and hit Empty."

"Is everything lost?"

Libbie was still smiling. "I know a few tricks," she said. "I've just undeleted that folder and put it back where it belongs."

And with that she handed the laptop back to the disbelieving Alice.

"You mean... It's all there now?" Her mind was racing. She didn't recall deleting anything, but she must have done it. You could do all kinds of dumb things when you worked late nights right through the weekend.

"Thank you so much," Alice said. "Yet another reason to be grateful we have you."

"Hell yeah," said Tom. "That was impressive work. You really are a godsend, Libbie."

And just for a moment Alice felt a twinge of disquiet. Jealousy, even. The way he looked at her. The way he said those words. The body language of how he sat, twisted toward Libbie and almost imperceptibly *away* from Alice.

"I'll just mail this file," she mumbled, fixing her eyes on the screen.

She knew it was stupid to react like that. Seeing things that weren't there. Tom wasn't like that.

He was just making the extra effort to show their joint appreciation. Perhaps over-compensating for something. It was nothing.

By the time she'd dispatched the file to Michael Tuckett, the moment had passed. Tom was polishing off the rest of his mammoth portion of cheesecake and Libbie was doing something on her phone.

"Thanks again," said Alice. "And my apologies for that. Too much stress for a Sunday evening!"

"You need to look after yourself more," said Libbie. "Working so hard. All that responsibility. You need some *you* time."

Alice laughed. "That's going to have to wait until after I've landed Mapleview!"

"I mean it," said Libbie. "You need to chill. Hey! What are you doing lunchtime tomorrow? Working through, I guess? I have yoga class at twelve-thirty. How about you join me? I could pick you up at Pierson Newport on my way to the yoga studio. I really got into yoga this year. It keeps you so centered."

She was right about lunchtimes, of course. Alice worked through most days. She couldn't imagine anything much worse than forcing yourself into yoga pants and pretzeling yourself for an hour in the middle of the day.

But the girl was so keen and she'd been so helpful just now. Alice reminded herself that Libbie was new in town, had no friends here, and it was the least she could do to help her find her feet.

"That sounds great," she said, ignoring the incredulity on Tom's face.

She met his look and said, "If I'm doing that, I won't have time to get to the bank to sort out paperwork for paying the construction crew. You'll have to do that. Can you manage it?"

Her words were perhaps a little sharper than she intended, hinting at old frustrations she'd thought suppressed.

He hesitated, and in that moment Alice was aware of Libbie watching them closely. He said, "Yeah, sweetie, sure. I'll take care of that. Whatever you want."

And then he reached for his plate again and scraped up the last remnants of the cheesecake.

CHAPTER 12

Alice looked in her element as she emerged through the double glass doors of Pierson Newport's head office. Energized by her work, perhaps, and by an even temporary escape from her dull suburban existence with Tom.

She wore her hair pinned up at the back of her head, a few strands drifting stylishly free across the temple and forehead. Makeup on point but not excessive. Smart gray pantsuit and modest heels. Every inch the aspiring modern executive. Every inch—

And who was *that?*

A tall guy was at her shoulder, skinny and slightly stooped, with unkempt hair an indeterminate shade of mid-brown that would blend right in with Alice's mundane interior decorating preferences.

He was looking at her with blatantly obvious puppy-dog eyes.

Libbie raised the camera from her lap, zoomed in close on the two, and let off a rapid series of shots.

If she'd been a sensitive, caring kind of a person she'd wait in the car for Alice to find her and avoid the risk of embarrassing her in front of her worshipful friend.

Instead, she climbed out of the car, gave a cheery wave across the wide paved area in front of the building and called out, "Hi there, Alice! Over here."

The two came over and Libbie stepped forward easily to air-kiss either side of Alice's face. Stepping back, she said, "So who's your good-looking friend?"

The guy actually stepped back. She'd embarrassed him. Such an easy game.

Alice grinned and turned to indicate the man. "This is Walter, a colleague of mine. An old friend. Walter, this is Libbie. She's our—"

"Perfect tenant!" they finished in unison.

"Oh, too sweet!" said Libbie. "You even finish each other's sentences. Are you sure you two are just colleagues?"

Alice laughed again. She seemed to be in a good mood today. It was funny seeing her in such a different setting. Did Alice even realize how much Tom seemed to oppress her?

And this guy... well, he clearly didn't have the same effect.

"Walter's just a friend," she insisted. "He's a gamer. He doesn't have room in his life for anything beyond that, and I certainly don't have room in mine for more than one geek!"

She was referring to Tom's figurine collection. Libbie liked that they'd reached the stage of shared in-jokes. It meant she'd got inside the barriers.

It was so much easier to destroy from within.

"So, Walter, are you working on the Mapleview account, too?"

He shook his head, clearly relieved to be on safer ground again. "Oh no," he said. "I'm just a back-room kind of a guy. Alice here is the high-flying superstar."

"Oh, Walter."

The look between them, the connection, the easy exchange of praise and false modesty. How amusing!

"Oh, you two," said Libbie. "Are you *sure* you two aren't more than just colleagues? I mean Tom's nice, but talk about chemistry!"

She kept her tone light and laughed carelessly at the end, just to be sure they knew she was joking. They both laughed in response, which was good. She loved planting seeds on such fertile ground.

"Really, no," said Alice, but Walter had briefly opened his mouth to say something first of all.

Libbie fixed him with a look and waited, knowing a guy like him would have to fill such an awkward silence.

"Well," he started before Alice stepped in to rescue him.

"We went out a couple of times," she said, chuckling. Briefly, she squeezed his arm before letting go again. The two really were good together. "Way back. Long before I got with Tom, and Tom knows all about it. He teases Walter about the one that got away every time they see each other. The running joke is that it's never clear whether he means I was the one who got away, or that Walter had a narrow escape."

Libbie laughed dutifully. *God*, these people were easily

amused.

"You kissed! Please tell me you kissed."

They all laughed again.

"It wasn't a success," said Alice. "Oh, don't look at me like that, Walter. You were there too!"

He shrugged. "I guess we found out we're more like brother and sister than anything like that," he said.

"Listen, we're going to be late for our class," said Alice. "Catch you later, Walter? Thanks for your help this morning."

Soon the two of them were in Libbie's Toyota heading across town.

"Walter was helping you?" asked Libbie. "I thought he wasn't on the Mapleview pitch?"

"Not officially, but he's my go-to sanity check. I'm always running things past him."

Libbie smiled and said nothing, storing all this up.

"Look, I'm sorry I was late just now. This Mapleview pitch is swallowing up my time. It's the biggest deal I've ever worked on and they've made me the lead. The company has millions at stake. It's make or break, literally."

"For the company, or you?"

"Both. I have a shot at vice president if this goes well."

"Heady stuff."

"It really is."

They pulled up at the yoga studio a short time later, a

squat square industrial-looking building in a row of similar commercial units.

Libbie looked across at her passenger. "You're not feeling this, are you?"

Alice had been so *polite* about this, right from when Libbie had first mentioned it last night. She clearly hated the thought, though. It was tempting to pretend not to notice and make her go through with it. The thought of an hour watching her trying and failing the simplest positions was funny beyond belief.

But sometimes it was better to build bonds.

Libbie leaned closer. "You want to know a secret? I hate it too, even though I know it's good for me. I never was much of a gym bunny. All those sweaty women..."

"In sweaty yoga pants..."

"Whoever looked good in yoga pants?"

"Not me."

"There's a place two doors down," Libbie said conspiratorially. "Wholefood. Mostly vegan. I imagine they'd have plenty of options suitable for you. I still feel bad about that cheesecake."

"Oh, don't! You saw the look on Tom's face. He loved it."

She had seen that look. It had been almost as funny as the look on his face when he'd stood gaping out of the window the night before.

But she didn't say that. Sometimes bonding was so much more valuable than easy victories, no matter how much fun.

~ ~ ~ ~

It was funny spending time with Libbie alone. The dynamic was different to when it was the three of them, and it was undeniable Tom added a different tension to the mix.

Today, Libbie seemed more relaxed. Teasing Alice about Walter. Reading her well enough to spot that Alice really had no desire to spend her lunchbreak doing yoga with a group of sweaty strangers.

And she was being so sensitive about the food! Alice could have assured her it was fine. Knowing that the combination of skipping a meal and exercising might tip the balance, she'd checked her blood before coming out, so she knew everything was good. But she hadn't wanted to risk either patronizing her, or making her feel she was being educated on the subject, so she'd let it pass. This organic place wasn't at all bad, in any case.

They sat at a table on the terrace outside. The weather was still fine for this late in the year. Who'd have expected to be eating outside so close to Halloween?

At one point, she caught herself smiling fondly at her new friend. They really had bonded today.

"What is it?" asked Libbie. She'd spotted the look.

"Oh, I don't know. Sometimes you get so carried away with life you forget what the simple pleasures are like. Things like this. The sunshine, having lunch with a friend."

Libbie smiled shyly at that.

"So what's your story? Why the fresh start in a town

you don't know?" Libbie looked suddenly defensive, so Alice rushed to add, "Please, don't tell me if you prefer not to. I wasn't being nosy. I just wanted to get to know you a bit."

"No, that's fine." Libbie smiled again. "Small town like this. Stranger comes along. I get it. It's not so exciting, though. I grew up in the Big Apple with folks who bounced around from job to job, apartment to apartment. Soon it was just me and my mom, and then... well. Foster care isn't exactly all it's made up to be, and it's not made up to be very much."

Alice felt a heavy wave of sympathy for the girl. She was probably not much younger than Alice, but right now she seemed young and fragile, a true waif. It was easy to fill in the gaps in her story. An orphan—at what young age?

Such a harsh way for a kid to grow up.

"That sounds... tough."

Libbie smiled. "It *makes* you tough. You learn to stand up for yourself. To give as good as you get. Some of the things you have to deal with..."

Alice hated to think just what kind of things Libbie was referring to. She'd read the stories, seen the documentaries. It was an entirely different world from the privileged one she herself had grown up in. Right now, she felt a little bit nauseous, and it wasn't a blood sugar thing.

"You went to NYU?" she said, probably a little too brightly.

"I worked my way up. I guess my childhood was character-building. You could say all the knocks made me who I am today. I stood up for myself, got out of the system as soon as I could. Worked my way through odd jobs around the city, just like my folks had. And yes, somehow managed to scrape my way into NYU and pull myself up by my bootstraps."

"Listen, you want to see something really exciting? Tom and I have an investment property on Whitetail Lane. That's just the other side of downtown from here. Why don't we swing by there on the way back and I could show you around?"

Libbie looked genuinely impressed at this. "I can't wait to see what you're doing with the place. You've made such a lovely job of your own house, and my apartment. If you want, maybe I can take some pictures of the work in progress for you? I have my kit in the car. It'd be nice to get some photos of you there."

"That'd be great. And when the place is finished and we've decided whether to sell or rent it, maybe you could take some more for us? A paid job, obviously. It'd be good to get a professional in and show it to its best potential."

"I'd love to."

Only a short time later they were on site. Franco Vialli and his crew were sitting out back in the sun with their lunch when they arrived. Immediately, he leaped to his feet and insisted they'd been working flat out all morning and this was the first time they'd stopped.

Alice laughed at his fiery show of defensiveness and assured him she wasn't spying on him. Even as this was happening, Libbie had her big Nikon out and was taking pictures of the exchange.

"You want to see the place? Come on, let me show you around."

She took Libbie's arm and led her into the building, mindful of Franco's warnings about all the dangers of roaming around a live construction site.

All of a sudden, they were like two schoolgirls on an adventure. Alice hadn't had so much fun in a long time. And it felt good to be showing this place off to Libbie. It made her see it all as if for the first time, and that was exhilarating.

"This really is impressive," said Libbie, Alice's excitement mirrored in her eyes. "You must be thrilled with it all. I couldn't quite imagine doing something like this. Such a big investment. Such a big risk for you and Tom to take! I could never imagine trusting a guy to anywhere near that extent. That's so special."

Libbie smiled.

It was. Special. The trust they had.

The trust they had everything staked on right now…

CHAPTER 13

Libbie pulled up outside the Granger residence. She couldn't get that smile off her face. She was having such fun!

She reached for the camera and flicked through the photos she'd taken today. Pictures of Alice with the dark horse Walter. She was pleased. She'd captured that look between the two of them. She could do a lot with a photo like that.

And pictures from the investment property.

Alice flirting with the Italian construction site manager.

Alice in the half-built kitchen. Alice in the den. Alice in the master bedroom.

Alice, Alice, *Alice.*

She was glad she'd taken the trouble to invest in some decent camera gear before coming here. She'd never used anything more than an iPhone for snaps before this and hadn't known one end of a DSLR from another. It was amazing what you could learn from YouTube, though.

She'd put together a good—and convincing — portfolio, too. All compiled from Google Images and a few good stock photo sites.

She was nothing if not methodical and thorough.

As she sat there, rain started to spot on the windshield. About to make a dash for her apartment, she paused.

She'd seen movement at the far side of the house. Tom. Every inch the dull suburban drone trying to look cool in his black skinny jeans and mid-brown, tastefully distressed leather jacket. He had a half-shell motorcycle helmet tucked under one arm while he stuffed an envelope into an inside pocket with his free hand.

"Hey," Libbie called, getting out of the car and not minding the rain at all now. "Going somewhere?"

He jumped. Why did he always look so guilty when caught unawares?

"Oh, hi there. Just heading downtown. Need to take care of some paperwork at the bank."

"I thought all that was online these days."

"They need signatures." He shrugged.

Libbie looked up at the heavy gray sky and held a hand out, palm up. "Listen, do you want a ride? I'm heading into town anyway. I have some things to do, too. I don't imagine it's much fun riding that Kawasaki of yours in this kind of weather."

Let him wonder how she knew what kind of bike he rode. It was always good to sow a few seeds of curiosity.

"Come on," she pleaded in a lighthearted tone. "It's nice to talk to people. I don't know many people here yet."

He was too polite to say no. Of course he was. That, and he clearly enjoyed her company.

After he'd put his helmet away, he climbed in beside her. She smiled, and paused, letting the moment draw itself out just a fraction longer than was comfortable.

He looked at her, looked away, looked back again.

"How was yoga?" he asked, grasping for conversation.

She fired the Toyota's engine and laughed. "Oh, *yoga*," she said, drawing air quotes around the word with the first two fingers of each hand. "We didn't quite make it to yoga. Not really Alice's thing."

Tom laughed. "I was surprised she said yes last night."

"She was just being polite. You two are too sweet. You've been so kind to me. We got as far as sitting outside the yoga studio then went for lunch instead."

Tom laughed again. "No cheesecake, I hope."

He was teasing her. That was good. It meant he was relaxing.

"No cheesecake! We went to a wholefood place. All organic lettuce. And more organic lettuce. I'm sure Alice thinks I need to diet." She took one hand off the wheel and ran it down the curves of her body.

"Oh, she wouldn't mean anything by that!" Tom assured her.

She smiled and he blushed. They both knew he'd been looking as she ran that hand down her body. This was going well.

"We came by your investment property after lunch. That is such a cool place! You must be really excited. I told Alice how impressed I was. I could never imagine taking on that kind of financial risk with another person.

You must have staked everything on it."

"And *then* some," said Tom.

"Things must be very tight." Of course they were. Nobody rented out their basement for laughs. And she'd flicked through some of the bills in the letter rack in their kitchen.

"Oh yeah."

"So much must depend on Alice."

She saw a tensing of the muscles in his jaw. No other response than that. A sensitive point, then. The fragile pride of a kept man.

"It's good you two are so close." She kept her voice light. "That's so sweet to see."

~ ~ ~ ~

He couldn't work her out. She really was the perfect tenant. Friendly. Helpful. Considerate.

She was easy to be with, easy to talk to. And then, every so often, she would say something in all innocence that triggered Tom's deepest fears.

Yes, the investment place was a huge financial burden and risk. He and Alice had debated it at length before committing. In truth, Tom would have been far happier consolidating efforts on their own place rather than taking on a new risk, but Alice had convinced him, as she always would.

And now...

"When I picked Alice up she was with a guy. Laughing

and fooling with him. She really is such a friendly person, isn't she? She could get on with just about anybody. If I didn't know that of her I'd have been sure they were a couple!"

"A guy?" His mind was racing.

"Hm. Good-looking, in an off-beat kind of a way. Name was Wilbur or Walter or something."

"Oh, Walter!" He relaxed a little. "We've known Walter for years."

"That's nice. That explains why they were so easy with each other. Alice said they've been spending a lot of time together lately. That big account she's chasing. Walter's not officially on that one, but apparently he's been going out of his way to help her with it. I thought that was really good of him."

It was.

Of course it was good of him. Walter was that kind of a guy.

Nothing was too much trouble for Walter. Particularly where Alice was concerned.

Tom glanced across at Libbie. She was concentrating on her driving, clearly oblivious to the seeds she'd sown.

He cursed himself for thinking this way.

For doubting his wife.

Libbie was right. He and Libbie had committed to a lot together. It was stupid to start doubting things now.

"How about I treat you to coffee and a donut?" asked Libbie, as she pulled up into a parking space. "I know you don't get to satisfy your sweet tooth too often at home."

"Oh, I couldn't. I just need to do the bank thing and then head home. Really. Thanks for the ride. I'll be fine from here."

"I insist. You guys have been so kind."

He hesitated, his hand on the door handle.

A few minutes later, they sat in a coffee shop, rain streaming down the windows.

"I bet you're glad you didn't come on the bike."

He nodded and took another bite of his donut.

"I hadn't imagined you on a motorcycle, but that jacket and helmet kind of suited you. I bet you look at home in the saddle."

"Oh, I don't know. It's just a way of getting from A to B."

"Said no guy ever when he's talking about bikes!"

He felt flattered by the attention, and with a flash of guilt he realized he was enjoying the novelty of being with someone new. Since making the shift to homeworking, he didn't really get out much at all.

He looked up from his coffee. She was studying him, a strange look on her face. Intense.

"I like this," she said.

He took a sip. Swallowed.

"Being out with a guy again. Maybe I should consider dating again."

He allowed himself to breathe. At first, he'd thought she was actually hitting on him, but then last comment made clear that she was talking in generalities.

She enjoyed the *concept* of being in the presence of a guy. Not this particular guy. And she was thinking in terms of dating *someone*, not focusing her attentions on Tom.

"What about that guy the other night? Doesn't that count?"

She tutted at him disapprovingly. "That was a one-off. An aberration. I told you to put that out of your mind." She paused to moisten her lips. "Looks like you found that hard to do."

"I..." At first he thought she was cross with him, but now realized that, of course, she was teasing him.

He recalled hearing a horn outside, looking out and seeing her lit by the streetlights. Her dress pulled down. That guy's hands on her.

"You're seeing it now, aren't you? I'm shocked."

He didn't know what to say.

Then she laughed and reached out to put a hand briefly on his forearm. "I'm only kidding, Tom. Covering my embarrassment, I guess. Don't think anything of it, please. Listen, you go and do your bank business and I'll meet you back at the car when you're done. And I promise not to remind you about what you saw that night."

And then she winked, stood, ran her hands down her waist and hips to smooth her clothing and turned to walk out of the coffee shop.

She was a bit like a force of nature, Tom decided. She blew into your life, turned things upside down and then left you wondering exactly what you'd just encountered.

Storm Libbie.

He was smiling, though. A storm that was a breath of fresh air, perhaps.

He knew Alice felt the same. It was nice that the two had been for lunch and got to know each other a bit.

He crossed the street and went into the bank.

He didn't believe Libbie had things to do in town. She was just giving him a ride to be helpful.

Slowly, the queue edged forward.

It was a shame he hadn't gotten to ride the bike today. He'd been looking forward to it. But Libbie had been right, the rain had come down hard as they drove in.

He reached the front.

"And how may I help you today, sir?" asked the clerk.

"Hi there. I just had some paperwork to drop off. I believe it required signature in the presence of bank staff." As he spoke he fumbled in the inside pocket of his leather jacket.

Funny. The pocket was empty.

He was sure he recalled slipping the envelope with the paperwork in there. Had he missed the pocket and the letter dropped to the ground? If so, it was no doubt lying in a sodden mass in a puddle back at home.

"Sorry, I…" He checked the other inside pocket. Nothing.

Behind him he heard angry mutterings. People impatient not to spend what remained of their lunchbreak standing in line in a bank.

He smiled apologetically in answer to the woman's

impatient look. Checked the pockets of his jeans. The outside pockets of his jacket.

Still nothing.

"I'm sorry. I was sure I'd brought it with me."

He checked the inside pockets again.

"Excuse me, but are you going to be here all day?" That was the woman behind him in the queue. Looked like a librarian. Voice like a trucker.

He smiled at her again.

"I…" He felt panic welling up in his chest. Something as simple as this and he'd screwed up! One simple form. One damn signature.

What was Alice going to say? They'd have to complete the form again. Bring it in another day. Explain to Franco why payment was delayed and hope that wasn't going to cause a problem.

"Well?"

This time he snapped an angry glare at the woman and she shrank back, then turned to the guy behind her, muttering angrily.

"Sir? If there's nothing I can help you with right now, I'm going to have to suggest—"

He shook his head and stalked off, not waiting for the clerk to finish his sentence.

What had he done with the form? How could he have been so careless?

~ ~ ~ ~

Outside, Libbie sat in the car, smiling to herself about how successful today had been.

And now there was Tom, striding back toward her as if impatient to be in her company again. How sweet.

He opened the door and leaned in, eyes searching the car's interior.

"I don't suppose..." he began, then started again. "You didn't see an envelope in here, did you? Might have fallen out of my pocket."

"An envelope? Why no, I'm sorry. Was it important?"

"No. No, not really. I can deal with it another time. No sweat." He smiled wanly and she saw just how hard it must be for him to force that smile.

"You good to go now, or was there anything else?" she asked.

"No. All good. Let's get out of here."

"Let me just get rid of the trash," she said, indicating her empty coffee cup with its plastic lid, sitting on the car's dashboard.

She stepped out of the car, breathing deep. A shaft of sunshine burst through the clouds as she moved over to a trash can and deposited the cup. The paper cup, and its plastic lid concealing the ripped-up remains of an envelope containing an Authorization to Transfer Funds form.

She was going to break these people. Slowly, step by step.

Then she turned back to the car and Tom forced another pained smile.

The day was just getting better and better.

CHAPTER 14

By evening, that little escape with Libbie seemed so long ago to Alice. Sneaking away from the office for lunch, and then the little adventure as they detoured so she could show off the Whitetail Lane property. Such a release!

But now…

Sitting in the big easy chair in the den, trying to ignore the sound of the TV. Struggling to concentrate.

She'd shown Michael Tuckett a draft of her pitch for the Mapleview account and he hadn't been impressed.

She'd thought it was coming together nicely, but he'd torn it to shreds.

"Those charts and graphics look pretty," he said, "but anyone can see it's just window-dressing. The figures are cosmetic and unsubstantiated. You're telling the story you think your audience wants to hear rather than telling them what you *need* them to hear. There's a difference. Or didn't they teach you that in business school?"

That had stung and he'd known it had as soon as he said it, from the look on his face. Tom had been a favorite of Tuckett's. He'd started at ground level and worked his way up, and Michael had taken him under his wing. The older man had always said he saw something of himself in Tom, a young man made good.

Which was in complete contrast to Alice, who'd joined the company at a higher level, straight from business school.

The subtext behind Michael's criticism was that if only Tom hadn't blown it at Pierson Newport, he'd have done a far better job on this bid than Alice had.

Or maybe that was only what *Alice* heard in his criticism. She knew she shouldn't take it personally. He was just trying to get the best outcome possible for the company. And he was right. She'd only shown Michael a draft and she'd known it needed work. She should have waited until it was as good as she could make it before showing him.

And so now she was sitting at home, still working on the document, while Tom watched something mindless on TV.

She'd wanted to talk to him about it, but when she got home he'd seemed distracted. Focused on cooking, and not open to conversation.

Even when they'd broken to eat, he'd seemed closed in.

Maybe that was her, too, though. Maybe *she* was really the one who didn't want to talk. Didn't want to admit to herself that even after a year out Tom might have something to bring to the pitch that she couldn't offer.

So instead of sitting at the table to eat, which was their normal time to catch up with each other's days, they'd filled plates and eaten in front of the TV. And now Alice sat staring at her screen, wishing she wasn't so bone-weary all of a sudden.

She needed to focus, damn it!

She needed to get this *right*.

"Sweetie? You interruptible?"

She hated that. What if the answer was no? She'd already been interrupted!

"Sorry. Later."

"No. It's fine, honey. What is it?"

He'd moved from the far end of the couch to sit nearer to her, leaning forward with his hands gripped between his knees.

"I went to the bank today."

And this was supposed to be news? She bit back on that response. She was tired and irritable, she knew. That wasn't his fault, it was her.

"Yes, hon'?"

"Those papers. I couldn't find them."

"So why did you go to the bank?"

That was her first response: logic, trying to work out why he would go to the bank if he didn't even have the papers. Then: he hadn't *done* it! One simple job and—

"No, I *had* them. I'm sure I had them. But when I got there… Well, I didn't anymore. I could've sworn they were in that envelope you left on the console table by the door. You did put them in there, didn't you? You didn't take them with you by mistake? You were the one who'd originally been going to the bank."

"You're saying it was *my* fault? You didn't check the envelope. Are you telling me you took an empty envelope all the way to the bank?"

"No! I mean… I don't know what I mean. I'm just trying to work it out. I was sure I'd taken that envelope, and the papers were inside it. I don't know what happened."

It took so much effort not to be angry with him. Not to let her wellhead of frustration burst out across him. But she knew that wouldn't be fair. She took a deep breath.

"Right, let's work through this together. Do you remember picking up the papers?"

He nodded. "I did. In the envelope. I checked they were inside."

"And you put them… where?"

"My inside jacket pocket."

"They couldn't have fallen out?"

A shake of the head. "I remember checking them again, to make sure they were secure."

"And when did you check them again?"

"In the bank, I think. When I went to hand them over to the clerk."

"Could they have fallen out on the way? When you were on your bike?"

He looked briefly sheepish, then shook his head again. "No. They were secure. I just can't work it out. They *must* have fallen out somewhere."

Alice sighed. She could hardly work it out *for* him.

He was staring. He'd noticed the sigh. It had been

hard to miss. And now he thought she was judging him, which she was.

One simple task…

"I don't know what you expect from me, Tom," she said, letting some of the frustration come out in her tone. And the tiredness.

Was she supposed to do everything herself?

"I'll get another form."

"You didn't even pick up another form when you were there?"

"I was confused! I didn't know what to think, everything happened so fast!"

He had no right to be getting angry with *her*. She wasn't the one who'd screwed up. And he hadn't even picked up another form.

"Really, Tom. I don't know what to say. Don't worry, though. I'll do it myself. I'll call Franco to apologize and I'll take time out from work to get another damn form and I'll stand in line at the bank when I have a million and one more pressing things to be doing, and…"

She sensed a darkening at the edges of her vision. A flush of heat across her cheeks and forehead.

She knew what it was immediately, and from the look on Tom's face he'd read the signs too.

When had she last checked her blood sugar? She couldn't remember. She knew she needed glucose now, though.

"You just sit there, sweetie. I'll get your stuff."

"No. Don't bother. You've done enough today." She stood unsteadily and waited for her head to stop spinning. "I'll do it myself."

She found her bag on the console table by the door, and rummaged inside it as she headed to the bathroom.

For a mad moment, she imagined pulling that missing envelope out of her bag, but she knew that wasn't possible. She hadn't taken it with her. It wasn't her *fault*.

She almost didn't make it. Her head was swirling, her vision blurring. But stubborn determination not to have to rely on Tom in the middle of a row carried her through.

She pushed the door shut then went to wash her hands. Breathing deep, she steadied herself before finding a glucose tablet and swallowing it whole. It was the fifteen-fifteen rule. She needed fifteen grams of carbohydrate to raise her blood glucose and then wait fifteen minutes to see if she was back to normal.

It was a thing she'd done a million times. A thing Tom had done for her. A part of her life. *Their* life.

She sat on the edge of the bath, waiting for her vision to clear and her dizziness to ease.

She wouldn't admit to herself that she didn't really want to go back out there now.

That she didn't know how to pick up again after a row like that.

Was it her fault? His?

She knew the bank thing was his fault, of course, but the row itself?

It would be easy to say it was a hypo thing. When you were a diabetic, you could blame blood sugars for just about anything and nobody would dare contradict you.

Above anything else, she was disappointed in Tom. One simple thing. That's all she asked.

She was working so hard to keep them afloat, and he couldn't manage one simple thing?

She'd thought they were strong. A team. But a team was only ever as strong as its weakest member. She hated herself for even thinking that. And hated that circumstances had led her to think it.

She couldn't do all this again. Not now. Not ever.

She couldn't face another year like last year.

Another *incident* like last year's.

She didn't think she could stand it.

And she knew their marriage couldn't.

CHAPTER 15

Never go to bed on an argument. That was the one piece of life advice his pop had given him.

The old man's words had kept coming back to Tom that night, as he lay by Alice in the darkness. Her back was turned to him, a gap between them. They'd mumbled goodnights, but no kisses, no contact.

He'd been concerned about her. The blood sugar thing. It wasn't like her to screw up like that, but she'd done it a few times recently. The stress of work, he supposed.

And he was hardly helping things with his forgetfulness.

He must have slept eventually, because when he awoke daylight was streaming in through the gap in the curtains and he was alone in the bed.

When he went downstairs, Alice was taking trouble to busy herself at the coffee machine.

How long was she going to be mad at him?

"Hey," she said, twisting and smiling awkwardly.

"Hey, sweetie."

"You sleep?"

"Not much. You?"

"Probably about the same."

"I'm sorry, sweetie. I messed up. I shouldn't have tried to blame you."

"*I'm* sorry. I was unfair to you."

"Your blood sugar…"

She shook her head. "No. We can't blame that. I've been unfair to you a lot lately. I've been tired. Stressed. Over-reliant on you."

"I've been worried about you. That you might be over-doing it."

"I don't want work to come between us."

"Hey, you promised me business-class! Don't try backing out now." He winked. Smiled. He always knew he could win her over with a wink and a smile.

"You want to haul your ass over here so I can show you I'm sorry?"

Tom paused, as if weighing up the offer, and she looked around for something to throw at him. All she found was a dishtowel, and by the time it was mid-air and heading in his direction, he was halfway to her.

He swiped the towel out of the air and then he had her in his arms. It felt so damned good!

They kissed and he lifted her back up so that she was half-sitting on the kitchen unit. The kiss lasted. He wasn't going to let go of this moment in a hurry.

Eventually, he leaned back, still holding her, and said, "So just how sorry *are* you?"

She laughed and pushed at his chest. "I have to get to the office. I'm running late already."

He gave her his best kicked-puppy expression and she laughed again.

"Maybe later," she said. "We need to make more time for each other, don't we?"

"We do." He kissed her again and it felt like the old days.

"And don't worry," he added. "I'll call Franco and explain. He won't be as sympathetic to me as he would to you, but I'll take it on the chin. My fault. My responsibility. And I'll go to the bank again."

"I love you."

"Damn right you do. Now get that gorgeous ass in to work and earn me business-class, you hear?"

She laughed and wriggled free, and as she squeezed past him he slapped that gorgeous ass just because it was there and it was so utterly perfect. Suddenly, everything was right with the world again.

He took a coffee upstairs to the guest bedroom, which he used as an office. Once he'd flipped open the laptop, he checked his inbox. The job he'd been expecting had come in overnight, so he reached for his Bluetooth headphones, ready to start work.

It was dull stuff, mostly transcribing long legal reports from bad recordings, but it kept him busy and paid at least a little toward the mounting bills.

Best of all, it was low-stress and low on responsibilities. The work came in, he did it and checked it through, and then he sent it off again. Lives didn't depend on it. Businesses weren't made or broken on the back of choices he made about the words he'd heard or misheard, and how to punctuate them.

Minimum wage. Minimum responsibility. It wasn't perfect, but it suited him just fine right now.

It was safe and steady.

Just like Tom.

Or just how he wanted to be.

He lost track of time, working on automatic, so when the doorbell chimed he didn't notice it at first. Then the sound penetrated his cloud and he jumped in his seat, realizing he'd already heard that sound a couple of times and someone must really be wanting his attention.

He went downstairs, opened the door and found Libbie.

He smiled in greeting. He still couldn't work out how he could be simultaneously genuinely pleased to see someone and just a little on edge in her presence. That girl sure had a strange effect!

"Tom. I can call you Tom?"

"Of course you can. Only Alice calls me *sir*." The joke didn't sound right, but it was too late now.

"Listen, I hope you don't think I'm being cheeky, and please feel free to say no to me, but I have a commission this afternoon. I've just been to check it out and I think I need some help. I figured you're at home all day, so maybe you'd be interested in coming out and lending a hand? I could pay. Not much, but it's something. I know things are tight."

He was sure she didn't realize how comments like that hurt, the implication that he might do just about anything for a few dollars. It hurt because it wasn't far from the truth.

And he always hated when people thought that because he worked from home he wasn't really busy and could drop whatever he was doing at a moment's notice.

But the girl was new in town, and stuck, and this was one of her first commissions here, and…

"Sure," he said. "No problem. You don't have to pay me, though. Happy to help out."

"Oh, thank you so much!"

And before he knew it, she'd stepped forward and planted a brief, wet kiss on his cheek. "I'm so grateful!"

He shrugged, smiled, didn't know where to look, his cheek still burning.

It was like he'd thought when he opened the door and saw who was there. Libbie Burchett, like nobody else he'd known, could make you smile at the same time she made you painfully uncomfortable, but she never failed to make things at least interesting.

~ ~ ~ ~

That afternoon tested the balance between smiling and painful discomfort almost to breaking point.

"So what's the shoot?" Tom asked as they pulled up in Libbie's Toyota in the parking lot by the high school sports facility.

"Oh, some local kid. She wants to get into modeling

and she wanted some portfolio shots. Her parents are paying, and they might turn out to be good contacts, so I'm happy."

They gathered together Libbie's gear from the back of the car and walked around the corner of a building. The football team was going through their moves out on the field, all grunting and testosterone, and down in front of the bleachers about twenty cheerleaders were leaping and kicking.

"Funny," said Tom. "So many people say they wish they could go back, but can you imagine actually living through all this again? I'm so happy not to be a teenager."

Libbie squinted at him. "You can never escape it, though, can you? It stays with you wherever you go."

Tom grunted. He always felt uncomfortable visiting schools, all the memories triggered. He was very glad to have left all that behind. Getting older was good for something after all.

"So what's the plan?" he asked brightly.

"There she is," said Libbie, waving as one of the cheerleaders broke away from practice and came toward them.

"Hey, Marissa," said Tom.

"You know each other?"

"Marissa's a neighborhood kid," he said.

"Mr. Granger." The girl looked at him, then away again, that teen awkwardness. "Libbie. Thank you so much for this. I didn't realize Mr. Granger was helping. That's cool."

"Come on," said Libbie. "Let's head over this way. I want to get the other cheerleaders and the football practice in the background. Every guy's fantasy, isn't it? Sports and cheerleaders?"

She nudged Tom playfully as she said this. He didn't know what to say. It made him uncomfortable, particularly because Alice sometimes teased him about Marissa having a crush on him.

And there she was in her tiny cheerleader outfit, blonde hair in a long ponytail, bare arms, and mile-high legs.

She was sixteen. *Blossoming* would be the word.

He didn't think of her that way. He wasn't like that. But she'd reached the age where she pressed a lot of biological triggers.

Why had he come here?

"You okay, Tom?"

"Sure, sure." Had Libbie picked up some of his discomfort?

"So. Just give me a minute." Libbie squatted over her camera bag, taking out a swanky looking camera and fitting a lens. "You get that reflector there, Tom? See the one? Just unfold it and get in low. I want to bounce the light back up. Can you do that?"

Tom did as he was told, holding the reflector so it bounced light up from ground level, softening the shadows cast by the strong afternoon sunlight.

"That's it. Just go down a bit more, can you?"

He was aware of Libbie at his shoulder as he kneeled,

leaning in close to get the angle. And Marissa striking a pose, one leg held high.

"Less smile, okay? Think sexy. Try not to feel awkward. Remember you want to be a model, Marissa. So think of someone you like."

The kid looked straight at him.

Oh God, she looked at him!

"That's perfect, Marissa! Hold that thought. That perfect balance between innocence and desire."

Tom watched the footballers. Running at each other. Bouncing off each other.

"Hey, Tom. Just a bit closer. Just be careful where you're looking."

He couldn't remember feeling so uncomfortable. Ever.

He should tell her to stop. He was sure she was oblivious to his embarrassment. Just doing her job. The constant stream of chatter and wisecracks must all be part of a shoot like this. Putting people at their ease. Keeping their minds occupied.

He met Marissa's eye then and smiled awkwardly.

She smiled back. Awkward too. Shy.

"Perfect! That's the look I want. Knowing. Adult. And yet innocent."

Libbie was in closer now, her leg against his side making him very aware of her presence.

"That's perfect, isn't it, Tom? Now, Marissa, let's try something different. Try standing with your back to us. Then twist at the waist to look back, right into the camera. Give me that same look you had just now. And Tom: in close at the side, bouncing the light back into the side of her face. That's good. That's perfect. That's the one."

And so Tom did as he was asked, because he was too polite not to, and that painful discomfort was tested to its absolute limit.

CHAPTER 16

Rusty approached the Granger house later that afternoon. The weather was good for the time of year. Someone had said something about global warming, but he didn't know about that.

All he knew was that the sun was warm this afternoon. He liked to keep things simple in his head. Clear.

Like cutting grass. You do a good job. You get it just right. And then you do the same again a week later. You know what to expect with grass and flowers.

Not like people.

Maybe that's why he didn't have many friends, and rarely kept the ones he had for long. You never knew quite what to expect with people. The Grangers were different though.

Mrs. Granger was different.

She treated him kindly. She remembered things about him that other folk forgot. Mr. Granger, too. They were good folks.

He could earn more elsewhere, he knew. Uncle Rick always wanted people at his garage. Even the fast food places in the mall paid better rates, although he knew greasy food and the acne that still peppered his face were not a good combination. Money wasn't everything though.

Give him grass and flowers and trees any day. And the Grangers.

The Grangers got him, like other folks never did.

He liked it simple like that.

He did his usual round of the garden first of all. The Boston ivy growing over the shed needed trimming, but not at this time of year when the deep red coloration was so vivid. The grass needed cutting, although the growth was slowing now as fall progressed. The flowerbeds all needed attention. Dead-heading to keep the flowering going as long as possible. Cutting back the herbaceous perennials to ground level. Pruning and shaping the woody varieties. It was the time of year when suddenly there was a lot of work to do.

He knew the Grangers were too busy to manage it all, which was why he'd volunteered. Mrs. Granger with her high-flying job downtown. Mr. Granger so important he'd left a similar job to go freelance last year. They were good people to be around and he had the stupid hope that some of their success would rub off on him some day.

He came round to the side of the house where the paved path led to the door to the basement apartment where that new girl was living now.

He didn't know what to make of her. She was hot. There was no denying that. The kind of hot you stored up in your head for those quieter moments and then felt guilty about later.

But there was *something* about her.

Like when Marissa Sigley or her cheerleader friends spoke to you and you didn't know where to look or what to say. She had that about her.

The house was built so the basement was part below ground and part above, so the apartment benefited from a row of little windows at ground level. Rusty had never set foot in the place until that day he'd helped Libbie move in. It was nice. The kind of place he could imagine himself in one day. That big flatscreen. And the almost cave-like sense of isolation. Of shutting the noisy world away.

That would be cool.

Checking the flowerbeds by the house, he couldn't help but see in through those windows, triggering memories of that day.

When he saw movement inside, he was startled.

He hadn't known anyone was home. He felt guilty for snooping even if he hadn't been, not really.

But Libbie was down there in the den. Kneeling over something on the floor, her perfect ass pointing at him in a way that made him uncomfortable all over again.

She liked to wear her jeans tight. He'd noticed that about her before. Couldn't help but.

He couldn't quite see what she was doing. There were papers spread out on the floor. Pictures. Wasn't she supposed to be some kind of photographer?

He looked away. Bent over a clump of asters and picked at a few flower heads going to seed. You could keep these in bloom way past Halloween if you treated them right.

He tried to stop thinking of the new tenant. The way she'd been kneeling.

He moved along, looked in through the next window. Saw better what she was doing. Scratching at something with a small implement of some kind.

At a photograph.

Weird. Was that the kind of thing photographers did? Scraping at images to somehow make them better? He remembered seeing an old movie once where a guy had been in a darkroom, printing a picture from a big enlarger and shaping shadows with his hands to change how it printed. Rusty liked art and that image had stuck with him. That you could change things like that, just by shaping light.

That wasn't what she was doing, though. He could see better now. See that she was gouging viciously at a photograph.

At the face of the person photographed.

It was a repetitive, obsessive movement, as if it was somehow therapeutic. Like scratching at an itch, Rusty thought. And you'd carry on scratching even when it started to hurt. When it started to bleed.

That wasn't just anybody in the photograph.

You couldn't see the face any more, but the guy was wearing a white baseball jersey.

Mr. Granger was the only person Rusty knew who wore a white baseball jersey. His wife teased him about it whenever he wore it, but he still did.

If Mrs. Granger ever teased Rusty about something like that, he'd never wear it again.

The Grangers' tenant, Libbie, was scratching Tom Granger's face off that photograph. Scratching it so hard she must surely have gone through to the carpet by now.

Rusty struggled to understand what that might mean. Why would she do something like that? Did she hate him?

What kind of a person would do that?

Rusty backed away from the window, careful now not to pass across in front of it in case she saw him.

But what he hadn't worked out was that in doing so he passed in front of the sun. He only saw too late, when his shadow passed across the floor, right by where Libbie kneeled.

Still, he thought he'd gotten away with it.

Then he saw her body tense, her head turn.

He didn't dare move, because he understood enough about physics to know his shadow would move too.

So when Libbie spun and peered out of the window into the sunlight, her eyes narrowing in the glare, he was standing right there in full view.

~ ~ ~ ~

He waited what felt like several long seconds until she looked away again, then half-walked and half-ran away from the house.

She might not have seen him. And if she had, she might not have recognized him.

They'd only met that one time, after all. Rusty knew he

wasn't exactly the kind of guy that stuck in folks' minds. A wallpaper kind of a guy, his mom had called it, although she'd been talking about someone else when she said that.

He went to the shed and let himself in. Closed the door and leaned against it.

He'd cut the grass. Lose himself in the noise of the mower. Try to forget the world. *Her*.

He went to the mower, checked it over. He kept the motor in good shape. He was good with engines. Uncle Rick had taught him lots. That was why he kept saying he should work at the garage with him.

The smell of engine oil was soothing. The way it mixed with the smell of old grass cuttings. Nothing else smelled quite like that.

He didn't know if he heard the sound of the shed door first, or was blinded by the bright sunlight as it swung open. Maybe they were both at the same time. And he didn't know why he was worrying about that when *she* was there. Standing in the doorway, like a cut-out silhouette.

"Rusty," she said.

So she *did* remember him.

"I never did thank you properly for helping with the move."

He was confused. Had expected her to be angry, not nice. Not... that tone to her voice. That special kind of nice.

"It was nothing," he stuttered. "Jus' bein' neighborly."

"I like that."

She took a step so she stood just inside the shed. Suddenly the place seemed smaller.

"All this work you do," she went on. "It must make you so *strong*. I bet the girls love that."

He swallowed. Nobody ever spoke to him like this. Not in real life.

She said nothing more and so he felt he had to say something to fill the silence. "I don't know about that."

Another step.

She was hot. Scary, too. He didn't understand that. Didn't understand how it made him feel.

He swallowed again.

He didn't want to be here.

He wanted to run.

"Listen," she finally continued. "Was that you I saw outside my window just now? Don't worry if it was. It's just... I was working on a secret project. Did you see what it was?"

What should he say?

He shook his head, then shrugged. "I didn't see anything," he said. "I was fixing the flowers. And that sun... it's bright." He remembered her squinting. She'd believe that.

"I don't want anyone to know about my project just yet. It's a surprise. It's art."

Art. He understood photography. And he understood painting things so they looked like the real deal. But there was a whole lot of other stuff folks called art that left him way behind.

Was that what she'd been doing? Art?

He wanted to believe her. Things were simpler that way, and he liked that.

But he'd wanted to believe that when she'd come into the shed just now and started talking in that way that nobody had ever spoken to him before... well, he'd wanted to believe that too, but he didn't.

"I guess," he said. He hoped she was convinced by that.

He just wanted her to go. He wanted to be alone in this shed with the smells of engine oil and old grass clippings, and nothing more complicated than that.

"Do you promise not to say anything? You'd hate to spoil the surprise, wouldn't you?"

"I guess." Again, as if they were the only words he had left.

"Because if you do spoil the surprise you'll be in a lot of trouble, Rusty. Do you understand that? You'll make Alice sad and she'll never want to speak to you again. You're lucky she talks to you at all, kid like you, but if you make her upset she'll hate you. Downright hate you."

"I guess." He understood that. She wasn't being nice to him at all. She'd only been pretending when she came here. She didn't *like* him.

For a moment, he closed his eyes and visualized what he'd seen. Her kneeling. That repetitive movement as she gouged at the picture. Then he opened his eyes again and saw her still studying him. He didn't know what he'd seen. Didn't understand what she'd been doing.

Art. Whatever.

They weren't things he understood.

He glanced at the mower and said, "I have to get going."

Keep it simple. Do his job and leave.

Don't get involved in what you can't figure out.

Just carry on and hope the mad woman leaves you alone.

CHAPTER 17

The house was in darkness, apart from the glow from the big flatscreen. Tom sat on the deep leather sofa, Alice beside him, turned so her feet were in his lap.

"You feeling relaxed now?" he asked, rubbing gently with both thumbs at the arch of one foot.

"I'd be feeling a lot more relaxed if you didn't keep asking me," she said, poking him in the ribs.

She wore sweatpants and one of his t-shirts. She said she felt like a hobo, but he knew she was comfortable dressed down like this. He thought she looked just great.

"How was your day?" she asked.

The TV was on a talk show. Something they rarely watched, but getting Alice just to stop was such a rarity these days, he'd found whatever TV show she'd shown a hint of enthusiasm for and settled for that.

"Oh, you know," he said. "Transcription's hardly gripping work, but it keeps me in hookers and cocaine."

She slapped at him. It was an old joke, and a sensitive one, given how little his transcription fees would ever actually pay for.

"I sorted out the bank stuff," he told her. "Then I called in on Franco and groveled. I said I'd see if Rusty wanted to go and help out. They could use some extra hands."

"That's good. Rusty's a sweet kid and he needs the income. Thank you for that."

Alice seemed a bit distracted tonight. He thought it was because she'd rather be working. He'd insisted she needed to unwind, and maybe because of their conversation this morning she'd acquiesced. She was the one who'd said they needed more couple time and she'd confessed that she found it hard to relax.

He switched to her other foot and was pleased when she let out a long groan of release. He could feel the tension slipping away from her.

"That good, sweetie?"

"Hmmm."

The doorbell went and Tom cussed under his breath. That thing seemed to be going all the time now, and it always seemed to be their perfect tenant.

Maybe she needed to back off a little. She was starting to come across as a bit needy. Especially when he had his gorgeous wife's legs in his lap and she was clearly enjoying so much the way he rubbed at her feet and up around the ankles.

"I'll get it," Alice said. Perhaps she'd sensed his instant tensing at the sound of the bell.

He started to object, but she'd already swung her legs clear and was standing.

"Get rid of them," he told her. "Whoever it is. I was just about to start working my way up."

"I could tell."

He'd been right. It was Libbie, again.

He heard the voices, liking the way Alice seemed to perk up when she saw who it was. He tried to tune it out, but then he heard the name *Marissa* and immediately listened more closely.

"…just came by to thank Tom for how good he was at Marissa's shoot today."

"Shoot? He hasn't told me about that part of his day yet."

Laughter, then: "Marissa Sigley. Her parents hired me to help her with her portfolio. She's interested in modeling. She's a natural. She was really good. Although I must say I was a bit shocked at how, well, *suggestive* she wanted to get. I've never done that kind of glamour stuff before, if you know what I mean. I know guys have a cheerleader thing, but…"

"And Tom helped you with the shoot?"

"Oh yes, he was great. It really helped that there was someone there who Marissa knew. He really helped her relax and let go of her inhibitions. Not that she had many of those!"

Tom was cursing himself again. He'd been going to tell Alice about the afternoon. He just hadn't gotten that far in his account of the day yet. He hadn't been hiding anything, but now she'd think…

"Did the pictures come out well?"

"Yes, I think so. I'll show you them sometime, if you like? And Tom, too, if you think he'd like to see them?"

"Maybe not tonight."

"That's good. Anyhow, I just wanted to thank him. Would it be okay if I had a quick word?"

Moments later the two appeared in the den. Tom couldn't work out the look on Alice's face. He wasn't sure he wanted to.

"It's Libbie," she said. "I'll leave you to it."

"Sorry," said Libbie, as the door closed. "I just wanted to thank you again for this afternoon."

"That's fine," said Tom. "You're welcome."

There was something a bit odd about her tonight and he soon found out why.

"I just wanted to ask…" she said, hesitating. "Rusty. He has a thing for Alice, doesn't he? Has he ever tried anything, you know, *rough?*"

She was back on that again. She was the one who'd warned them about the dangers of adolescent crushes. If anything, *she* was the one who appeared obsessed. But then what she said next stopped Tom in his tracks.

"He… He made a pass at me today."

"What?!"

"After we'd gotten back from the shoot. You went out again, so I was all alone, and he was there staring through my window. When I went out to confront him, he got strange with me."

"What do you mean by strange?"

"He kind of reared up over me. He's a big kid. Strong. All of a sudden I was very aware that I was alone with him."

"Did he do anything?"

"No. No, nothing like that. He just kind of stared at me as if he wanted me to know I was at his mercy. Then... then he told me he liked me. It sounds stupid when I say it out loud like that, but he said it in a *way*. It scared me. Then he just stood there while I backed away. When I got into my apartment I locked the door, but when I looked out the window he was still standing there, smiling."

"You want me to have a word with him?"

"No, please don't! It sounds stupid now I've said it out loud. I was just scared. I'd hate to think he'd done anything like that to Alice, too. I just wanted you to know, that's all."

Just then Alice reappeared. Libbie made her excuses and rapidly left.

"Well that was odd," said Alice, coming back to join Tom on the couch. "Were you going to tell me about your little erotic photo shoot?"

"It wasn't like that!" Tom protested. "And I was just about to tell you when she showed up."

"Yeah, yeah. You say that now that your sordid little secret's out."

She was joking about it, he knew, but it was all coming out wrong. He didn't like being out of control like this. Stuff going on, so much he felt he had to chase just to keep up.

"You need to learn to say no to people," Alice said. "You're way too nice sometimes."

"It's just one of those things," he said. "Libbie asked for help. I didn't quite know what it was going to be. It was a bit weird, to tell the truth. The kid's only sixteen, you know. The photos were all pretty tame, but still…"

Later, in bed, Alice brought it up again.

They were just snuggling down. Tom had looped a long arm around her and was thinking about where they'd left off earlier, when the doorbell had rung. He was just nuzzling into the side of her neck, when she said, "So is it true? What Libbie said? That all guys have a cheerleader thing?"

"It's kind of designed that way, isn't it? Bare legs and shaking those pompoms." He sounded defensive, and he knew it.

He rolled onto his back. If he tried anything now she'd assume he was thinking of cheerleaders. Of Marissa Sigley.

"I'm not jealous," she said. "Not really. She's kind of cute. Marissa."

So he was right. That's what she was thinking. She was joking, he knew. Teasing him. But it was the kind of teasing that made him uncomfortable right now.

Particularly after what Libbie had said earlier about Rusty. A sure reminder of her warnings about the dangers of adolescent crushes… and obsessions. He remembered what it was like to be a teenager. The mood swings. The feelings you don't understand. The constant horniness.

It was easy to imagine that taken to another level.

He found it hard to believe Rusty behaving the way Libbie had described, but can you ever really know another person?

"You're quiet."

They were in bed. Wasn't it normal to be quiet?

Alice had clearly sensed the tension in him, that he was still lying there awake.

"Just something Libbie said earlier. Got me thinking."

She turned to face him, drawing one leg up across his thighs.

"She doesn't feel comfortable around Rusty. It just… well, it made me concerned about you, given that he likes you so much. If he makes Libbie feel that way, then what about you? Has he ever, I don't know, *intimidated* you? Made a pass?"

At least she didn't laugh. "Oh, Tom," she said. "Rusty's a sweet kid. Libbie just doesn't know his ways. He's awkward around people and he's big. That easily comes across the wrong way if you're not used to it. It's nothing."

"You'd tell me if there was anything? That's not the kind of thing to keep to yourself. Things escalate quickly when you're dealing with obsession."

"Tom. Just slow down, okay? Don't run away with this, just because you've gotten something into your head. You know this kind of jealousy isn't healthy. We don't want to go there again."

Again. One word like a slap.

He *cared*. There was nothing wrong in that.

Maybe it was primitive, the hunter-gatherer protective thing. But that didn't make it wrong.

Would she rather he didn't?

He bit down on the responses, though. He'd only sound defensive.

"Tom?"

"I'm fine," he said. "I just wanted to be sure there was nothing."

"Don't obsess about Rusty, you hear? He's a good kid. There's nothing."

He reached down, found her leg, and squeezed.

"It's not all getting too much again, is it, honey?"

That slap repeated. That word. *Again.*

"The stress. The money. The construction. The tenant thing—you were never comfortable letting a stranger into our space, but I kind of pushed it on you, didn't I?"

"I'm fine."

"That's lots of triggers. And now the jealousy…"

"I'm fine."

"You don't think you should see someone? Just to be sure? You don't want another breakdown. *I* don't want to see you hit that kind of a place again."

Again.

"I'm fine."

He pulled away from her, and she actually flinched.

Swung his legs out to sit on the edge of the bed.

He stood.

"Tom?"

He went across to the door and paused.

"Tom?"

"I'm fine."

And then he walked from the room.

CHAPTER 18

Tom tried not to let his frustrations show.

Franco had messaged them first thing, said there was a development on site and they needed to come and see and make some decisions. It sounded ominous.

Tom had wanted to head straight out, but Alice, already at work, had insisted they come together, which meant waiting until she was free at lunchtime. Convenient for her, yes, but it meant Tom had to interrupt his day rather than getting the site visit over with and getting down to his own work.

He tried hard not to dwell on how his work always seemed to come second.

It was only natural. She was shooting for VP and he was just a keyboard monkey, chasing peanuts.

Whatever.

He was fine.

They didn't talk much after Tom picked Alice up at the office and headed on to Whitetail Lane.

They pulled up at the curb behind Rusty's beat-up Mitsubishi.

"He's working here already?" said Alice.

"Yeah, he seemed keen. College funds."

The kid was a hard worker and it seemed he'd do anything for the Grangers. On another day he'd have made a joke of that, given his wife that old smile and wink, had a bit of fun. But not today.

Her concerns last night were in danger of pushing him too close to the edge. It was like her complaint that keeping on asking if she was relaxed didn't exactly relax her. He was fine, but pressing him about the state of his mind and whether the stress was getting too much... well, that was the one thing guaranteed to push him into an unstable place.

He didn't want to go there again.

Not ever.

"Hey, Rusty!" he called, waving to the kid.

Rusty was unloading a flatbed truck, lifting big sheets of drywall off the back, ready to move them into the building. When he paused to wave back, one of Franco's guys snapped something at him and he jumped back to work.

Just then Franco came over, wiping his hands on his jeans before reaching out to shake.

"Kid doing all right?" Tom asked, nodding in Rusty's direction.

Franco nodded. "He's okay," he said. "We have to be careful, you know. He's not properly licensed or insured for this kind of work, but the guys like having someone lower than them to boss around, you know? Makes 'em feel superior."

They laughed. Maybe some hard work on a

construction site would do Rusty some good. The kid tended to shy away from the world if he could get away with it. Tom had worked construction to get through college and it had been the making of him.

"So is this just a progress report, or what?" asked Alice, taking the lead.

"Let me show you."

Tom glanced at his wife. This didn't sound good.

They went in, putting on the hard hats Franco handed them. Tom helped Alice balance as she stepped over some debris—she hardly had the shoes for this—and she smiled at him.

They went up the stairs and through to what was going to be the back bedroom. In contrast to downstairs, where they were already starting to fit out the drywall and woodwork, up here was still more like a demolition site. The entire ceiling was down, exposing old beams and wiring.

And daylight.

There shouldn't be daylight coming in at that angle.

Franco was watching them, waiting for the questions that would come.

Instead of questions, though, Alice simply said, "Tell us."

"It's the woodwork in the entire back section of the roof. Everything looked fine from outside, and even from inside the loft space in the early inspections. But once this lot came down and we opened it up. Well... none of the timbers are sound. Been exposed to leaks for too long. We'll strip it down to solid wood and replace the bad, but you're looking at a whole new section of roof up there. None of that was on the plan."

And so none of it had been budgeted for.

"You got a ballpark figure?" asked Tom.

Franco shook his head. "I called you soon as we found it. I'll need to get someone up there to see just how far the damage goes. I'll get you figures soon as I can. Give you a price for the minimum fix, and one for the best job."

Franco always worked that way. Tells you the least you can get away with, and then follows up with a *But if it was me, this is how I'd do it properly.* Up to now they'd always gone with the *But if it was me* option, because Franco was good and they wanted to do it right, but now... Tom struggled to see how even a minimum fix was going to be achievable.

They'd have to pay for the roof, of course, but if they did then that might mean halting the interior fit until Alice made vice president. Or until Tom found something better than piecemeal freelancing gigs from home.

He was starting to feel a little nauseous. He didn't dare look at Alice, didn't want to know where her head was racing.

He couldn't help but feel somehow responsible, even for something beyond their control like this.

On the way back down Alice made her own way over the pile of debris.

~ ~ ~ ~

Libbie was outside. She seemed to be everywhere these days.

But Alice smiled when she saw their tenant and that shifted a weight inside Tom a little, so he could hardly complain. Maybe they needed a few more friends in their lives again, to stop them getting too closed in on each other. The ever-present Libbie really had been a breath of fresh air.

He stood by as the two women kissed cheeks in greeting, and then had that awkward moment when he realized he didn't know the appropriate way to greet her. Shake her hand? Sketch an awkward wave in the air?

Then she stepped forward and planted a surprisingly firm peck on his cheek.

"Hey, you guys," she said. "I was out here on a project, remembered this was where you had a place so swung by, and what do you know? I saw your car here. How's the work going? It looks good."

Tom and Alice simultaneously grunted an almost identical laugh, then stopped and finally met each other's gaze. Alice smiled. Tom smiled back and he felt that weight lift a fraction more.

There was a reason he was with Alice.

Lots of reasons.

He turned to Libbie again. "Oh, you know. Things go well and then the roof falls in."

"Literally." He shared a look with Alice again as she said this. Back to finishing each other's sentences.

"There's a hole," he explained.

"In the roof."

"Oh dear. That sounds expensive." Libbie had a knack for making exactly the observation that twisted the knife a little more.

"I was thinking about what we said the other day," Libbie said, addressing Alice. "About how maybe I could take pictures of the place for when you want to rent it out."

Or sell it, Tom thought, but didn't say out loud.

"Maybe I could take some pictures of the work in progress? Pictures of that nasty hole in the roof, to show how bad it was, in contrast to just how good you're going to make it."

"You won't need your flashgun," Tom said. "There's plenty of natural light coming through!"

"Tom, would you be a dear and get my camera bag from the trunk of my car? Alice can give me a progress report."

As she spoke, Libbie slipped her arm through Alice's and the two of them looked so easy in each other's company Tom found himself heading off to the street without even questioning it. How did he always end up running around after the women in his life? Was he too nice, as Alice had implied last night? Too much of a pushover?

Libbie had parked her Toyota right behind Tom's car. He pressed the trunk release button on the key fob Libbie had handed him and found the bag. Maybe he should look for work as a photographer's assistant. He had the experience now.

Heading back, he passed his car, then Rusty's.

That was when something caught his eye.

A book, lying on the front passenger seat of the Mitsubishi. One of those car books mechanics had, photographs and schematics of all the different engines for the various years and models of a car.

And sticking out of the book, like a bookmark, was a full-color printout. The part sticking out revealed a lurid image, like something from a magazine.

Bare flesh. Limbs tangled, splayed.

Even at first glance through the car window Tom could see it was a fake, a clumsy, unskilled Photoshop collage, an image no doubt taken from the internet with the faces changed.

The unmistakable acne-pocked face of Rusty himself on the guy. And Alice's face on the woman.

What the…

Tom controlled the anger.

He'd learned to do that. How to block the first rush of thoughts. How to control the breathing, and by doing that control the thumping heart and the rush of angry blood.

He waited. Not looking at that obscene image.

Waited.

And then he went back to the construction site.

"Rusty? You got a minute?"

The kid was back at the truck, dragging another sheet of drywall free.

"Sure, Mr. Granger. Right with you."

Tom waited, and then as Rusty approached he turned and walked farther away from the site, and the curious ears of the crew, so that Rusty had to keep walking to follow him.

He didn't want to do this in front of Franco and his men. Didn't want to do it in front of Alice, Libbie.

"Sir?"

"Rusty." The kid flinched when Tom stopped and met his look again, clearly sensing something bad. "I want you to listen to me very carefully. Okay?"

"Sir."

"I don't want you here again, on my property. You understand? And I don't want you back at the house either. Cutting grass, tidying the trees. Whatever it is that you do. I don't want you anywhere near our house and I don't want you anywhere near my wife. Do you understand?"

He saw the kid's jaw working, but no words coming.

He saw Franco standing in the doorway, watching them curiously.

Saw Alice and Libbie standing nearby.

Alice took a step toward them, and said, "What is it, Tom? What's going on?"

"You want to show Alice your book, Rusty? *Engines for Beginners*, or whatever the hell it is?"

Still, Rusty stood there, his jaw working silently.

Alice was the one who followed the direction of

Tom's gaze, went to the beat-up old Mitsubishi before he could stop her.

Saw the book, the picture.

Rusty followed and now the words came. "But... What's that? I didn't do that. You have to believe me Mr. Granger. *Mrs.* Granger." The last came out more as an anguished cry than words.

Alice said nothing, just looked from the book and across to Rusty, then back again.

"But..."

"Stay away from us, you hear me?"

The boy met Tom's look again, tears welling in his eyes.

"I..."

"Stay away."

Tom was aware that Libbie had joined them now, her arm hooked into Alice's again.

That should be him. He should be comforting his wife, reassuring her that this had been dealt with, that he was in control.

But it was all he could do not to punch Rusty in the face. The kid had size over him, but Tom had no doubt he could take him. He had the power of sheer, indignant rage on his side.

He didn't though. He was in control. He was on top of his feelings, just as he'd learned.

So why did he feel like the bad guy right now, as Libbie comforted his wife and Rusty skulked off around the side of his car?

CHAPTER 19

Alice wanted to leave it at that. Yes, she'd seen the disgusting thing Rusty had done with that picture. And yes, her mind had pushed deeper and she'd known what that meant: it wasn't just a picture. The boy had spent time selecting just the *right* pictures to use, time imagining this, putting himself in that imaginary, perverted scenario.

With her.

She knew this was yet another confirmation of Libbie's warnings about Rusty. The dangers of adolescent obsession.

Not adolescent, she reminded herself. He was a senior at high school. Eighteen years old. A kid in the body of a big, strong man.

A dangerous mix.

But she'd seen the horror on his face when Tom had confronted him. The absolute shame that his private actions had been exposed.

Right then he wasn't a man, he was a small frightened child found out.

Before Rusty had fled with a screech of wheels, Tom had demanded he hand over the picture. That seemed to be when her husband's attitude hardened. Seeing the picture close up. Holding it in his hands.

"I'm going to talk to Bill and Ruby." Rusty's parents. "I'm going to make sure they put a stop to all this."

And so now, early evening, they were standing on the porch of Rusty's home, waiting as someone fumbled with the door from the other side.

It was Rusty.

"Mrs. Granger, Mr. Granger. Uh…"

"Bill, Ruby," said Tom, addressing Rusty's parents, who stood beyond him in an interior doorway.

Alice had never been inside their house before. Like Rusty, they were quiet people, kept themselves to themselves.

She didn't get to set foot in the house tonight, either.

"Tom, Alice? Why, come on in," said Bill.

"No thanks," said Tom. "We won't be long. We've just come to ask you to keep your son away from us. Away from our properties. Away from Alice."

"Rusty?"

The boy had backed away into the shadows of their entrance hall.

"What is it, Rusty?"

"It's this," said Tom, waving the shocking printout at them.

Rusty's parents came forward, examining the paper, then looking up at Alice, horror written large across their features.

166

"No!" Alice snapped. Bill and Ruby had always come across as a bit slow, but they were looking at her as if that photograph was real.

"Your boy faked this picture," said Tom. "Pasted his face onto it. And Alice's. He's obsessed. You need to put a stop to this or the police are going to be involved."

"Rusty...?" That was his mom, staring at him in horror.

"Mom! It's not... I didn't..."

"Don't deny you're obsessed with my wife." There was steel in Tom's voice.

Rusty didn't deny that part. Instead, he said, "I didn't do that picture. I ain't never seen it before."

"It was in your car. In your book."

"I didn't put it there! Hell, I don't even know how to make a picture like that."

"Language." Alice almost laughed out loud, that the boy's mother should latch onto his language at a time like this.

"Sorry, Mom. I mean... I didn't do that."

The kid was on the edge of tears again, just as he'd been earlier today. For an instant, Alice even believed him. Could this be some awful kind of misunderstanding? How could that even be possible?

"Keep him away from us."

Tom took her hand, turned, and started to walk. Rather than make any more of a scene here, Alice went with him.

And as they walked, she thought, *Is that someone standing there in the shadows? Somebody watching us?* Or was that her imagination? Paranoia taking over.

She told herself to snap out of it.

In a world where everyone around her seemed to be losing their mind, she couldn't go losing hers too.

~ ~ ~ ~

They lay in bed, a cold space between them. Even so, she could sense the tension in Tom's body.

Her words didn't help ease that. "You don't think you were a bit harsh with Rusty? Humiliating him in front of his folks like that? He's only a kid, despite how he looks. He doesn't find it easy with people, and this kind of thing is never going to help."

"Harsh? You say it as if this is somehow my fault. I didn't make that picture. I'm not the one obsessing over someone twice my age. This kind of thing can get dangerous. It has to be stopped."

Silence.

Then he added, "I can't believe I'm hearing this. I can't believe you're still soft on him, even now."

"You saw how upset he was."

"Good. He should be upset."

"You're being unreasonable."

"You should never have encouraged him."

"Encouraged? Is that what this is? You're blaming *me?*"

"You always had a fondness for him."

"Don't, Tom."

"He sensed that. Took it as encouragement."

"Tom."

More silence.

"Would you just listen to yourself, Tom. You're being ridiculous."

"You should never have encouraged him. He probably saw all that as some kind of flirting, even. To someone like him, that's an open invitation."

There it was. Jealousy. Distrust. Over a goddamn *kid!*

"I did not do that, Tom. I never would. You know that. I trust you, and you should trust me just the same."

He didn't say anything. He didn't have to. She knew where his mind had taken him.

"You know nothing happened that time, Tom. We've been over all this. You know your jealousy got to be too much."

The time she was referring to was triggered at a party Pierson Newport had hosted last year to celebrate winning another big contract. The incident had all been a misunderstanding. Nothing more than that.

An entirely innocent situation he'd walked in on. He'd claimed to believe her at the time, but he'd been unable to let go. She didn't know about green-eyed, but she'd learned then just how much of a monster jealousy could become. They'd worked through it, though. Buried it in the past.

Or so she thought.

She tried a different angle. "It's no good deflecting, Tom. This isn't my equivalent of the cheerleader thing."

"Cheerleader? What do you mean?"

"Well... just because guys fantasize about cheerleaders, it doesn't mean we're all like that. It doesn't mean I've ever had thoughts about sleeping with an eighteen-year-old."

"You think I...?"

Marissa Sigley. The photo shoot.

"It's flattering that she likes you. You don't need to feel guilty about it. But it's not fair to transfer that onto me and assume *I* might feel that way about a teenager. Unless you really *would* sleep with a sixteen-year-old?"

He flinched away from her. Turned to sit on the edge of the bed, just like last night.

"Do you see now?" she said, sitting too, drawing her knees up to her chest. "Do you see how it is to be accused of something so ridiculous? A *teenager*? No, Tom, I never encouraged Rusty. And yes, I think you over-reacted, just like you always do. And yes, I think you need help, because you're losing your grip all over again, and it scares me. It scares me far more than some spotty kid who's been playing around with Photoshop."

She turned, stood, pulled her long night-shirt down over her legs, and walked past him, out of the bedroom.

~ ~ ~ ~

The night air felt good. Cool. Refreshing.

Alice pulled her long cardigan about herself, glad she'd pulled on sweatpants before stepping out onto the porch.

If you're going to storm off, make sure you're at least comfortable first of all.

She smiled. That was the kind of lame joke Tom was always making, when he was well. A joke, a smile, a wink.

"Thought you might appreciate this."

She hadn't noticed Libbie there, standing down in the shadows. She came up onto the porch now, and Alice saw she was holding a bottle and a pair of cut crystal glasses.

"A single malt? Glenmorangie? How did you know that's my favorite?"

"I'm just *that* good." Uncannily, she said it with a wink and they laughed.

They sat, Alice on the swing and Libbie on the wicker bucket-seat. Like an old married couple.

Alice took a sip of the single malt. She and Tom had been to the distillery near Inverness one time, when they took their honeymoon in the Scottish Highlands. Tom hated scotch, so for every tasting Alice had finished his, too, and he'd ended up having to do the driving the rest of that day.

"Want to talk about it?"

"You should be a therapist." Libbie had a way of opening people up, getting them to drop their guard.

"What is it, Alice?"

"Oh, just Tom. That thing with Rusty, the photo he made. Tom insisted we go round and tell his folks."

"That can't have gone well…"

"About as you'd expect. Tom got angry. The parents were confused. Rusty was mortified."

"Funny, Tom never struck me as the possessive type. You two are such a sweet couple, and he seems so kind and calm. He couldn't have been more helpful on the shoot the other day. That was so generous of him."

"You'd be surprised." Alice took another mouthful, let it sit on her tongue before swallowing. Savoring the burn.

Libbie said nothing and Alice was reminded of her observation of how good their tenant was at drawing things out of people.

"He is," she said. "The possessive type. Jealous."

Still Libbie said nothing, and Alice went on. "About a year ago. It got bad. He got it into his head that, well, that something had happened. That I'd cheated on him. I hadn't, of course. It was all entirely innocent. But once the idea was planted in his head, well… I don't know how long he'd been feeling that way. How long he'd been looking for something. He got a bit fixated."

Libbie leaned over to top up Alice's glass.

"It was a rough time. He kind of lost his grip a bit. Lost perspective."

"You've hinted at things," said Libbie, clearly picking her words with great sensitivity. "You mentioned your lives had changed a lot in the last year. Tom's career switch. The pressure on your finances, just as you were buying the second property."

Alice nodded. Took another drink. She said, "Yes, that's the diplomatic way of putting it. The public line.

Tom had a meltdown. It nearly destroyed him. Me. Our marriage. It wrecked his career. I don't think he ever quite recovered."

"And did you? Your marriage?"

"I thought so."

"Until now."

"Until now. I hate to see it happening again. To realize how much I'd been fooling myself, how close to the surface all this stuff still was."

"Was this how it was before?"

"It was. It started with a few stray comments. A few too many questions. Things I didn't notice at the time, but saw clearly in hindsight. Then it escalated. The jealousy. The suspicion. The anger. I can see it all now, just the same. And it scares me. I can't go through that again. I can't lose everything."

"You won't lose *everything*," said Libbie softly. "You still have your friends. You still have me. I've only known you a short time, Alice, but it feels like we've been friends for so much longer. We're going to be friends forever. I can tell that now. And I won't let anyone hurt you."

Alice smiled. She wished she could believe that.

"Another drink?"

"Hell yeah!" And she leaned over for a refill, surprised that her glass had emptied so quickly.

CHAPTER 20

Libbie didn't sleep much that night.

Her head was spinning, thoughts rushing. All this was so exciting! She'd never thought they'd be so easy to play.

Rusty was a bonus. That dumbass lump of a kid, all hormones and cougar fantasies. A real gift from the gods.

It had been so funny, every stage of the way.

Finding just the right pictures to montage together. A stealth shot of Rusty to paste over a porn actor's face. Searching her extensive library of Alice images for that O of surprise to paste over the chick—such a porny look on her face, when taken out of context.

Tom's reaction to the picture couldn't have been more textbook. She hadn't even been sure he'd spot it lying there in Rusty's car—he wasn't exactly the brightest penny in the pile. But not only had he seen it, the red mist had descended. He'd gone after Rusty, then to defend himself he'd made sure Alice had seen the picture, too.

Perfect.

And then, the icing on the cake, he'd hauled Alice to watch him lay into the kid's parents!

That had been fun to watch. Standing back in the darkness, seeing the look on Alice's face, the agony of discomfort.

Everything was coming together. She was so close to her goal!

It was worth a night of very little sleep, when your wakeful mind was filled with all that.

And now she stood by the air duct, listening for sounds from above. Waiting for Alice to leave.

Her cellphone trilled, buzzing in the pocket of her jeans.

Damn.

Who would be calling her so early?

When you had no friends or family, a phone call was nearly always official or trouble. And if it was official, that usually meant trouble anyway.

She checked the screen, but the number was withheld. It would be a nuisance call, or something official, coming through a switchboard that shielded the source number.

"Yes? Hello?"

"Hi Libbie. This is Dr. Holt. How are things?"

"Dr. Holt."

As she'd feared: official *and* trouble. Dr. Holt was one of the few people whose measure she'd struggled to find. Whenever she thought she'd gotten the upper hand with him, he would sidestep and come at her from a different angle. It went with the territory, she guessed.

"I'm good," she said. "I've moved out of New York. Small town life suits me. I'm getting involved with the community." Oh yes!

"We don't have a change of residence listed."

Damn. She should know not to get clever with him.

"Sorry. It's only temporary. A change of scenery. My permanent residence is unchanged."

"And how are you coping with the stresses of everyday life, Libbie? As I always say, nobody knows the inside of your head like *you* do. You're the best person to spot the warning signs. Are you doing that? Are you sticking to the self-monitoring routine we established?"

"Oh yes. I am, absolutely. I have my ups and downs, but none of the trigger points we discussed. I'm doing real well, Doc. Trust me."

She wished he'd get off the line. Every conversation with him was a series of traps. Traps with serious consequences; he was the one man who could have her recalled for further treatment.

"That's good, Libbie. You have to remember that this is a lifelong commitment on your part. You never know when another episode may be just around the corner. That's always going to be a concern."

"I know, Dr. Holt. Believe me, I don't want that to happen again. I just want a quiet life. I just want to find the things that make me happy. Is that too much to ask?"

Things like her scrapbook and all the small victories that were mounting up into a landslide—one that would smother and destroy perfect Tom and perfect Alice.

"No, that's not too much to ask at all," he said. "It's good to hear you speaking like this. I'm glad you're doing well."

"Oh, I'm doing very well. Now if that's all? I have to

be somewhere."

She'd heard the door upstairs, looked out the window and seen the wheels of Alice's Ford Focus rolling away.

Yes, she had to be somewhere, doing the things that made her happy.

Which apparently wasn't too much to ask at all.

~ ~ ~ ~

"Hey, Tom. You okay?"

He looked rough, standing in the doorway, holding the door as if about to slam it shut again in her face. He clearly didn't want to see her. Probably didn't want to see *anyone* right now—she wouldn't take it personally.

"Oh. Libbie. Look…"

"Listen, I hope I'm not overstepping here, but I care about you guys. You're the sweetest couple. I… I heard your voices last night. Raised voices. I just wanted to be sure that you're okay. I know things have been a bit stressy around Alice recently, with the Mapleview pitch and all. And that business with Rusty…"

Yes, she'd heard the raised voices, but only because she'd been listening in at the air duct. She didn't explain that part though.

His shoulders slumped. If she knew about the row then that put her on the inside of this, in his mind. He could talk.

Or at least, she hoped he felt that way.

"You want to talk?"

177

Still he hesitated.

"Why not come downstairs? Change of scenery. I have a pot of coffee on. And I went by Zak's earlier." Zak's was a local bakery, Tom's guilty secret when he was working from home.

He followed her down, pulling a sweater down over his head before smoothing his mussed up hair.

"It was nothing," he said, as she opened the apartment door. "Just a few tensions hitting the surface. We don't fight."

"It's fine," said Libbie. "I know what it's like. I love Alice to bits, but she's all or nothing, isn't she? I've seen how hard she's working. That must make things very hard for you."

"Behind every great woman…"

"…There's a great man." He smiled now.

She took the jug from the coffee machine and poured two cups. The box from Zak's was on the breakfast bar. Cream-filled donuts, Tom's favorite.

"Does it bother you that you fought last night? You know, given how you say you never ordinarily fight."

"We're good. Just a lot going on."

She loved that he was still in denial, or at least lying about it to her. That meant his inner turmoil was so much more intense.

Enough to tear a guy apart.

"That's good to hear. You two are so perfect together. You're so good, Tom, supporting her when she's clearly so stressed."

She could see his shoulders lifting. He really thought she believed that. Believed another person saw that Alice was wrong and he was right.

So easy!

"It must be tough, though, when you know you're in the right, and you're only trying to do the best thing."

He took a bite of his donut. "These are so good," he said.

The guy had such a sweet tooth—another side of him he kept suppressed around his wife. If everything else failed, Libbie figured, she could lead him to a slow, slow death through obesity and heart disease. Death by donut and cheesecake.

"You been together long?" She knew how long, to the day. Sometimes you didn't ask questions for the answers, though. Sometimes you did it for the effect.

"Married a bit over six years," he told her, and she saw from his expression that just being reminded of the good times made him so much more aware of how bad they were now.

"That's sweet."

"It's a whole lot sweeter than that. We've known each other since we were kids. Overlapping friendship groups, then we were friends for real, right through high school."

"Childhood sweethearts!"

"Not sweethearts. We didn't date back then. Just friends. That all came later."

"But still… It's like you were fated. Always meant to be a couple. I knew you guys were right together.

Whatever happened last night clearly was just a blip."

That pained look on his face again. It was like kicking a puppy, both incredibly easy and every blow hurt.

"We drifted apart, though. Went away to college in different towns. Lost touch. Dated other people. Nothing ever felt right, though, with anyone else. It was as if the benchmark had been set too high."

"Aw."

"And then we hooked up again. Same line of work. Professional circles overlapping, like history repeating. We even ended up working for the same firm for a time."

"You guys!" She wondered if she was laying it on thick before deciding it didn't matter.

"I love her. Always have."

"That's clear." Would it be rude to puke now?

"I don't want to force her away again."

"Again?"

He faltered. Met her look, then looked away. He hadn't meant to say that.

"We had difficulties before now." He seemed to be picking his words carefully. "Like you say, Alice is all or nothing, and sometimes I can be too. We've hit some lows together. Battled through the hard times. But we came through. You know what they say. If it doesn't break you, it—"

"—leaves you scarred for life and vowing revenge?"

He paused for a moment, long enough to pick up the jokiness in her tone, and then they both laughed.

"Sorry," she said. "I was fooling. I don't mean to belittle what you're saying. You two are clearly meant to be together. It is such a beautiful thing to see."

"I really do love her."

"That's… reassuring." Now it was Libbie's turn to mirror the look he'd given earlier, the one that said too much had been given away.

"Reassuring?"

She didn't answer. And just as he'd done earlier, she avoided his look, knowing it would make clear to him that she was hiding something.

"Oh, it's nothing." And when, in the entire history of people saying *Oh it's nothing* did it ever turn out to be nothing?

"But…?"

"Really."

"What is it?" That hint of irritation in his tone was perfect. She knew he'd be willing to shake it out of her rather than let it lie.

"Just…" She was milking it now, she knew. But that desperate look on his face was just too delicious.

"It's Alice," she said. "But it's nothing."

She had him dangling. Waiting.

"Alice and that guy." Leave him to fill in the gaps.

He was taken aback. "Walter?"

That hadn't taken him long at all.

"It's just… I was puzzled. The other day. When we

met up for lunch. I was messing with one of my cameras while I waited. And then the two of them came out—but out of a different building than the one I was expecting."

She had her laptop nearby. Flipping the lid up, it came up with the picture she'd preselected.

Alice. Walter. That look of intimacy in their faces. Their bodies about as close as they could be without touching.

Standing in the lobby of the Easy Day Hotel.

"I'm sure it's innocent," she said. "I didn't want you to see this. The hotel's just across the square from Pierson Newport and it has meeting rooms and conference facilities. I'm sure they were there on business."

"Pierson Newport has meeting rooms." Tom's voice was low, controlled. As if he was having to work real hard to keep it that way.

"It's just… You're such a nice guy, Tom. Honest, down to earth. The kind of person who sees the good in others so much they sometimes overlook the bad, if that makes sense? I'd hate to see you get hurt."

He was still staring at the screen.

"I'm sure there's an innocent explanation. Maybe Pierson Newport are going to use the hotel's conference facilities for a big meeting about the Mapleview account or something? I know Walter's been helping on that, even though it's not his area."

It was like Chinese water torture, every word another drip. Every suggestion of innocent explanations a reminder of the alternative.

"Are you okay there, Tom?"

Staring.

His eyes caught the light differently now, the film of moisture thicker, threatening to spill over.

Still staring at the picture on the screen.

Alice and Walter, their bodies so close, their eyes locked. So much more subtle than the porn star O of surprise she'd given Alice on that other picture. This look was more intimate, more personal. More loving.

Even if she said so herself, it was a work of art.

And as they say, the camera never lies.

But the photographer does.

CHAPTER 21

The day didn't start well for Alice, and then it only got worse.

Her head hurt. Lack of sleep, and the exact opposite of a lack of whisky. Libbie coming by with a full bottle of Alice's favorite scotch had been just what she needed at the time, but now she regretted it. That girl had a subtle way with the refills!

And Tom's glowering mood this morning hadn't helped.

Why was it okay for him to storm out of their room in the middle of the night, but not when she did it the next night?

She knew better than to expect reason and logic from him when his mental balance swung like this, but still... That didn't make it fair, or easy to deal with. She was going to have to confront this. Find a way to tackle it without him blowing up again.

Tom needed help.

They both did.

Alice and Tom had always known they would be together forever. They had plans. They talked about what they would do in their retirement, the trips they would take, the dream home where they would live.

That was how it was going to be.

Everyone saw them as the model couple.

You're too sweet was how Libbie described them.

She couldn't imagine a future life that didn't have Tom at its center.

And it scared her that she was starting to wonder if she would have to do just that.

She was early in the office, as she always was these days. Sitting at her desk, watching the main open-plan area filling up. Catching the occasional eye, the smiles and nods. The smell of freshly-brewed coffee and overpriced muffins. People knew she was working hard and they knew what a difference the Mapleview account would make for the company.

It felt good to be at the center of things. To have people's respect and support. Working in the corporate real estate sector wasn't exactly a spectator sport, but this was as close as it came.

It was nice to have something she was good at. For a time, she even managed to push aside her fears for her marriage and her concern for what was going on in her husband's head.

When her desk phone rang and it was Ruth, she didn't think much of it. "Mrs. Granger? Mr. Tuckett's asking if you'd mind stepping through for a brief meeting."

"Oh, sure. I'll be right through."

Michael Tuckett was her boss right now, but if she stepped up to VP they'd be on equal terms. That would take some getting used to after all this time with the company, but she was starting to believe that she deserved the opportunity.

Right now though, she found him intimidating, sitting there behind his wide oak desk, fixing her with gray eyes from beneath tangled eyebrows. His hair was thinning, his jowls generous, and his body seemed almost melted into the seat as if he'd grown in situ.

"Mr. Tuckett?"

He nodded at a seat, and she sat.

"Everything okay, Alice?"

The big boss guy never started a conversation like that unless something was wrong.

"Sir?"

"At home? Your health? Because there must be something to explain your performance on Mapleview."

She felt sick. Felt her vision blackening as if she were about to faint.

What was he talking about?

"You're running behind schedule."

That wasn't fair. Tuckett himself had agreed to a revised schedule when the Mapleview people had requested changes and then had been late on delivering their figures. She was bang on the *new* schedule, and he knew that! And she'd been working all hours of the day, night and weekend to achieve that.

"And when I asked for an interim report, you sent an unfinished draft."

But that was the *nature* of an interim report, particularly when it was requested at the last minute. The clue was in the word *interim*.

She resisted the urge to justify herself. She understood this wasn't a debate.

"And even then there are key elements missing. Overlooked or forgotten, I don't know. If that kind of sloppiness gets through to Mapleview, at best they'd take it for incompetence. At worse, fraudulent misrepresentation."

"Sir?"

"The Deer Island amortization. Completely ignored. That skews the whole representation. All the projections are thrown off-kilter. I don't know where your head is, Alice, but it's not where it should be."

Deer Island? But she'd spent half a day on that. Yes, she'd drafted the projections in a separate spreadsheet because it was such a complex element, but she knew it was integral to their business case. She'd fed those calculations back into the draft report. She knew she had.

Michael Tuckett wasn't the kind of man who wanted excuses or explanations, let alone contradiction. He wanted things done *right*.

But she *had*.

"I'm sorry, Mr. Tuckett. I'll need to check that report. Get it right."

He nodded, clearly not satisfied. How could he trust her work in the future?

"I don't want this happening again. If we lose financing on this one, that hits us across the board. Just like last year."

That was so not fair. She had never let this company down.

But she knew… this was not a debate.

"Don't disappoint me, Alice." His tone was softer now. She knew he had a heart, even if it was mostly made of stone. "I wouldn't have put you on this if I didn't think you were the right choice. Don't make me question my judgment."

"Sir."

When she walked from his big corner office, she felt everyone's eyes on her. Burning into her. How did they all know she'd screwed up? Had word gotten around somehow? Had they heard the exchange?

Or was it simply that it was so obvious in her face and the way she walked, defeated, back to her own office?

She'd run those figures. She'd included them in the report.

She knew she had.

But when she sat at her desk and pulled up the report she saw immediately that Tuckett was right.

It wasn't obvious at a glance, unless you knew what was missing, but it was a serious oversight. It made the projections look so much better. It made it look as if she'd been window-dressing the report. Deliberately misleading by omitting a big risk factor.

She didn't understand.

"That sounded bad," a voice said, making her look up.

Walter stood in the doorway of her office, leaning casually on the frame. So they'd heard. They'd all heard.

"I screwed up."

"That's not like you."

"I've had a lot on my mind."

"You're the juggler." An old joke between them. Walter insisted he'd never known anyone as adept at juggling different tasks and responsibilities as Alice.

"I rushed things. The interim report. I missed some figures."

"That's even *less* like you."

She'd been preoccupied. Tom. The Whitetail Lane project. The business with Rusty. She didn't need to burden Walter with all that, though.

"Maybe I'm just not cut out for operating at this level. Maybe I should take a lower profile behind the scenes."

"No," he said, smiling, coming into the office and nudging the door closed behind him. "*I'm* the backroom guy. You're the superstar. I thought we'd established that?"

That made her smile, at least.

"So what went wrong?"

"I don't know. I really don't. A whole set of figures missing, skewing the projections so it looked like I was presenting a falsely positive view of our pitch. I don't get it."

"Did you submit the right file? An earlier version, perhaps?"

She should have checked for that. She checked the file's properties now. It was the current version, the version she'd considered ready to hand over.

"A corrupt file?" she floated, clutching at straws.

"Files don't corrupt like that," said Walter. "File corruption is random. It doesn't neatly excise chunks of reports and tidy things up so you'd never know they were missing."

She knew immediately what he was saying. "Only people do things that neatly."

Was there jealousy within the company? Someone who might want to make her look bad?

Walter nodded. "Does anyone else here have access to your files?"

She shut her eyes for a minute and considered the question. Pierson Newport had shared cloud storage, but every member of staff at Alice's level had a secure private area. "No. It's password-protected. No-one can get past that, can they?"

If anyone knew, it was Walter. He shrugged. "If you've been careful with your security, you'll be safe from any casual intrusion. But most security can be cracked if you know what you're doing, though."

They both knew she wasn't a computer whiz like him, but she knew enough to follow safe practice.

"Anybody else have access? Maybe from your home laptop?"

Again, she knew Walter well enough to read between the lines. Tom knew the Pierson Newport systems, and he might easily have a grudge, but he'd never do anything to sabotage her big project! She could have all kinds of doubts about her husband, but never that.

"Libbie," she said, instead.

"The perfect tenant?"

"It sounds stupid."

"But?"

"You're right, I do have access to the files from my laptop at home. The other night I was working at home but some files had gone missing. An entire folder—the one that contained the interim report and all the associated documents."

"And Libbie?"

"She studied computers at NYU, something called… Interactive Media and Technology, I think. She used to work on an IT help desk. She recovered the files for me."

"There's no such thing…" He waited for her to finish the sentence, but she wouldn't. *As a perfect tenant.* "Ali, do you trust her?"

"She's sweet. She's thoughtful and considerate." And somehow Libbie Burchett seemed to pop up at the center of just about everything that was going wrong in Alice's life right now.

Always there to offer support.

Always there to help.

To sympathize.

Always there.

"You want me to dig?"

She nodded. She wanted Walter to dig.

She wanted him to reassure her she was being paranoid.

She wanted to *know*.

CHAPTER 22

She couldn't stay at the office that day. Everyone watching her. Talking about her.

If Walter had heard the ass-tearing Michael Tuckett had given her, then everyone else must surely have done so, too.

She knew what a cutthroat business this was. When Tom had left last year, they'd all been lining up to take his place. Like vultures, even before he'd officially left the company.

She could feel that now. One false move, and who would be first in line to sweep in and volunteer to relieve her of Mapleview? Lloyd Cooper? CeeCee Jonson? Even Jilly Tuckett? Michael had been scrupulous about not showing his daughter any favoritism but Jilly was thrusting and hard-working, and just waiting for her big chance.

Alice hated the paranoid turn her mind had taken recently. She'd never been like this before. She told Ruth she had a blood sugar issue and needed to be home. She could work from there. She hated using the diabetes as an excuse, but it was all she had right now. Sometimes you had to use all the tools you had at your disposal.

And she needed a change of scene. A change of

atmosphere.

Sitting at home in the kitchen, she found herself staring blankly at her laptop screen. She really felt as if she were burning out.

She found the Deer Island figures. She had to put this right.

It was harder working with such big spreadsheets on a small screen, but she was glad she'd come home.

She should take a break. Make something to eat. She'd told Tom she'd get dinner, even though that was his job. He was the one with the flexible working pattern. And he was a better cook. But it felt like a principle thing. She could do it all.

She didn't need him.

So he'd gone out to work in the yard. A principle thing, too, making the point that they didn't need Rusty.

They'd get past this. They had to.

She stared at the screen, the columns of figures. Tried to piece together the steps she'd taken before to include this in the main report.

It was soul-destroying redoing work she knew she'd already done.

Her heart sank when there was a knock at the door, shattering her concentration. She ignored it. Tom was in the yard. He could deal with it.

Moments later a dark shape appeared at the kitchen door. A sharper knock.

She went to answer it. Libbie. Of course it was Libbie.

"Hi," said the girl. "Sorry to disturb you. Are you working?"

Alice forced a smile. Seeing Libbie in the flesh, she felt instantly guilty for her paranoia earlier. The accusations she'd made to Walter. She remembered last night on the porch, the scotch.

"Oh, it's fine," said Alice. "I just brought some work home. I was feeling a bit rough. Blood sugars." Repeating the lie.

"I hope it wasn't the scotch!"

Alice smiled at their shared secret. It was strange how it seemed impossible to think anything bad about Libbie in her presence, but in her absence it became possible to doubt.

"What can I do for you?" Alice asked brightly. Perhaps too brightly.

"Oh, it can wait, if you're working."

"No, no. What is it?"

"I'm probably just being stupid, but I can't work out the heating in the apartment. It doesn't seem to be working. Perhaps Tom could take a look? He probably has more free time than you right now?"

"No, it's fine." She didn't need to rely on Tom.

Outside, she pulled her cardigan more tightly around herself. The weather had finally taken a turn for fall, a chill wind whipping around the corner of the house.

"Oh, it's cold!" Alice muttered as they paused at the apartment door. "No wonder you want your heating to work."

The apartment temperature seemed comfortable enough, but if the weather stayed this way it was going to get cold soon.

Alice looked around. It was funny seeing someone else's imprint on the place. The way it had subtly changed. Libbie had camera gear spread out over the dining table, as if she'd been cleaning lenses or whatever it was photographers did to maintain their equipment.

"Sorry about the mess," Libbie said, as if following Alice's gaze.

Libbie went across to where a big scrapbook lay on the table beside an array of lenses and swept it up into her arms. "A private project," she explained. "Ideas. Plans."

"That's nice."

Libbie smiled and went through to the bedroom to put the book away.

Alice went through to the kitchen. The heating unit was fixed to a wall between two cupboards. She checked the LCD display, trying to remember how the apparatus worked. It seemed to be okay. No warnings about pressure. No error messages. The timer seemed to be set correctly, too.

"How are things?" asked Libbie. "I don't know how much you remember telling me last night, but I know things are tense between you and Tom."

Alice glanced away from the unit's display. She hadn't drunk *that* much.

"We're good," she said. The thermostat seemed to be set correctly.

"That was quite a fight."

Was it? Perhaps. But it was over. They were good.

She returned her attention to the display. "Aha!"

"You've found it?"

"That slider there." She indicated a control at the side of the unit. "Somehow it had gotten flipped from Automatic to Manual, so the heating hadn't come on." She pushed it back to the Automatic position and instantly the heater roared to life.

"Oh, thank you so much. I know Tom would have fixed it too, but I'm so glad it was you."

"Oh?"

"I mean. Well, single girl. Not that I mean anything by that, of course. It's just, after that photo shoot…"

"The one with Marissa?" Instantly, Alice's mind was racing. Libbie clearly hadn't intended to say any of that, but now she'd started…

Libbie nodded. "He was asking earlier if I had any more work lined up with Marissa. I think he was hoping to assist again. I'm sure it's nothing. He's so helpful, isn't he?"

"He can be, yes."

"And the photos came out real nice. I was just sorting through the prints before I came to find you."

Alice followed her glance, across to the table. The scrapbook had been resting on a card folder, from which a few prints stuck out a short way.

"That's good."

"I'm trying to pick the nicest ones, maybe leave out

one or two of the more racy shots."

Alice felt sick. "Can I see?"

"No." She said it too quickly, and seemed to realize that. "I mean… it's just a few silly pictures. Not interesting at all."

But Alice had moved out of the kitchen to the dining area. She reached for the card folder. Slowly flipped it open.

The first photo showed Marissa leaning forward, hands on knees, pouting at the camera and showing far too much cleavage for a sixteen-year-old.

The next showed her kicking one leg out, her arms stretched high, a photo that emphasized all the lines and curves that this kid so unfairly possessed.

And the next showed her standing in Tom's arms. She had one leg drawn up, the knee high, and Alice saw her husband's arms looped easily around the girl's waist. Every guy's wet dream come to life.

"I'm so sorry," said Libbie. "I didn't mean you to see that. It looks far worse than it was. They were just fooling around. It's harmless. Really it is."

Utterly harmless. Seeing your husband with a nubile cheerleader wrapped around his waist.

Oh yes. Totally harmless.

CHAPTER 23

Tom knew Alice had come home from the office, but they'd barely even seen each other, let alone spoken, since her Ford Focus had pulled up by the house.

She'd said something about a headache and needing some peace and quiet, and that had been it. She'd settled at the kitchen table with her laptop and a look like thunder on her face.

Was she still mad with him for some reason, or had something happened at the office?

Now wasn't the time to ask, so he left her to it.

He was still waiting for the next two transcription jobs to show up in his inbox, and normally when that happened he'd give himself some quiet time with the TV with a donut from Zak's. Not today, though. Whatever was going on with Alice he didn't want to add to her stress by breaking that peace and quiet she'd come home for.

He went outside. Found his way to the tool shed at the side of the house and let himself in.

It had been a while since he'd set foot in here.

He'd consider himself an outdoor type, but not the kind that rolled his sleeves up and got dirty. Hiking and mountain bikes, yes, but he couldn't remember the last time he'd fired that big mower into life. Gardens were... well, while it was Alice who always took the lead on interior décor, outside they'd always relied on someone like Rusty.

That damn kid!

How could he be so dumb? Okay, play out your fantasies on a computer. Tom had no idea what kids did these days with all the technology at their disposal. Porn on tap, and there was any number of things you could do with a graphics program.

But leaving it out in full view in his car like that? *Jesus...*

Rusty came across as a bit slow sometimes, but Tom had always put that down to his manner and awkwardness. He'd thought him smarter than that.

To his credit, though, the kid knew how to look after his tools. The smell of fresh oil in here was almost overpowering and that mower positively gleamed, it was so well-maintained. All the tools were lined up neatly on the workbench, or hanging from hooks. All the empty pots and boxes of fertilizer or whatever else gardeners used were perfectly arranged, any labels facing out.

Was that the sign of some kind of obsessive personality, though?

He shook his head and turned. Grabbing a lawn rake, he strode back outside.

He'd always thought he was a good judge of character, but right now his take on people was all over the place. Swinging from realizing how much he missed having Rusty around the place, not just for the work he did but for his lumbering-giant charm, and then finding ways to confirm his suspicions about the kid.

He started to rake at the leaves on the back lawn. The grass was still neat and trim from the last time Rusty had mown, but it was covered with a layer of red and golden leaves from the maples and oaks that surrounded this part of the property.

Every time he'd managed to drag a good number of leaves into a pile, a gust of wind scattered them. There must be a knack to this. A secret. Like getting someone else to do it.

"Hey, Mr. Granger. That looks like hard work. Doesn't Rusty usually do that kind of thing?"

Rusty would do a job like this swiftly and efficiently. Of course he would.

Tom bit back on the resentment and turned. For some reason he'd expected the annoying reminder of his own inadequacy to have come from the ever-present Libbie. The voice hadn't registered until now, when he looked up and saw Marissa Sigley.

Even though the weather had turned cold, she wore cutaway denim shorts and a floaty top that clung in all the places Tom didn't want to be looking.

"Marissa," he said. "Everything okay?"

"I'm good thanks, Mr. Granger."

"But…?"

She shrugged and smiled, in a way that would get her what she wanted in almost any situation.

"Am I that obvious? My folks are out and they made

me promise I'd decorate the house for Halloween, but you know what I'm like with heights... I actually came here hoping to persuade Rusty to come and hang the high-up stuff for me, but..."

"It's a tough call," Tom told her. "Carry on making a fool of myself trying to rake leaves in the wind, or spend some time in a warm house helping a neighbor."

"Oh, Mr. Granger, thank you! My hero."

He fixed her with a look and she laughed. She'd been joking. Marissa was one person whose measure he still had. While Alice and Libbie made digs about her having a crush on him, Tom knew Marissa was smarter than that. Maybe she did, a little, but he knew it was a game she played. She did it teasingly, knowing how others would see it. A bit of fun.

And right now it was something of a relief to let her play her games, have a laugh, and do something nice for someone.

He leaned into the tool shed to deposit the rake, smiling briefly at his concern that he might have put it back in the wrong place.

"Halloween?" he said, as they headed out to the street. "Is it really that time already?"

"I know, right?" She said it as a question, and for some reason that made him feel old. The kids even *spoke* differently these days.

He realized she was studying him closely. That made him stall for words, and that in turn made him feel like a prize fool. He remembered Alice's—what were they? Jokes? Teasing? Accusations? The assertion that all guys had a cheerleader fantasy.

She'd joked more than once in the past that the only reason he followed the Browns was for the cheerleaders because you'd hardly follow them for their football, would you?

Marissa had said something, but he'd missed it, his mind wandering.

"What?"

"I said you seem quiet. Are you sure you're okay to help out? I don't want to get in the way if you have deadlines or such."

He smiled. "Did I look like I had a deadline?"

She laughed again. She did that a lot around him, he realized.

"So, are you serious about modeling?" he asked. "I hadn't realized until the other day."

She shrugged, tossing her long blonde hair back as she did so. "Oh, you know," she said, as if he'd have asked the question if he'd known the answer.

"You need to be careful. It's a tough industry, from what I've heard. Easy to get exploited."

"I guess. I haven't really given it much thought. It just came up in conversation and Libbie said I was a natural. I kind of liked it. Weird, but cool, if you know what I mean."

He didn't, really, but he let it go.

"Would you do it again?"

"Are you asking?"

He laughed awkwardly, looking away. He hadn't meant

it like that and she knew it. Playing her games again.

When they came to the house, Tom saw that Marissa had already made a good start on the decorations. There was a giant inflatable pumpkin on the porch, bats and skeletons hanging in the windows, fake cobwebs sprayed around every pane of glass. Warning signs littered the front yard, and right by the path a fake hand appeared to be clawing its way out of the dirt.

"This is great," said Tom. "I love it!"

Marissa actually blushed at the praise.

"So what's left to do?"

"Inside," she said. "I wanted to hang the ghosts and bats from the ceiling, but that means going up a ladder and, well…"

"Heights. I take it when you're cheerleading you're not the one they throw about from the top of the pyramid?"

"The flyer? No, I'm too big for that." She kind of straightened up as she said this, and Tom had to look, reminding him of just how long-limbed and full-figured she was.

Damn. Maybe Alice was right. Maybe he was just like every other guy on the planet.

He cleared his throat. "Shall we… uh…?" He nodded toward the door, and then followed her into the house.

She already had a ladder out. Within minutes, he was up there stretching to hang fabric ghosts from the ceiling of the double-height den on hooks that were already in place from previous years.

"Be careful, Mr. Granger!"

"It's fine." He looked down to smile reassurance at her, and in that moment felt the ladder wobble. It was nothing, a split-second adjustment, but she'd seen it, and cried out.

"It's fine," he said again.

When he climbed down, she was there at the foot of the ladder, poised as if about to throw herself into his arms.

It was shock, he told himself. Nothing more than that.

"I… I thought…"

"I was fine. I was in control."

He saw her frame relax, her shoulders dropping a little.

"Oh, Mr. Granger. I don't know what I'd have done. You're so cool about it." A pause. A flitting of those blue eyes towards his and then shyly away again. "You're so cool about most things."

And in that moment, Tom realized he'd got it wrong again. His reading of people. Earlier he'd thought Marissa was the one person whose measure he still had. He'd seen through her knowing games, her teasing. He'd thought the flirting was just a ploy to put herself at the center of things.

He'd thought he understood.

But no.

She meant it.

As she looked at him with those big eyes, it was with an adolescent passion similar to how Rusty looked at Alice.

When Libbie had instructed her to think of someone she desired, back at the photo shoot, Marissa had looked at Tom. It hadn't been a game. It had been an involuntary reaction.

She really did have a crush on him.

And right now the two of them stood toe to toe. Her eyes were on his, her body visibly tense again. For a brief moment, he let himself respond to all those triggers, to a girl who had become a beautiful woman, to the attention and desire, to the simple fact of being *wanted*.

He stepped back, bumping clumsily against the ladder.

"No, Marissa," he said. "Just no."

For a split second, she looked as if she might debate the point. Some inner cunning telling her that all she had to do was push a little harder and he would be powerless before her.

Then she slumped, her frame sagged, and she stepped back. She turned away so he couldn't see her face.

"I'm sorry, Marissa, but there's a fine line between fooling around and doing something that's just plain *wrong*. I'm a married man and you're sixteen. You're great. I really like you, and I'm glad to be part of your life, but that's all it could ever be. You have to know that, okay?"

He wondered if she would try to bluff it out. Claim she didn't know what he was talking about. He'd take that. He'd take the embarrassment on his part if that was the best way for her to save face.

But no, instead, she said, "I'm sorry, Mr. Granger. It's stupid, I know. You must hate me."

"I don't."

A flicker of a smile, then.

"At school... They're all just kids. It's so frustrating. Everyone's so immature."

"You'll get through that soon, Marissa. Believe me, nobody ever truly wants to be sixteen again after they've survived it."

She smiled once more.

"Are we good?" he asked.

"We're good."

"Do you have any more ghosts?" The incongruity of the question broke through the tension and, after a brief pause, they both laughed.

When the time came to leave, Marissa put a hand on the door to stop him. "I hope you don't think badly of me, Mr. Granger. I was stupid. I got carried away. I don't know what got into me. I think maybe it was the other day when I saw you and Libbie together, and you were kind of flirty. I guess it's different with someone like her, isn't it?"

"It's no different at all," he said. "There are lines not meant to be crossed."

And as he backed away down the porch, then turned to walk away, he wondered just how true that was. If even Marissa had detected something between him and Libbie, how dumb was he being?

Yes, Libbie was beautiful and she was strangely exciting to be with, too. Challenging and... stretching.

But he wasn't alone in thinking that. Just look at how Alice's whole demeanor changed when she was in

Libbie's company.

As he'd told Marissa, there were lines you just don't cross. He hadn't crossed any with Libbie, had he? They hadn't done anything wrong.

The trouble was, even in his own head, he sounded way too defensive.

How many secrets had he kept from Alice since Libbie had burst into their life?

He hadn't told her about the photo shoot, although that was only because Libbie had told her first. He'd been planning to mention it at some point. But would he have told her how awkward it had gotten, as Libbie involved him in it more and more?

And the other day, when Alice had quizzed him about how he'd lost that bank form, she'd asked if it might have fallen out of his pocket when he rode his bike into town. He hadn't told her that Libbie had driven him and he didn't understand why he'd felt the need to keep that secret. Because Alice would misinterpret it?

All the little conversations he'd had with Libbie. All the shared confidences.

Were these things actual secrets, or simply things that had gone unmentioned for innocent reasons?

He couldn't answer that honestly. He didn't know.

But perhaps the simple fact that he was even having this internal debate provided an answer of sorts.

CHAPTER 24

Alice couldn't work.

It had been bad enough before. Redoing tasks she *knew* she'd already done. And always with the nagging feeling that it would be so easy to overlook something this time, because in the back of her mind she'd know she'd done it all already.

She knew she couldn't afford to make any more mistakes. Michael Tuckett had made that perfectly clear. She already felt as if she was on borrowed time, and there were several people waiting in the wings to take the Mapleview account over.

It was a deal that could make a career.

But equally, it was one that could break a career too.

Hers.

So she'd come home, hoping she could find some kind of focus in the familiar surroundings. And then Libbie had come along. Shown her those photographs, albeit reluctantly.

There was no un-seeing those images.

She knew a photograph was only ever a snapshot of an instant in time. Photographs really could lie, or mislead. An instant that looked suggestive when frozen in time might only have been fleeting, a passing moment in a jokey photo shoot.

Without context, there was no difference between a person's face when they sneezed and when they orgasmed. But Alice had seen those images. They were ingrained in her mind.

It's nothing at all.

That's what she kept telling herself.

She knew how unhealthy jealousy could be. How such thoughts were not so much a vicious circle as a vicious *spiral*, leading you ever downward into a pit of paranoid suspicion and obsession.

A spiral she'd witnessed in Tom, so she should know better now.

Should know not to let those thoughts swirl around, dragging her down.

But she'd seen the way he looked at that girl. Seen the look in his eye.

And she'd seen Libbie's photographs.

She stood away from the computer, went across to the kitchen window. The wind was whipping at the trees now and Tom had clearly given up on raking the yard.

She wondered how much he'd enjoyed doing Rusty's work. Had he been trying to make some kind of point? Showing her that they didn't need Rusty around the place?

Well, his efforts didn't seem to have made much difference to the yard. Leaves still layered the grass, debris accumulating in corners. Flowers needed dead-heading.

Usually, you could at least tell when Rusty had been working, but there was no sign of Tom's impact on the garden this afternoon.

She knew she was judging him harshly. Punishing him in her head at least, for his indiscretions—even if they only existed in her head too.

"Oh, Tom," she sighed out loud. She didn't mean to take it out on him. To doubt him.

She then came to a decision not to be so hard on him. It was so easy to lapse into negativity and doubt.

As if on cue, she heard the front door, and moments later Tom appeared in the kitchen.

"Hi, sweetie," he said. "How's it going?"

"Oh, you know," she said with a shrug. She guessed it was pretty obvious from the abandoned laptop and the way she stood at the window tightly hugging herself that her afternoon had not gone well.

"I was surprised you were back so early today."

She hadn't explained about the hard time Michael Tuckett had given her, or her fears that she was screwing up big time. She didn't want to go into that now, either. It was as if saying any of that out loud made it more real.

They had so much at stake!

"Where have you been?" she asked instead.

"Oh, I went round to the Sigleys' to help with their Halloween decorations."

"I'm surprised Bob and Carol needed help," she said carefully. She knew Marissa's parents worked long hours out of town.

"It was just Marissa," Tom said. "She asked me to help out."

"And so you did."

She saw his whole body stiffen then. His eyes flitting from side to side, not meeting her look. He couldn't have looked more evasive if he'd tried.

Now, when Alice closed her eyes, she saw those photos again. Marissa leaning forward suggestively as she pouted into the camera. Marissa standing with one leg drawn up across Tom's front, his arms looped around her waist.

Every guy's cheerleader fantasy.

And every wife's nightmare.

"Are you fucking Marissa Sigley?"

He looked as if he'd been slapped.

She couldn't tell if he was more shocked at the cursing or at what she'd asked, or if his mind was simply racing to work out what to tell her. How *much* to tell her.

"Of course I'm not," he said. He was keeping his voice steady, trying not to inflame the situation.

"But you'd like to." She didn't even know what she was accusing him of. "She's a teenager, Tom. Sixteen." As if he didn't know.

"Don't do this."

This. The jealousy thing. The thing *he'd* done with such style last year.

That's what he was accusing her of now, in his very restrained way. Over-reacting.

But this was different. She'd seen it. She'd seen the photos. It wasn't like last year at all.

Last year...

The party at Pierson Newport. Tom had been drinking, but as always Alice had held back. When you're a diabetic it becomes second nature to watch—and count—everything that goes into your body. The drinks. The food. You don't lose control.

Walter had been drinking, too, and that's what had led to the whole thing.

Alice had seen a light in one of the side offices and gone to investigate. Nosy, she knew. Suspecting an office affair, or at least a party fumble the two participants would live to regret. She'd thought it might be Lloyd Cooper and Jilly Tuckett.

She wasn't proud to be snooping, but hey.

It was Walter, though, sitting at his desk on his own, staring intently at the big screen as his hands raced over the keyboard.

He started guiltily when she appeared, and for a moment she thought he might have been watching porn. Maybe that rapid typing had been him sending instructions to some girl on the other end of a webcam.

It was worse than that, though.

"You're playing *games?* And what's that... SwelterificJones? What does that even mean?"

"I'd had enough to drink. I needed to get away. And anyway, it's not just a game," he said awkwardly. "It's an interactive online community. I have friends in Taiwan, India, Australia. It's not a game. And... that's my avatar.

My screen name."

"SwelterificJones?"

"It's just one of those things. A name I picked up. It's kind of cool. If you're into the gaming scene."

She just looked at him. She was most definitely *not* into the gaming scene.

How had she known him all this time, even dated him a couple of times, and not known this about him?

She was standing at the corner of his desk, and he'd stood up when she came in, and now they stood there. It was a weird moment. In a movie it might have been a moment when star-crossed lovers finally kissed, they were standing so close.

But in reality, they'd kissed once, a long time ago, and the chemistry had been non-existent, and so now it was a different kind of intimacy. A moment of understanding where Alice realized that they'd each had their own reasons for escaping the hubbub of the party.

And that was when Tom had walked in.

He'd seen Alice slipping away, had been curious, had followed. And now he stood in the doorway staring at them as they stood toe to toe, the moment poised.

~ ~ ~ ~

And now…

Now Alice had every reason to be jealous, whereas back then Tom had merely walked in on two people in an office, doing nothing inappropriate.

Back then he'd let his mind run with it, filling in the gaps, elaborating.

He'd advanced across the office and Alice had stepped in his way, fearful of what he might do.

"It's nothing, Tom," she'd hissed at him, and he'd backed down. Poor Walter hadn't even realized what Tom was so mad about. Later, though, Tom had been unable to let it go. He'd quizzed her repeatedly, demanding to know why she'd been alone with Walter, what they'd been going to do if he hadn't butted in.

And he'd started checking up on her. Reading her cellphone messages when he thought she wasn't looking. Reading her emails. Following her, even.

They'd argued repeatedly, but how do you argue with paranoia fueled by irrational jealousy?

Don't do this.

And now he was accusing her of doing what *he'd* done: getting swept by jealous paranoia.

"There's nothing to be jealous of," he said, facing her across the kitchen. "Don't let yourself get carried away. Please, Alice."

"Just because you did, that doesn't mean we all think that way."

"I was wrong. I was the one who *did* get carried away. I let it tip me over the edge. And when I realized how badly I'd screwed up, the only thing I wanted was to make it right again."

That was true. Desperate to make amends, he'd focused on material things. The plans they had for the house, their future together. All of that took money and so he'd thrown himself at work, pushing himself so hard he eventually burned and crashed.

He'd said at the time that all he wanted was to make her happy, to make her love him again like she had before.

She told him she'd never stopped, and that was when he'd quit Pierson Newport and finally agreed to go to therapy. The start of his recovery. The start of *their* recovery.

The whole thing had been an extended psychotic breakdown.

It wasn't like this at all.

This time she'd seen the looks. Seen the photos.

And now he'd come back from the Sigleys' place, guilt plastered all over his features.

He turned and walked away.

She hadn't expected that. She'd expected him to at least stand his ground.

She went after him, through to the den where he stood idly rearranging his friggin' figurines.

"You're working too hard," he said softly. "You're wearing yourself out. It's making you more… edgy."

"Don't you dare turn that on me too," she said with a tightly controlled voice.

That was *his* thing. The irrational jealousy. The overwork to the point of breakdown.

"Don't you *dare* say this is all in my head because I'm under too much pressure."

"I'm scared for you, Alice. For us. You're working so hard. The strain's obvious to everyone. It's all work nowadays."

"I'm committed," she said. "I'm taking my opportunities, not running away from them. Not running away from the world."

Like you did last year. She didn't say that last bit. She didn't have to.

She saw him fighting not to speak. That damned restraint he'd learned, that had forced him to walk out of the kitchen just now rather than engage in this petty, damaging argument.

She didn't hold back though.

"One of us has to be out there, fighting the fight," she said. "We can't all hide away with these shitty figurines."

That seemed to hurt more than anything else she'd said.

"They got me through," he said softly. "Gave me something to focus on. My escape."

"Escape!" she snarled. She reached out and picked up one of the small china figures—that strange one Libbie had presented him with as a gift—and hurled it across the room at him.

Surprised by her own action, she stared as the thing struck a doorframe and tumbled to the floor.

Tom stared at her, then turned and walked out again.

Go on, run away. Escape again.

She didn't say that out loud either. The fact she even thought it was bad enough.

~ ~ ~ ~

He didn't know where he was going, just that he needed to not be *there*.

Needed to not see the look in Alice's eyes.

The distrust. The anger. The frustration.

The disappointment in *him*. That, more than anything, was something he needed to get away from. Last year he'd let her down. He'd lost his grip on the world and he'd almost lost the love of his life. He'd never wanted her to look at him that way again.

He didn't even understand what he'd done this time.

Was it a sin to be the nice guy? That pushover who always goes out of his way to help other people?

Maybe.

It was a lack of judgment, he knew. He shouldn't have dismissed Marissa's feelings for him as mere fooling around on her part. He certainly shouldn't have gone to the Sigleys' place when Marissa was there alone. Particularly when they'd just been through dealing with the over-zealous desires of *one* teenaged admirer, that foul-tasting business with Rusty.

Stupid.

He knew how close to the edge Alice was. The strain was telling and he'd been doing all he could to support her.

He shouldn't have let this happen.

He found himself outside on the porch. The wind was still whipping noisily around the house. Somewhere wind chimes clanged loudly, dissonantly, and the trees roared like rushing water.

It wasn't fair. He was doing his best, but it was still a struggle to hold it all together.

Once you've been through one major breakdown, you're always aware of just how close you might be to the next. Alice couldn't put all this on him.

She'd messed up with Rusty. Encouraging him when she should have known better. Not deliberately, of course, but still, she should have recognized the signs better.

And Walter. That thing Libbie had told him about the two of them emerging from the Easy Day Hotel. The photo she'd taken. He was sure there was an innocent explanation, just as there had been that time at the Pierson Newport party.

But it tapped into his vulnerabilities. The fears he tried so hard to suppress.

What if he wasn't enough for Alice? What if she'd never got over that sense of disappointment in him she'd shown last year?

He knew he shouldn't be thinking this way.

He went out into the darkness of the yard. Felt the coldness of the wind against his face and breathed deep.

He knew the business with Walter was entirely innocent. He understood that the only reason his brain was focusing on it now was some perverse kind of tit for tat: if she can accuse *him*, then maybe the hat fits both ways.

But also he was very aware that Alice and Walter, even

in their innocent, professional friendship, had a particular kind of intimacy Tom felt estranged from. An easy understanding. A familiarity with the inside of each other's heads.

And in some ways that was even worse than anything physical. It was untouchable. Irreproachable.

It wasn't *fair*.

All of this.

The accusations. The blindness she had to what he did for her, and to his own on-going struggles.

He loved her. So damn much.

And he feared that even that might not be enough.

It was maybe a minute or two later that he sensed more than saw a figure in the darkness.

Libbie. Doing her thing of hanging back, unsure whether to intrude or not. Somewhere between stalker and the model of diplomacy, he thought.

"Hey," he said, acknowledging her presence so she no longer had to make that choice.

"Hey. Fighting again?"

She knew when to talk straight, too.

"You heard." Not a question. Their voices had been raised, only a floor separating them from Libbie's space. "Sorry if we disturbed you. We're not usually this way."

"You've said that before." A pause, then: "So has Alice."

How many times had they fought recently? Probably more times in the last month than in all the time they'd been together. Even when things had gotten really bad inside Tom's head, he and Alice had mostly remained solid, rarely erupting into full-blown argument.

"Yeah, well… There are a lot of strains at the moment. At work."

"You don't have to make excuses for her."

He paused, peering through the gloom at their tenant. She wasn't usually so forthright in her assessments.

"I'm not making excuses—"

"It's okay."

How had she come to be standing so close all of a sudden?

Close enough to put a hand on his chest. Her touch was both soothing and invigorating at the same time.

"You want to talk? Come down to the apartment, Tom. Have a drink. Try to let some of it go. I'm a good listener." Her hand still rested lightly on his breastbone. "I'm good at providing comfort."

Did she mean what he thought…?

"I'm fine."

"I can tell."

Her hand, still on his chest.

He reached up to remove it, but instead his hand simply came to rest on hers, feeling the cold smoothness of her skin. Pressing it harder against him rather than removing it.

His throat felt dry. His heart far too loud.

Her hand moved now, but instead of pulling away he felt the bones and tendons shifting as her grip closed on a bunch of his shirt.

"Sometimes you just need distraction, Tom."

Pulling him closer, until he felt her breath warm on his face.

It would be so easy to kiss her.

He knew the feel of those lips already. Her kiss, in greeting or parting, her lips soft on his cheek. That brief intimacy.

It was only a small leap to imagine how those lips would feel against his own.

Distraction…

So easy.

She was stretching up toward him now, so that he felt some of her weight being taken on his shirt, where she gripped it so tight.

Why not? Alice already thought the worst of him. Was continually disappointed in him. Thought he would stoop so low as to screw their sixteen-year-old neighbor. Why not just confirm her expectations? Seek comfort. Distraction.

Libbie's lips against his were soft, just as he remembered them. Slightly parted.

The contact was tender, almost gossamer-light at first, and then—

He jerked back. So abruptly that he pulled her with him as she still clung to his shirt. They staggered, him taking a step back, her stumbling forward against him so that he suddenly, briefly had her in his arms. He felt the way her soft curves fit against him, molded to his shape.

Briefly, he knew what it was to hold her.

Then she righted herself, straightened, staggered back, and released his shirt.

"I... I'm sorry," she said. "Oh my goodness, I'm so sorry! I don't... I don't know what..."

"It's okay. It's fine." It wasn't. But that's what you say when you're the good guy who only cares what other people think.

Even when you're the good guy who'd just come so close to crossing a line that could never be uncrossed.

Not even crossing it for good reasons, if there could ever be a good reason. Not crossing it for desire or passion or love, but crossing it for what? Revenge? Some pathetic impulse to self-destruct?

"It's fine."

Say it often enough and maybe you'll believe it.

"Are you sure you're okay?" she asked. "I really didn't mean to... I got carried away. Lost all perspective."

"I'm fine. Are you okay?"

"I am."

"Good."

"Fine."

They'd run out of bland, meaningless things to say, and so now simply stood facing each other in the gloom.

Tom turned, went around the corner of the house to

where she'd parked, but then realized she was gone.

He didn't know what to do. It was only early evening, although the darkness made it feel later. And here he was, a grown man standing in his own yard, scared to go back inside his own house and nowhere else to go.

What a mess.

What an unremitting, goddamn mess.

CHAPTER 25

Alice got in the car and drove.

When Tom had stormed out, the house had felt so incredibly large and empty without him, in complete contrast to how claustrophobic it had felt moments before when he was still there.

She couldn't bear to be there alone.

When she got in the car she didn't have a plan in mind, but now she decided she would head to the office. It was long enough after normal office hours that it was unlikely anyone would still be there. Maybe she'd find that peace and quiet she'd sought and failed to find at home. Even if she only managed an hour working on refining the pitch that would be more productive than the rest of her day.

Traffic was slow as she hit downtown. Everyone else finishing for the day. Heading for home. Happy families. Relaxation.

She leaned forward and thumbed the stereo, flipping through the stations before turning it off again.

Nothing was going to please her right now.

Least of all Tom.

Had she been harsh with him? Maybe. She was aware

she'd let loose tensions that had been building up for some time now. All in one mad rush. No wonder he'd looked so shocked!

And she couldn't help thinking that if those tensions had been brewing for so long, that wasn't exactly the healthiest of signs.

Had she even been right to stick with him last year? A clean break then might have been far simpler. She'd been close at the time. Close to just walking away. But you can't walk away from a sick, broken man. Particularly one you love.

She couldn't believe she was even thinking like this.

Thinking almost wistfully of the life she might have had if she'd washed her hands of him back then.

She'd have gotten through the pain, come out the other side. She'd be healed by now, moving on. Instead, she was fighting the same old battles. The jealousy. The insecurities. The erratic, thoughtless behavior.

She couldn't believe he'd gone to Marissa's house, even if it was entirely innocent. Most likely it *was* innocent. He'd hardly have admitted that's where he was if he'd been up to anything, would he?

She didn't know what to think.

It seemed that everywhere she turned something was going wrong in her life. Work. Home. The renovation at Whitetail Lane. Rusty and Marissa.

And it seemed her relationship with Tom was at the heart of it all. If not the source of all the problems then, sadly, it didn't seem to be part of any of the answers either.

Had she finally stopped loving Tom?

Asking that question was bad enough, but not having the answer broke her heart.

~ ~ ~ ~

Michael Tuckett was just emerging from Pierson Newport when Alice pulled up in her parking space. He saw her immediately, and for a moment almost looked as if he was going to blank her and turn away to his own car.

Instead, he stopped. Waited.

The look on his jowly face was like a storm waiting to break.

Alice couldn't look him in the eye. Instead, she fixed her gaze on his thick, tangled eyebrows.

"Alice."

"Mr. Tuckett." Not on first name terms yet. Maybe not ever.

"Ruth's made a time for us to sit down tomorrow. I didn't know your vanishing act would be over today."

You have a meeting or a consult with Tuckett when things are going well. A *sit down* sounded ominous.

"I'm taking it off you, Alice. Mapleview. It's my fault. I shouldn't have pushed you into it. You're not ready."

She felt sick. She felt blackness creeping into the edges of her vision.

"Sir?"

"I've briefed Jilly and Lloyd on taking it over already.

They have access to all the documents."

Lloyd was the company golden boy. It had been a close thing between Alice and Lloyd for getting Mapleview the first time around.

And Jilly. Michael Tuckett's daughter.

"Mr. Tuckett, I've been home all day working on the pitch. Will you at least look at what I've done? I think we're close to having a final proposition to put forward. I've worked so hard on this!"

"I think we're close too, Alice. And Lloyd and Jilly will be putting it forward. We need to win this one. And when we do, the entire company will benefit. It'll be a team effort and your work won't be overlooked."

Gold-plate it all you like, but Alice still knew grade A bullshit when she heard it.

It wasn't a team effort. She was being swept aside. She'd done most of the work but she wouldn't get any credit, or any of the rewards. She certainly wouldn't get VP. She'd be lucky to still be working at Pierson Newport by the end of the month.

This was a cutthroat business and Michael Tuckett had just wielded the knife.

"I'm sorry, Alice, but sometimes the hardest decisions have to be taken. It's not easy."

"You have to make the right choices for the business," she said. She even managed a flicker of a smile. She couldn't afford to burn this bridge completely. It was all she had.

"Get your head down, Alice. Regroup. Come back fighting. That's the Pierson Newport way!"

"I will, sir."

"Good night, Alice."

"Sir."

She watched him walk away.

She almost went back to her car, then, but instead, keyed her way into the building and headed for her office.

She would show him.

She hadn't been lying when she'd said the pitch was close to completion. She'd done a lot of work on it, and once she'd reincorporated the missing elements she could show it to him, force him to at least give it a glance.

Regroup. Come back fighting.

Oh yes! Just bring it on, Mr. Tuckett. Bring it on.

There was only one other person still in the office. As she entered the open-plan area, Alice saw the familiar screen glow coming from Walter's side-office.

She went over to stand in his doorway.

"Waiting for everyone else to go away, before it's time to play?" she asked.

She knew he was sensitive about his hobby. People could be cruel. She felt honored that she was just about the only person who could get away with teasing him, because he knew there was nothing mean behind her words.

He looked up now, his face lit by the screen. Smiled. "You know me so well."

"I didn't want to disturb you, but I sure could use some of that whiskey you keep in your desk right now."

"Whiskey? What whiskey?"

She said nothing, just fixed him with a raised-eyebrows look.

"Oh swell," he said. "And here I was thinking that was my little secret."

He reached down to the second drawer and produced a bottle and two plastic cups.

"It's not single malt," he said.

"I don't care if it's discount turpentine right now."

"That bad?"

He poured two good measures, then topped up the first and handed it over.

She nodded. "Michael Tuckett's just told me I'm as good as fired."

Walter's mouth fell open.

"He's taken Mapleview off me. Given it to golden boy and his little baby."

"Lloyd and Jilly? Terrific. That's just so damn... terrific."

"I was surprised my keycard even worked to let me into the building, or that my name's still on my office door. Not for long, I'm sure."

"So what are you going to do?"

"I'm going to nod and smile and hope things work out, is what I'm going to do. And in the meantime I'm going to carry on finishing off my pitch in the hope he can be convinced to reconsider. I don't have anything else."

"I wish I had some good advice. Or even bad advice. Anything."

"You can tell me where you got that screen-name from."

Walter looked surprised for a moment, then laughed. He'd never told her any more than that it was a cool thing among gamers to have just the right avatar name. She still remembered his embarrassment when she'd walked in on him at that office party and found out the guilty secret that he spent his spare time playing games on the company's high-speed network.

"It's what I was called at school," he said. "It was cruel then. A bullying thing. I reclaimed it, made it my own."

She'd worked that much out already. "What was it? Some kind of ironic superhero name? SwelterificJones?"

"Nothing as glamorous as that. I was never the most articulate kid. I struggled to find the right things to say. So when I had to respond to something quickly I'd say something like *swell*, or *terrific*. Add my surname, and there you have it. Swell-Terrific-Jones."

She smiled. She should have known it would be something simple like that. Now that he mentioned it, even now he said *swell* and *terrific* a lot more than most people.

"That's... terrific," she said.

"Swell."

They each took a long sip of their drinks. She was only vaguely concerned that the alcohol would mess with her blood sugar levels. She had bigger problems tonight.

"This whole thing's pretty damn swell right now, isn't

it?"

He nodded. "Don't worry," he told her. "You'll turn it round. Remember, you're the superstar. You've got this."

"It sure feels that way."

Now she remembered them standing like this in her own office a couple of days before, positions reversed: her at the desk and Walter at the door. "You remember saying you'd do a bit of digging into our perfect tenant for me?" she asked him. "I don't suppose…?"

She wanted a distraction. But if she thought she might get some kind of reassurance that at least one area of her life was not descending into turmoil, she was sadly mistaken.

She knew something was up as soon as she'd asked the question. A cloud passed over Walter's features.

"I don't know," he said. "I'd been meaning to talk to you about that, but… well, you've been busy, and then today you went home before we got the chance to talk."

"What is it?"

"It's nothing, I'm sure. I just haven't dug deep enough yet, or in the right places."

She knew that wasn't true. Walter knew where to dig. And he was *good*.

"And?"

"I can't really find anything of any substance about her. That in itself is odd. Everyone has a big and usually very messy digital footprint these days. Everyone leaves an online trail. Usually the problem is that there's too much to wade through, not too little. But I can't find a work history for her, or a school history."

"What?" Alice whispered.

"I can't find drunken vacation snapshots, or embarrassing video clips friends have posted on social media. She has a Facebook profile, but it's only the bare bones of one. The privacy on her social media profiles is tight, but even when you sidestep that there's not really anything to see."

Walter was tapping at the keyboard as he spoke, as if he was going to show Alice something, but then he let his hands fall.

He continued, "There really is nothing to show. It's weird. It feels manufactured, like those fake profiles you hear about. You said she's a photographer?"

Alice nodded.

"So where's her online portfolio? There's nothing at Smugmug, 500px, Zenfolio or any other places you might expect. She has minimal presences on Flickr and Instagram, but if you look at the images, well... it's hard to pin down, but they don't *feel* right. Too generic. The pictures don't feel like they were all taken by the same photographer, if that makes sense?"

"What about school? She went to NYU."

"That's what she told you. Interactive Media and Technology. But that program is only available at NYU Abu Dhabi. Has she ever mentioned living and studying abroad? Why go all that way to study something she could have studied stateside at a different university? It hardly seems likely, does it? And that campus only opened for real in 2010. How old is she? Early thirties? Wouldn't she have been studying for her degree before then? It doesn't add up."

"So what does that mean?"

"I don't know. It could be as simple as you've misremembered her school, or the precise title of her degree program. It could mean she has some strange family reason to have done her degree late and in a distant country. It could be that she's a very private individual and she uses all the tricks she learned in her degree to protect her social media presence from prying eyes like mine."

"Or it could mean she's lying."

"Have you heard of Occam's Razor?"

She had. It was a rule that stated, simply, that when faced with more than one explanation, the simplest explanation was always the most likely one.

And according to Occam's Razor, Libbie Burchett had been lying from the very start.

CHAPTER 26

Tom watched his wife leave. Standing in the shade of the garage, he wondered if she was even going to come back.

She looked so lonely, walking to her Ford Focus. So vulnerable.

She pulled the door shut softly, as if hoping not to draw attention. Not wanting confrontation. *More* confrontation.

She sat quietly inside for a long time. She looked as if she had her arms folded across her chest, hugging herself, but the dim lighting made it hard to see. Was she crying?

He should go to her, but his feet were rooted to the spot.

The engine fired and the lights came on, not shining directly at him but still dazzling. Had she seen him? He didn't know, but the car started to pull away regardless. Moments later she was gone.

He was shivering. He put it down to the cold wind, nothing more. He went back inside.

He couldn't believe she'd actually said it out loud. The accusation. That he was sleeping with a sixteen-year-old.

Did she realize how offensive that was? How much it

hurt? That would be so many levels of wrong.

He didn't know if she actually believed it, or was doing it for some kind of effect. To shock him out of his own jealous behavior, perhaps.

Either way it hurt like a punch to the gut.

And one of the reasons it particularly hurt was how close it came to the truth.

Not Marissa Sigley, but... Just how close had he come to giving in to Libbie's advances?

He'd been angry. Frustrated. He'd found himself in that place where, when you believe you've lost everything, what more is there left to lose?

He closed his eyes and leaned back against the door, pushing it shut against the wind.

He'd kissed her.

Or she'd kissed him.

The semantics didn't matter. They'd kissed.

He could still feel that ethereal touch of her lips against his. The tightness of his shirt where her closed fist had bunched it against his chest so she could hold him close, pull him closer.

It had lasted a fraction of a second. So brief, it had barely even happened.

But it had.

They'd kissed.

He'd felt that surge in his abdomen. The rush of his heart. His body responding.

And in that fraction of a second, that *what the hell?* reaction. That *What have I got to lose anymore?*

"Come *on*, Thomas Granger!" The words came out in a hiss.

If he'd been able to slap himself he would have. He needed to pull himself together.

What mattered most? That he'd almost given in, or that he *hadn't?* That he'd seen what mattered and had resisted?

Maybe he was kidding himself, but he clung to that thought.

He loved Alice, damn it! Everything else was noise. He loved her.

He looked around, saw that damned figurine on the floor. For a moment, all his resentment focused on the thing, and he almost swept it up and put it in the trash. Then the OCD in him took over and he gathered it up, the figurine and the fragment that had chipped off the arm.

Maybe it was a metaphor. On closer inspection, the small porcelain figure looked old and worn, as if it had seen better days. But it had survived. Even with that fragment chipped off the arm, it could still be fixed. Made just as good as new, in fact. Just like their marriage. Surviving. Enduring. Fixable.

He went through to the kitchen and rummaged in the utility drawer where they kept scissors, string, glue, and old keys that no longer had a lock to fit.

He sat on a bar stool at the kitchen counter where the light was good and peered at the figurine.

The broken fragment was a near-perfect fit, apart from a flake of porcelain that was missing from near the shoulder.

Odd, though, the figurine appeared to have been repainted. A brown figure with a white jersey. The shirt even bore what looked remarkably like a Brewers logo. Had Libbie herself repainted the figurine to look like a Brewers mascot, or had she simply seen the shirt and thought of him?

Underneath the white, the figure of the smiling bear had originally been wearing orange.

Weird. He'd thought the figure was oddly familiar when Libbie had given it to him, but he'd been unable to place it. But now… That orange jersey.

Instead of gluing the fragment back into place, he went back through the house and upstairs to the spare room he used as an office.

A couple of minutes on Google was enough to confirm his suspicions.

The bear was a ghost from his youth, the mascot from the summer camp he'd been to in his teens.

Surely, this was some kind of freakish coincidence? Maybe an orange-jerseyed bear was a commonly used mascot for summer camps, not just the one he'd attended. There could be a million of these things in circulation.

And the paint job? Well, even Tom had taken it for a piece of Brewers merchandise when he'd first seen it. Libbie must have seen him in his team jersey and picked it for that reason.

What other explanation could there be?

~ ~ ~ ~

"I'm sorry."

They both said it at the same time, as soon as Alice stepped into the house.

Their eyes met, they hesitated, as if both still uncertain of how to move on from this shaky territory, and then they stepped toward each other and were suddenly in each other's arms.

"I'm sorry, I really am."

"I was stupid. Thoughtless."

"I was angry. Not at you, but at… *everything*."

He held her, felt her heart pounding against his chest. Breathed in the scent of her hair as he pressed his face down against the crown of her head.

"How did we ever let it get that way?"

She tilted her face up and he dipped his down and they kissed, a kiss they'd shared a million times before but rarely one that carried as much meaning as this one did.

He brushed her tears away with the tip of one finger.

"I think I messed up," Alice told him. "Everything. Us. This. Work."

"We're a team, sweetie. We *both* messed up." A wink. A smile.

She laughed, briefly.

"We're good," he told her. "Whatever goes wrong,

whatever we have to go through, we still have us." Saying it out loud, he even believed it.

They moved through to the kitchen and sat on bar stools swiveled to face each other.

"What's happening at work?"

Alice looked away as soon as he said this, and he knew it was bad.

"Michael Tuckett," she said, her voice so small he had to strain to hear. "He's taken the Mapleview account from me. Says I've made too many mistakes. I'm too big a risk factor. He's given it to Lloyd and Jilly."

Tom snorted. "Of course he has."

"He's right. I've been screwing up. I processed a whole batch of figures to include in the pitch and then somehow left them out. I still don't know how I did it."

Tom said nothing. She'd been showing the strain recently. Irritable and distracted. Had that transferred into her work? It wouldn't help anything for him to say that out loud, however.

"So what's the plan?" He reached out and squeezed her hand. Alice always had a plan, whatever went wrong.

"I almost finished the pitch anyway," she told him.

"So you might as well do so." Finishing her thought, just as they always did for each other.

She smiled. "Maybe he'll see he was too quick to take it off me."

"Maybe."

She clearly believed it about as much as he did.

Now, she reached across to where he'd left the broken figurine. "Sorry about that," she said. "Is it fixable?"

"A bit of glue, that's all it needs. But do you want to know the strangest thing?"

She said nothing, just raised her eyebrows, waiting for him to go on.

He took the figurine off her and held it to the light. "See here? Where the top layer of white has flaked away?"

She studied it, but didn't seem to understand.

"Orange?"

"Remember summer camp?"

While Tom had been a regular at summer camp through his teens, Alice had only gone a couple of times, so maybe the memories were less imprinted.

"The mascot," he prompted her.

At last, he saw the recognition in her eyes.

"I wasn't sure, so I checked on Google Images. There's no mistaking it. That's our summer camp mascot."

"But…"

"I know, right? It's almost certainly some freaky kind of coincidence. After all, it was painted in the same colors as my favorite Brewers shirt."

"But underneath…"

Not only could they finish each other's sentences, they could read the other's expressions, too, and Tom knew when Alice's mind was racing.

As it was now.

"What is it, sweetie? What's going on?"

"I don't know," his wife said slowly, as if measuring her words out one by one. "But…"

He waited. Gave her time to gather her thoughts before continuing.

"I've been talking to Walter."

He felt a surge of the old jealousy but clamped down on it. Of course she'd been talking to Walter. He was a colleague. A friend. Tom shouldn't resent that she had friends! He knew that, just as he knew that those jealous feelings were *symptoms*, signs of a problem and something to be fixed.

"About…?"

"Libbie."

He waited for her to go on. He could tell this wasn't going to be good.

"I was getting a little… *uncomfortable* about her. Some of the things she said and did. Walter offered to do some digging."

"What did he find?"

"Nothing. That's the problem. He should have found *something*. But her digital footprint is almost non-existent. He said it was like those fake Facebook profiles that try to friend you. She has an online presence, but it's only superficial. No substance to it."

"There must be something."

Alice was shaking her head. "No, that's the thing.

Think about it. Just how much do we know about her?
Go on, list them now."

"She's a photographer."

"With almost no online presence, and what she has is
a gesture at best."

"She came here from Manhattan."

"How many million people live in New York? What
do we specifically know that confirms that, or gives us
any more detail?"

"She…" He was struggling already. "She went to
NYU, didn't she? Some kind of IT course."

"That doesn't exist. Or at least, it only exists as a
recent course at NYU Abu Dhabi!"

"Abu Dhabi?" he repeated blankly. "That's impossible,
I checked her references."

Alice shrugged. "How easy is it to buy fake references?
I don't know. I'm not saying she did, just that we don't
know she didn't."

"What are you saying?"

"I'm saying Libbie Burchett, our previously perfect
tenant, doesn't seem to add up."

"But… why?"

Neither of them had an answer for that.

"What can we do?" Tom asked, instead.

"I'd hate to over-react," said Alice hesitantly.

"But if you think about it, everything started to go
sideways when she stepped into our lives, didn't it? Even

if there's nothing malicious going on, it's as if she's some kind of magnet for catastrophe."

"Rusty. Marissa. All the things going wrong at work."

"Us turning on each other."

"Or *being turned* on each other."

It was true. How much had all of Libbie's little digs and observations mounted up to feed the growing turmoil?

"We should ask her to leave," said Tom. "She's like a bad-luck charm."

"Or a voodoo doll."

Maybe that wasn't quite the right analogy, but he knew what she meant.

"She wouldn't go, though, would she? She'd want to know why, and what would we tell her anyway?"

"The truth," said Alice. "She's... Well, I think she's poison. Poison in the groundwater, contaminating everything she touches. We have to flush her out, Tom. The more I think about it the more sure I become."

He squeezed her hand.

"We will, sweetie. We will. It might take time though."

They both had a lot of professional experience in real estate and they knew that any legal move to evict their tenant might be a protracted affair.

"We should talk to someone as soon as possible, start things moving."

"And in the meantime, avoid her as much as possible."

Poison. That was as good a word for Libbie Burchett as any Tom had come up with.

And all you can hope to do with poison is flush it out of the system.

~ ~ ~ ~

Dr. Holt and his team of therapists had trained Libbie well.

That initial rush of anger. The sheer rage that made you want to lash out, destroy something. Someone.

They'd taught her how to recognize it the moment it was triggered. How to clamp down on it. Hold it in. Even when the provocation was at its greatest.

Like when someone said you were poison.

A bad luck charm.

When someone said they wanted to throw you out on the street.

She sat in the kitchen of the shabby, badly decorated apartment they so generously let her rent. The only light came from a lamp on the work surface. Shining down onto the scrapbook before her.

The only movement, the repetitive back and forward of one hand, clutching a pair of scissors that were inverted so the tip of the blade scratched, scratched, scratched on what had been the face of a man in a white Brewers jersey.

How dare they!

She fought to control the anger, the rush of thoughts.

So they'd seen through her. They knew she wasn't who or what she claimed. But they'd as much as admitted there was nothing they could do about it. She still had time, even if she had to speed up her timetable a little.

Still had time to destroy the oh-so-perfect Grangers.

For now, though, she contented herself with the scratch, scratch, scratch obliteration of Tom Granger's face in the scrapbook before her.

CHAPTER 27

Walter was an addict. If there was a Gamers Anonymous, he'd be there every week, trying to earn those medals, following whatever twelve-steps plan they had, all in the hopes of leveling up.

But no. Who was he kidding? That would mean he wanted to actually give up his addiction, and here he was, back in the office at the crack of dawn, having left some time after midnight.

The network connection here was fast, better than anything he might eventually get at home. And there was something about gaming in an office environment... something vaguely *illicit*.

He took his kicks where he could.

He knew he didn't have the looks or the personality. He didn't have the confidence. He was never going to be the star of the show. He was never the guy who got the girl.

Particularly a girl like Alice.

Of course he had a thing for Alice. He always had. Sure, they joked about those couple of dates, about their one kiss. He had the whole line about it being like dating your sister.

They were friends. He'd settled for that long ago.

Nothing creepy about it. Nothing stalkerish.

Walter was old school. He knew the rules. Knew the boundaries. Friendship with Alice was just about the best thing in his life, and he was good with that. That and gaming.

So here he was, first thing in the morning before anyone else had stirred, back in the office.

SwelterificJones, swinging back into action.

He sat back down at his desk with a double espresso. Another addiction.

The conversation with Alice last night had disturbed him. Yes, he'd done his research, digging into the online presence—or lack of presence—of her perfect tenant. But he'd thought it was simply a case of someone guarding their privacy.

It hadn't really shocked him until he saw Alice's reaction. Until he realized how his contribution was just one piece of a puzzle that seemed to be adding up to something far more disturbing.

Who *was* Libbie Burchett? And why had she infiltrated herself into Tom and Alice's life?

Was she a long-forgotten girlfriend with a grudge? Was she running some kind of elaborate scam? He couldn't work it out.

So now, instead of feeding his gaming habit, he opened up the folder he'd saved. The folder called *Perfect Tenant*. He'd saved everything. The few, mostly repeated images he'd found in her social profiles. A text file containing URLs and what few mentions he'd found of her.

Not much at all.

He tried a search again that he'd carried out the day before. Plucking one of the few images he had of Libbie and reverse-searching it.

He was wasting his time. The search results just came up with the handful of places he'd already found where that image had been used. Facebook, Instagram, nothing new.

Idly, he clicked to expand the search to similar images, setting all the search parameters as wide open as he could.

How many million results? How many young women with chestnut hair were there in the world? He really was wasting his time. Rather than broaden the search even further, he narrowed it by a few of the parameters he knew. New York—she'd mentioned NYU, and claimed to have moved from there, so maybe there was an element of truth in that.

He hit Return and waited.

When a gamer finds the hidden shortcut, or the easter egg a coder has left hidden as a joke, or simply when you're on a long unbeaten run, you get a particular kind of a rush. Something maybe only a true gamer really understands or recognizes.

Walter felt that rush now.

He'd hit the jackpot. He'd found the hidden trapdoor in Libbie Burchett's carefully constructed facade.

Only that wasn't her name.

Because of course it wasn't.

The picture on screen before him was of a girl of maybe fourteen or fifteen, but the baby fat and pigtails didn't disguise the fact that it was her. A boarding school photograph. An alumni page.

He started reading, pausing every so often to open a new tab with a related search. Digging ever deeper.

That rush... the thrill of discovery. The excitement at having cracked some near-impossible puzzle.

It didn't last long.

Within minutes it was replaced by the nauseous horror of what was unreeling before him.

"Holy shit."

He reached for his cellphone. It was early, but that didn't matter. He had to tell Alice what he'd found.

The phone rang through to voicemail. He considered leaving a message but didn't. She'd be in work soon. He would wait until then. Take her somewhere quiet for a coffee and tell her everything.

And in the meantime, he continued to scroll, continued to spawn new tabs with fresh searches, feeling the sense of dread growing steadily with every click.

~ ~ ~ ~

Alice was out early at the income property on Whitetail Lane.

She was standing, holding the look of Franco Vialli and biting back down on the angry retorts that bubbled in her head in response to his, "So? Sue my goddamn ass. Excuse the language, ma'am, but this is a construction site."

All around, his crew were gathering up their tools, loading supplies back into trucks, dismantling the scaffolding that until this morning had framed the front of the property.

"Wait, what's happening? On what grounds are you quitting the site and breaking our very tightly worded contract?"

"Failure to pay on schedule. Financial uncertainty. Changing the terms. You want me to go on?"

"Changing the terms? You're the one who keeps changing the terms."

"I didn't put no hole in the roof."

"But you were fixing it. Until this morning, that is."

"And now I'm not."

"Come on, Franco. I thought you were one of the good guys."

"I am. But I'm no patsy."

All those retorts rushed to the surface once again, but she clamped down on them. She needed Franco. She was in no place to hire a new contractor now.

"We were only a day late on the last installment. I thought Tom had smoothed that over with you?"

"That what he tell you?"

She wasn't going to get angry with Tom, even though her first response was to wish she hadn't left it to him again.

"A day late might not sound much to you," Franco

said. "But everything has a domino effect. You don't understand how precarious this business is."

She was in real estate. Of course, she understood the business.

And then she realized. He was just trying to screw them out of more money. He knew she'd struggle to hire someone new to pick this job up at this stage. And with that hole in the roof and winter approaching…

How many times had he done this?

All those times he gave them two quotes. The minimum job, and then the *But if it was me* quote for *doing it properly*. Had Franco been playing them from the start?

"How much? How much to get your crew to stay on site and finish this? How much to at least make that hole in the roof secure until we work something else out?"

Franco tried to look offended, but didn't quite manage.

Just then, her phone buzzed in her purse. She ignored it. She'd check it later. She had more important things to worry about right now.

Franco surprised her then. "It's not like that," he said in a softer tone of voice. "This business, a guy needs security. When you start to hear stories…"

"Stories?"

"About clients who aren't straight up about their financial position."

Was he accusing her of lying?

"When you hear about clients that don't have enough to cover their responsibilities, and who might be willing to string things along for as long as possible… And when they start getting late on payments. Well, it's always the guy at the end of the chain who pays, isn't it? I've been stung too many times before."

"Who's been telling you these things? Who's been lying about us?"

But she knew.

Who else would be spreading lies of the most damaging kind?

There was only one person who fit that bill.

~ ~ ~ ~

Walter waited, but Alice didn't show at work.

It was hardly a surprise, given the events of yesterday. Everyone had heard Tuckett bawling her out first thing in the morning, after which she'd feigned illness and gone home. And then later, when she'd come in and Tuckett had told her, effectively, that her time here at Pierson Newport was coming to an end…

Who would come to work the day after that?

If she was wise, she'd be searching for another job, but Walter knew she'd be working all hours to finish that pitch and make it good enough to convince Tuckett to keep her on.

When he was certain that she wasn't going to show, he tried her cellphone again, but nothing. This time he started to leave a message before stopping himself. What if Alice's voicemail had been compromised somehow?

He was reluctant to try her home landline, or even

Tom direct. He didn't really understand his relationship with Alice's husband. Superficially they got on, but there were always undercurrents. Since his breakdown last year, Tom seemed far too ready to blame Walter for things.

This was why Walter preferred his interactions with people to be online. As soon as things got complicated in real time, in the real world, he was out of his depth.

Email? That suited Walter's normal approach. In an email you could write everything down. You could re-read it over and over, fine-tuning it until you were sure it said exactly what you wanted to say. Unlike real life, where you only ever got one clumsy shot.

But email wouldn't work in this instance, for the same reason he'd cut himself off when he started to leave a message on Alice's voicemail. What if Libbie read it first?

He knew she was good with computers. She'd *fixed* Alice's computer problems and he was pretty sure from what he'd found out that she'd caused them in the first place. If she had somehow secured access to Alice's email, then that was not the place to lay down everything he had found out.

No, there was only one thing to do.

"Ruth?" he said into his desk phone, having punched in the number of the office administrator. "It's Walter. Walter Jones. I'm feeling rough this morning. Too many long days and evenings in the office." He was always there before everyone and leaving after they'd gone. She'd believe that. "I think I'm going to go home and try to sleep it off."

He'd go to Alice's house. She must be there. He'd tell her everything and they'd work out what to do from there.

And he didn't have any time to spare.

Alice's life might depend on it…

CHAPTER 28

Libbie seethed. Last night had been a mistake.

Trying to kiss Tom. Trying to seduce him. She'd gone off-script.

It might have been fun. Not the sex. The aftermath. The opportunities to play on Tom's inevitable guilt. Telling him she'd fallen in love with him. Setting up ways for Alice to find out. Getting Marissa to turn psycho with adolescent jealousy and indignation.

The possibilities were endless. And delicious.

But it could have gotten out of hand. All that was academic now, anyway.

They *knew*.

Or at least, while they didn't know the details, they knew she was playing them. They knew she wasn't who she claimed, that all she'd told them of her life was fake.

They wanted to get rid of her.

And worse, all this had drawn them closer to each other, not pulled them apart.

It was infuriating.

Frustrating.

It was time to take things up a level.

She waited until they were both out. Alice had gone to the Whitetail Lane site before going to work. Tom was still waiting for a couple of new jobs to come in, so he'd taken the opportunity to go to the mall before heading on to do the weekly grocery shopping.

Listening in via the air duct was priceless when it came to planning.

She hoped Alice was having fun at the construction site. The anonymous tip-off to Vialli had been fun. He'd sounded all too ready to jump ship. Late payments, difficult clients. It hadn't taken much of a push.

Alice might be able to win him over, of course. But even if she did, it would certainly cost her.

Such fun.

That would teach them to think they could get rid of her!

She paused on the porch.

Every time you let yourself into someone else's house, there was a heart-stopping moment when you had to commit.

You put the stolen key in the door, turn, push inside.

At that point, there's no disguising that you're doing something unlawful.

There are no excuses for doing something like that.

No possible justification.

She pushed the door shut behind herself and let a big breath slowly escape from her lungs.

She looked around and spotted the broken summer

camp figurine back in place in Tom's collection. He hadn't repaired it though. The sliver of exposed orange was almost imperceptible, and could easily have gone unnoticed.

It had been so funny, giving him something so blatant, so thinly disguised. Knowing it would be sitting there, right under their complacent suburban noses.

She headed upstairs.

She didn't find what she was looking for in the main bathroom, but in the master bathroom she struck gold.

A mirrored cabinet, one shelf loaded with toiletries, the other with medication. Painkillers, antacids, and decongestants, which she ignored. But *there:* rosiglitazone and acarbose. Diabetes meds and paraphernalia. She'd done her research, knew what to look for.

She took the boxes and put them in the canvas bag she'd thought to bring with her.

In the bedroom, she started by going through the drawers, checking for any other stashes of diabetes medication, but there were none. The mini-fridge in the corner paid dividends once more. Vials of insulin, and other medicines she didn't recognize.

She removed these, put some in her bag and took the insulin through to the bathroom. Here, she drained the vials and replaced their contents with water from the faucet.

Alice might notice that her supplies were low, but she'd probably just think she'd forgotten to get the prescriptions refilled. She'd been so forgetful lately, hadn't she?

Downstairs, she searched methodically again. Finding more insulin in the fridge, she repeated the process of replacing the contents with water. She dumped an entire jar of honey into the sink. She found a bag of candy and stole that, too.

There was another medicine cabinet in the downstairs washroom and all the diabetes medications went into Libbie's bag. She confiscated glucose tablets and instant glucose gel tubes.

Libbie knew she had a short fuse. A violent temper. That was why she'd ended up in that appalling hospital, after all, wasn't it? That was what she'd spent those ninety days doing. Being coached in anger management, rage control, impulse curtailment.

The most important lesson she'd learned was how to convince them that she was a changed person.

But that short temper was only one side of the coin.

The other side was this. The slow burn.

A burst of anger was deliciously satisfying, there was no denying that. But the joy of a meticulously planned and executed plot was so much more rewarding!

The slow release was so much more satisfying than the instant gratification of an anger spike.

She wondered how Dr. Holt would feel if he knew that was one of her big takeaways from her time in his care?

She went back around the house again for one last patrol.

No more hidden stashes of pills. Nowhere else she might keep insulin, meds, and sugar. She'd have some in her purse, of course, but there was nothing Libbie could do about that.

She went back to the kitchen and tipped the contents of her bag out onto the big table. So many goodies! She swept them back up into the bag. She would dispose of them later.

Time to go.

That was when she heard the noise. Nothing obvious. Just a kind of thump and dragging sound. It might have been something shifting in the wind. Or it might have been someone outside, bumping into something, or stumbling and righting themselves in the gravel.

She went carefully through the house to the foyer. Paused.

There had been no more sounds.

She peered through the frosted glass of the side window. No sign of either car.

Tom was being boringly domestic today, but right now Alice was either still having a nightmare encounter with Franco Vialli at Whitetail Lane, or she'd gone on to Pierson Newport where she'd no doubt be having an equally nightmarish time, now that everything had gone so badly wrong for her.

That made Libbie feel good.

That made her feel very good indeed.

The sound she'd heard must have been the wind knocking something over. A neighbor.

She opened the door and Walter Jones was standing there.

Guilty, surprised, he took an involuntary step back, raising his arms defensively as if he thought she was going to attack him.

"Oh! Walter, isn't it? We met at Pierson Newport when I came to pick up Alice for lunch that time. Can I help you?"

Be confident. Occupy the space as if you own it, as if you're meant to be there.

"This is Alice's place," he said. "What are you doing here?"

She dangled the key. "They gave me this," she told him. "I check the mail for them and help them out around the place. We've become the best of friends."

She smiled, taking pleasure in the look of confusion that washed over his features.

He didn't believe her. It was a most unlikely claim for why she might have a key.

But like any decent, upstanding member of the community, even now Walter Jones desperately *wanted* to believe her.

Because to do otherwise would be to accept there was evil in the world. In *his* world.

"Alice never mentioned that."

"She'd have told you?" Libbie kept the innocent lightness in her tone, knowing it would throw him. "She tells you everything then? She told me you two were close."

"I… I mean no. I mean." He stopped, licked his lips, started again. "I saw what you were doing. I saw what you

261

have in that bag."

So he'd managed to summon the courage to confront her, but he was stalling already. Libbie stayed silent, still smiling. Let him grind to a halt.

Finally, she said, "Libbie's meds, you mean?"

He was trying to read her expression. Trying to understand. He clearly hadn't expected a confession of sorts.

"The meds, yes," he said.

Libbie waited. She kind of respected the fact he'd had the balls to challenge her, but really... He was out of his league. *Poor thing.*

"You can't take her meds. She needs them."

"That's why I have them. She's been so forgetful lately. You must have noticed. She asked me to do an audit and make sure she had the right ones. There are so many. I'm just taking them down to my apartment so I can Google them all."

For a moment, she thought she'd convinced him. But then...

"Is that why you were pouring insulin down the sink?"

He'd seen.

Damn it. How long had he been here?

She carried on smiling innocently. She'd run out of answers, but that didn't mean she had to let him know he had her.

And behind the smile her mind raced.

"They were past their expiration date. I was doing as

she asked."

She stepped out onto the porch, pulling the door behind her.

Stepped past him, down into the yard.

"I'm calling the cops," he told her. "Right now. What you're doing… it's not far short of murder. It *is* murder!"

She carried on walking away, as if she didn't care.

From the corner of her eye, she saw that he had his cellphone out, was waving it in the air as if to convince her he was going to use it.

Finally, she paused, twisting to face him. "You could," she said. "Or we could clear this whole thing up." She put a hand to the side of her mouth and called, "Tom? Are you down there? Do you have a minute? Walter's here."

Walter was studying her carefully.

"Tom's down in the tool shed," she said. "He'll confirm what I told you. I don't know what you think you saw, but it really is all entirely innocent." She called again, "Tom?"

She turned and continued around the corner of the house.

Walter followed, just as she knew he would. He might not believe Tom was there, but he'd want to be sure. And he didn't want to let her get out of his sight, either.

She'd hit a dog once. With a baseball bat. The thing had annoyed her, yapping all the time. Just wouldn't shut up. That was why she'd ended up in the secure hospital. One fit of rage and the bad luck that it had been in the view of a security camera.

It had been satisfying, though. Such a release! Such a rush of adrenaline and endorphins.

The judge hadn't been impressed when she'd asked if she could keep a copy of the security camera footage of the incident.

That was another thing Dr. Holt had helped her with. Inappropriate humor.

Another thing she'd learned to hide.

But if braining that damned dog with a baseball bat had been satisfying, this was something else entirely.

Her move was smooth, as if choreographed. A slight pause, a shimmy, a sidestep, and Walter had caught up and was level with her without even realizing it.

A swing of the foot, a hand in the back, just before that little stone step down onto the path to the apartment.

The extra drop of that step confused him. He put a foot out to catch himself but it came down in midair rather than on solid ground and he kept tipping forward with his own momentum.

He grunted. Twisted to gawk at her in surprise as he kept falling.

Even then, he would have been okay. A few bumps and bruises, no more.

So, to be sure, Libbie dived after him. She smashed into his back and followed him down.

The combination of his weight and hers smashed him into the paved pathway with far more force than he could have anticipated.

She'd grabbed his arms on impact, not enough to leave

marks but enough to pin them at his sides and stop him from reaching out to break the fall.

When he hit the ground it was with his face first, the side of his head.

She felt the slump of his body beneath her as the air was knocked from it.

Saw blood, pooling on the slab already.

Such a vivid color in the golden fall sunlight.

There was beauty in this. Very few people ever got to appreciate that.

The few seconds after he hit the ground, breaking her own fall, was like a divine pause. A moment to soak up the splendor of the moment, the emotional rush of a perfectly executed maneuver.

He was still breathing.

That would not do.

Without a further thought, Libbie took hold of his head, raised it, and smashed it down on the stone.

The crunch of fracturing skull and the soft, meaty thud that accompanied it were another thing few people ever got to appreciate.

This time he'd stopped breathing.

She took a few seconds more, taking in the details. The spreading pool of blood. The yielding mass of another's body beneath her. The sounds of wind in the trees, of birds in the distance. All the almost imperceptible things that added up to convey the sense of lifelessness where once there had been life.

He was dead.

She'd killed him.

She was smiling.

Careful, she straightened, checking the body beneath her.

She spotted a long chestnut hair on the back of his coat. Removing it carefully, she tucked it into a pocket. She couldn't see anymore.

She'd been careful with every contact—the hand in the back, the grip on his arms—making sure she would do nothing that would leave obvious signs of struggle.

She stood, still studying the scene closely.

He looked as if he'd tripped. That would look even more the case when she got Tom's lawn rake from the tool shed and arranged it carefully across the path. Let Tom take the blame, or at least feel the guilt.

Should she feel some kind of guilt? Remorse?

Walter wasn't part of this, after all.

She felt nothing, though, other than the satisfaction of a job well done and the after-effects of the adrenaline rush.

As she surveyed the scene one last time, the first flies started to crawl across the blood. It really had been an exceptionally mild fall. She wondered if it would last.

CHAPTER 29

Alice had thought she had Franco Vialli's measure. Thought he was doing a new variation on the whole *If you want it done better you have to pay more* routine.

Take the roof off just before winter, threaten to walk.

Blackmail.

It was plain and simple blackmail.

But she'd been mistaken.

She'd asked him his price and he'd still hesitated.

He really wanted off the job.

He didn't believe she and Tom had the funds to see the project through, and if funds ran out it was inevitable the contractor would end up out of pocket for time and materials.

When Alice had been arguing with him, she'd been convinced it must be Libbie who had tipped him off. Now though, driving away from the site, she felt less certain. It really was hard to believe that of her.

She knew Libbie was not what she seemed, but it was still difficult to accept there might not be an innocent explanation.

Was she running from some kind of trauma? That

might explain the fake personal history, the evasion. Everything else was circumstantial. Maybe she really did simply attract bad luck.

Her mind was rushing from one thing to another.

She'd planned to go on to the office after Whitetail Lane. Put a brave face on things. Act as if everything was normal.

But after the encounter with Franco, she couldn't take any more, so she'd decided to head for home. Work on the pitch there. Try to focus.

She thought she'd left things okay with Franco. She'd assured him that the recent late payment had been a glitch, not a shortage of funds. She'd blamed Tom and felt instantly guilty for doing so, even though it *had* been his fault. Franco had laughed, as if it was easy to believe, which made her feel even guiltier.

He said he'd at least get the roof covered and secured while they waited for her and Tom to make some decisions about what to prioritize. The unspoken assumption behind that was that in order to fix the roof they'd have to put other elements on hold. From today, though, the site was going to be on hiatus.

The project was not going to be finished with the funds they had available. And if Alice lost her job as well as the Mapleview account, then she didn't know how they would ever pick the project up again.

Maybe Tom would get his way and they'd sell the Whitetail Lane property—not how he'd envisaged, but as an incomplete project, at a knockdown price.

They'd be lucky to recoup their investment if they did that.

She wondered if Franco himself might even buy the place from them. Maybe that was what he'd been angling for all along, taking the project to a critical juncture and then bringing it to a halt.

She felt exhausted. Drained by the whole thing.

She'd need to check her blood when she got home. Make sure that wasn't at least part of the reason she was feeling so bad. Sometimes a hypo gave her a real sense of dread. If so, then maybe things weren't so bad after all.

She actually laughed at that as she drove.

To any onlooker she must've appeared insane.

As she swung into the driveway, she noticed a little silver Hyundai parked at the curb. The car looked vaguely familiar, but she couldn't place it. Didn't make the connection with who must be here already.

She parked, pausing to take a deep, steadying breath. She really did feel rough. Maybe it was all starting to catch up with her.

Up on the porch she hesitated again.

Something didn't seem quite right, but she couldn't work out what.

She listened, but heard nothing out of place. Just the wind in the trees, the calls of birds, the sound of distant traffic.

Was Libbie in? She hoped not. Last night she and Tom had agreed to avoid their tenant as much as possible. However, in the light of day, she realized that was far easier in theory than in practice.

She went to the corner of the house and peered round

toward the basement apartment's entrance.

At first, she didn't register what she saw.

The clumps of tall asters in need of dead-heading. The border of shrubs leading up to the surrounding trees. The flat, paved path.

The body, lying sprawled in the path, just past the step down toward the back garden and the apartment.

She knew it was Walter immediately and realized then that it had been his silver Hyundai parked in the street.

His legs lay at an odd angle, one bent and crossed under the other. It was a position that could not have been comfortable.

His arms lay at his sides, which even then struck her as odd because if he'd fallen, wouldn't he have put his hands out first to catch himself?

A pool of blood lay around his crumpled head like a macabre halo.

Oh my God!

She rushed to him.

She paused for an instant, standing over him. Scared to go any closer and confirm what she saw.

He wasn't moving.

Not even the rise and fall of his chest.

She dropped to her knees. Reached out to his neck to check for a pulse.

He was still warm. What had she expected?

The blood pooled on the paving came from a nasty-looking gash in the side of his head, and when she looked closely, she saw that the wound was actually concave, as if the skull itself had been dented inward.

That couldn't be right.

"No… No…"

She couldn't find a carotid pulse.

How many years was it since she'd done that first aid course at the office? Too many.

She struggled to think what to do now, even as she fumbled in her purse for her cellphone.

She shouldn't move him, in case she did further damage. But how do you do anything for someone lying face-down?

She heaved at his body one-handed, half-raising him before losing her hold. He slumped to the ground again, and as he did so he gave a gruesome sigh.

Was he alive?

She knew he wasn't.

She knew that sound was just the air being forced from his lungs on impact with the ground.

"9-1-1? Yes. Listen… I…" Her head was spinning.

"What's your emergency? Please answer calmly."

"I found someone. A man. Walter. I think… he's dead. I think he hit his head."

"Is the patient breathing?"

"No. No, he's not. I can't find a pulse, either. Not at his neck. Not at his wrist."

"Is the patient bleeding?"

"He is. He was. His head. He's fallen and hit his head. Please send someone."

"Please give us your location."

She gave the address before going on. "Please. What can I do? He can't be dead... Walter can't be dead!"

Alice heard the voice, but not the words. She was aware of something strange going on with her senses, but couldn't work out what.

She felt dizzy again, so bad it felt as if her whole body was swaying as she kneeled over Walter's motionless form.

Walter!

She balanced herself with one hand against the ground.

She recognized the feeling. She'd been concerned even before she'd gotten home. Her blood sugar.

If she'd been on the brink even then, she knew *this* might easily have tipped her over. The fight or flight response as the body tries to flood your blood with extra fuel to deal with emergency. Extra sugar.

She was aware of the voice again. Of her own voice trying to answer. But everything sounded slurred. The bass tones booming, the higher tones whining like flies.

She rummaged in her purse.

She normally kept candy there, but there was nothing. She'd been so forgetful recently, even though forgetting about something as fundamental as candy and insulin was something she could never afford to do.

She turned away from the thing on the ground. From Walter.

Tried to stand, but only succeeded in stumbling forward onto her knees again.

If she had to crawl back to the house, she would do so.

She heaved her body forward. Felt the painful scrape of her knees on stone.

There was a lawn rake here, by the low step. Was that how Walter had fallen? Was it Tom's fault, like everything else?

She knew she shouldn't be thinking like that, but didn't care. All she could focus on was that last stretch of graveled ground before the double step up onto the porch.

The small stones on her shredded knees were agony, but a good agony, one that sent a rush of adrenaline that jolted her back to a vague semblance of alertness.

She pushed herself to her feet again.

She'd dropped her phone somewhere, but didn't care. She knew this was bad.

She wobbled forward, catching herself on the wooden post to the side of the steps up onto the porch.

Her purse! Thank goodness. She hadn't dropped that.

She fumbled inside it, tipping the contents out. Found her keys, and stabbed them third time lucky into the lock.

Alice pushed on the door and almost collapsed into the house, only catching herself on the table by the door.

The table had a drawer and she pulled at it, scraping at the contents. They always kept candy in there. *Last-minute candy* they called it. Put there so she could take a handful to put in her purse as she went out.

Why hadn't they topped it up?

She went to the kitchen drawer where they always kept a couple of tablets of glucose, and more candy. There was no candy, though, and the blister-packs were empty of pills, as if she'd used them all and then put them back here just to taunt her. Why would she do that?

The refrigerator!

There was glucagon, at least. One injection and catastrophe would be avoided. She was going to be okay.

How had she ever let herself get this bad?

She steadied herself, put a new needle in the glucagon vial and sprayed a two-unit air shot of the clear liquid to test it. Then she set up the dose, pressed the needle into a fold of belly and pressed the plunger.

The surge of relief was, in itself, exhausting.

That had been a bad one, she knew. A combination of her stupid complacency, her forgetfulness, and the fight or flight response to…

She remembered the sight of Walter outside, his body twisted, the pool of blood.

She wanted to cry but, strangely, was unable.

Her breathing was still ragged, her heart pounding.

She felt that blackness looming all around the edges of her vision. Felt the gathering heat in her head, the precursor to fainting.

The shot should have kicked in by now. She should be feeling *better* not worse. What was happening? Why wasn't she recovering?

Alice sat perfectly motionless and felt her whole body swaying.

She was going to black out. She knew it and there was nothing more she could do about it.

She didn't even have her phone to make another call to 911. She didn't have the energy to reach into the refrigerator again. If she could only get a mouthful of something sweet. That disgusting barbecue sauce that Tom loved could save her life...

Only the fridge seemed a thousand miles away, so out of reach. She tried to stand, at least to get out to the porch so the medics would find her when they arrived.

The blackness stole in, rushing across her vision, and she fell sideways out of the chair.

~ ~ ~ ~

This couldn't have gone better if Libbie had written the script herself. Which she kind of *had*.

She stood in the shade of the trees and watched Alice arrive. Saw the car pull up, saw the moment of hesitation as she found the body and still didn't believe what she was seeing.

The look of absolute horror on her face!

Not only that, but she'd pulled at Walter's body, let if fall again. Everyone who's watched enough *CSI* shows on TV knew that you don't disturb a crime scene. But Alice was too stupid. She didn't even *know* it was a crime scene, after all.

And when you think there's even the slightest chance the victim might still be alive, you do what you can. You grab at him. You pummel him. You try to turn him over and then let his body fall back onto the ground with that comical dead-meat-falling sound, don't you?

Alice had put herself all over that crime scene.

They wouldn't think she was responsible, of course, but she'd have destroyed a lot of the evidence that might have told the cops someone *else* was!

She followed as Alice half-crawled, half-stumbled her way back around the corner of the house to the porch and into the house.

Watched through windows that frantic search for anything that might save her, because by now it was clear even to Libbie's untrained eye that she was going into hypoglycemic shock.

Watched, finally, as Alice injected water into her belly in the belief it was glucagon.

So perfect.

So funny.

So *just*.

CHAPTER 30

For the first time in what seemed like forever, Tom felt as if he was taking control again.

As if *they* were taking control.

And that was the key thing. He and Alice were a team. When they pulled apart and isolated themselves, things started to go wrong. But when they pulled together, they were a unit. While they didn't think alike, they complemented each other. Their communication was fluid and often unspoken. As people often joked, they were the classic couple who finished each other's sentences.

They should never have lost sight of that. Of what they were.

He'd been out this morning. A trip to the mall for a new shirt and some of that Jean Paul Gaultier perfume Alice loved. A stop off for some groceries.

And a five-minute pre-consultation with Jason Grande, the real estate lawyer they'd used for the purchase of the Whitetail Lane property. Tom had called Jason's office first thing, and although his schedule was full the lawyer had offered a between-meetings chat to establish the procedure for evicting Libbie Burchett.

"So why the urgency? Why are you looking for the

fastest possible route when your tenancy agreement has an established three-month notice procedure?" Jason had stood there with raised eyebrows and what Tom took to be a man-to-man grin, before adding, "You haven't been a naughty boy, have you, Tom?"

Tom couldn't even object. Every time he closed his eyes he remembered that brief kiss. Remembered just how close he'd come to making the biggest mistake of his life.

He hadn't though. He kept telling himself that. He'd faced temptation and resisted.

"She's… erratic. She's creeping Alice out." It was hard to explain. "And then when we checked a bit closer and we found out about the fake identity—"

"Hang on, Tom. Fake identity? Are you telling me she lied in the lease? If you can confirm that, then the agreement is invalidated and you can just tell her to pack her crap and leave. What's her real identity?"

Tom had shrugged. "We don't know. Just that the identity she's using now is almost certainly a fabrication."

Jason had put a big hand on Tom's shoulder then. "Find her real name and prove she lied on that lease and your problem's solved," he said. "That's all you have to do."

Now, driving back across town, Tom's spirits were higher than they'd been in a long time.

He had no idea who Libbie really was, or what she was up to. It might easily be that she was escaping some past trauma of her own, as Alice had suggested. But it felt good that there might at least be a way out if they needed it.

It was time to move on with his life, he realized. To stop hiding.

He truly felt as if he was finally coming out the other side of his breakdown.

So maybe it was even time to put himself back out into the job market, rather than existing day to day on freelance scraps. He had qualifications, he had a lot of experience, and he still had some good connections.

He looked every so often. Guilty moments with the jobs websites, like that night Libbie had come around and asked him what he had on his laptop. Guilty because he'd never mentioned to Alice that he was looking, for fear of the desperately eager look she would get on her face as she grasped at the hope he was finally getting back to normal.

And there was a difference between those guilty checks to see what you were missing out on, and what was in his head now, the resolve that now was the time to take the next step.

He pulled up in the yard behind Alice's car. She'd said she was going into the office, but maybe that had been too much to face.

He felt briefly guilty again, that he should feel so buoyant when things around them were going so wrong, and when Alice's own career was in danger of nosediving. Would she think he was trying to reassert himself, taking the opportunity of her difficulties to make himself the main breadwinner again?

They would talk it through. She would understand. They were good when they were a team, he reminded himself.

He climbed out of the car.

Why was the front door open like that?

Had she just gotten home? Left the door so she could come back to get something from her Ford?

"Alice?"

He went inside. No sign of her.

"Alice? Sweetie?"

She was in the kitchen. Slumped over the big table as if she'd fallen asleep in the chair.

He went to her. He knew it wasn't right as soon as he'd spotted her.

"Alice?"

He crouched by the chair. Put a hand to the side of her face, felt that familiar clammy heat. Her breathing was shallow, her pulse fast.

He saw the diabetes paraphernalia on the table. The discarded syringe.

She'd given herself a shot of glucagon, so why hadn't it worked? Why was she in full-blown hypoglycemic shock?

Had she been too late? The shot should still have helped. Had she just applied it, in which case it was just a matter of time before it kicked in?

He knew the procedure. If he'd been with her throughout he'd know exactly what she'd tried so far and what he could do, but walking into the middle of it, he could only assess what was before him and make the call to 911.

He'd been through this with her before, but not for a couple of years. That experience didn't make this any less scary, though.

And he knew the risks.

He couldn't imagine a life without Alice. A life where he was no longer part of that team.

He fished his cellphone out of a pocket and was just about to key the numbers when he heard the wail of an approaching siren. He went to the kitchen window and saw an ambulance swinging into the yard.

Had she called herself? He hadn't noticed her phone among the clutter on the table. Maybe she'd dropped it on the floor.

He went to the front door, swinging it open just as the first paramedic was reaching for the bell.

"Sir? Can you tell us where it is? We're responding to a call about a possible fatality. Can you tell us where the body is located?"

His mind went blank and he stared stupidly at the man.

Finally, he managed to say, "Body?!"

He glanced back toward the kitchen. Alice had been breathing!

"She's through here," he said. "My wife. She's in hypoglycemic shock. Appears to have given herself a shot of glucagon, but there's no sign of recovery as yet. Through here, in the kitchen."

The emergency technician pushed through, a heavy bag swinging from one shoulder. A second paramedic loitered outside.

Body? Tom's mind still raced. He didn't understand.

From the kitchen, the first man called out, "Hey, Joey. Would you bring the gurney? We got a hypoglycemic shock, danger of full-blown hypo coma."

Tom felt sick. The other paramedic met his look, nodded reassuringly, then turned to open up the back of the ambulance.

And then stopped.

"Hey, Dwayne. You might want to come and see this."

"Ugh?"

"I think I found the body, Dwayne."

Another reference to a body… What was going on?

Tom hesitated, knowing his place was at Alice's side. Then he went out and joined the other EMT where he had paused at the corner of the house.

A motionless body lay just beyond the step. The man's legs were twisted. A big pool of vividly red blood had spread out from around his head.

It looked like Walter, but he couldn't be sure.

What had happened here?! Had Walter and Alice fought? Had that somehow triggered Alice's hypo?

Was it even a hypo? Had she been hurt too?

Tom turned and rushed back into the house.

The other paramedic was still tending to Alice. He flashed a look at Tom. "Listen, mister," he said. "I don't know what's going on here, but you have to just keep out of the way right now, you hear me? We have this lady to help and whatever my partner's dealing with out there. The cops are on their way."

"My wife. That's my wife."

"Okay, bud. Whatever. Let's just keep this calm, okay?"

Tom understood. There had clearly been some kind of incident outside—they didn't know yet if it was an accident. The EMT didn't know if violence had taken place, and here was Tom behaving erratically.

He felt as if he was going to burst with the injustice, and with the frustration. Still, he had to stay calm, do the right thing for Alice. He couldn't afford for the paramedics to be distracted right now.

He nodded, raising his hands, palms facing out. "Okay," he said. "I'll stay back here. I'll wait for the cops. Just do what you have to do for my wife, okay?"

The paramedic nodded and turned his attention back to checking Alice over.

When they arrived, the police officers treated him like a suspect.

"I don't even know what's happened," he protested. "I just got back. I saw my wife's car here, came in and found her like this. She's diabetic. She's in hypoglycemic shock."

The officer paused to glance at the EMT, who nodded in confirmation.

"I didn't even see anyone else was here," Tom went on. "Not until the other paramedic shouted. What's happened out there?"

"Guy hit his head," said the cop. "Or had it hit. We're open to all possibilities right now."

"My God." It still hadn't sunk in. "I think I know him. I think that's Walter Jones. Works with my wife at Pierson Newport. I don't know what he'd be doing here, though."

The two paramedics had lifted Alice onto a gurney now and were preparing to take her out of the house. Another team had turned up to deal with Walter outside.

"Listen," Tom began "I understand you have to look at all possibilities here. But that's my wife they're just about to wheel out. I need to be with her. When she comes out of this, she's going to be disoriented. She needs me."

He didn't think the cop was going to let him go. For long seconds, the guy stared at him, then he shrugged, and said, "Gimme a minute."

Tom watched him go outside and talk to another officer. There was some gesturing, some more shrugging, then the first cop came back. "Okay, Mr. Granger. You go with your wife. We'll take care of things here. We'll need to talk to you later."

"Thank you, officer." Tom nodded toward the side of the house. "What happened out there?"

"We've yet to ascertain that. But you folks really should take more care of your garden implements."

Tom didn't try to work out the cryptic comment. He was too concerned with Alice.

He watched as the paramedics wheeled her up through the back doors of the ambulance, and then, at a nod from one of them, he stepped in after her.

She looked pale as paper, apart from the heavy shadows under her eyes. Her skin looked slack, her breathing shallow.

He'd never seen her looking so sick.

And he'd never been so scared in his life.

CHAPTER 31

Libbie hung back. She desperately wanted to get involved, put herself at the middle of the drama. Not just so she could hear what they were saying and assure herself she'd not made any mistakes.

But simply to *be* there.

There's nothing quite like the buzz of life or death drama.

Alice going into shock.

Walter. Too late to save *him*.

Alice could easily die too. *Should.*

How funny for her to go into shock like that and give herself what she thought was a life-saving injection of… water.

And Libbie had done all of it.

She was good. Very, very good.

She forced herself to stay away though. Now was not the time to draw attention to herself. She knew Tom and Alice had turned against her. She would have to tread carefully.

And that meant holding back rather than getting involved.

So she hung back at Zak's. Ordered a coffee and sat at one of the four small tables at the bakery. Watched out of the window as the ambulance rushed past, then two police cars, and finally another ambulance.

That seemed a lot for an accident and a blood sugar drama. Had they worked out already that Walter hadn't just tripped and hit his head? That would sure spoil the fun.

She sipped her coffee. No rush.

Sometime later, one of the ambulances passed the other way.

Body or Alice? she wondered. Dead creep or Mrs. Boring?

There was only one way to find out.

At last, she allowed herself to stand and head outside. She'd parked out back and now she went around, climbed inside the dull, suburban Toyota and set off for *home*.

The cops had blocked off the drive, so she parked in the street behind Walter's Hyundai. A big officer built like a linebacker stopped her as she approached.

"You have business here, Miss?" he said.

She gave him her best wide-eyed innocent smile, with a hint of not-at-all-innocent pout. "Why, I live here, officer. What's going on?"

He was thrown, as she'd known he would be. That pout, the way she'd walked up to him, the way she stood, arms folded, framing her breasts. Even now she was unable to resist the easy old games.

"Miss, I'm afraid you can't go in here right now."

She liked the way he called her Miss, and not Ma'am.

"But officer!" She gazed past him, saw the cluster of uniformed emergency workers on the path to her apartment. "Oh my… What's happened? Who is that? I live here, in the basement apartment. Are Tom and Alice Granger okay? This is their house."

"The Grangers are fine," the officer said. "I mean… Mr. Granger's okay. Mrs. Granger was taken to the hospital. She just went in an ambulance. Both of them did, but it's Mrs. Granger who's in a bad shape."

"Oh dear. Will she be okay?"

Libbie put the back of a hand to her forehead, all B movie melodrama. She shouldn't be enjoying it this much, should she?

"I'm afraid I can't comment." He'd clearly just realized he'd said too much already.

"So who's *that?*"

"Ma'am. I'm afraid I'm going to have to ask if you have anywhere else to go right now. We'll contact you when it's okay to return."

Ma'am now. So he was getting formal, trying to assert his authority. But the good thing was that they didn't seem to be treating this with any great urgency, or suspicion. Already the other police cruiser was reversing out of the driveway. They didn't seem to be in any rush to get a statement from Libbie, or question her.

"Ma'am?"

"Oh yes, sorry. It's just all such a shock. I have errands to run in town. I can be out for a couple of hours. Would that be long enough? I'll give you my number. Just be sure to call me." She hesitated, then batted her eyes and added, "Any time."

He blushed and looked away.

Such fun.

~ ~ ~ ~

Late afternoon, she turned up at the hospital.

She wasn't sure about this. It could go one of two ways. Tom might take one look at her and demand she leave, his and Alice's suspicions about Libbie bursting out into the open in the drama of the situation.

Or he would be polite.

He looked up, interrupting that perfect tableau of Alice flat out in her hospital bed and him sitting at her side, clutching her hand.

After a moment of hesitation, he nodded and stood.

"Libbie," he said. "You must have heard."

"How is she?" she said, moving into the room. "How are *you*?"

He shrugged, looked away. He still seemed hesitant, so she stepped it up a level.

"Oh, Tom," she said. "This must be so awful for you."

She spread her arms, and he let her hug him. He was too polite not to. There was a moment of resistance, even then, and finally she felt his frame slump, and his arms go around her.

"Is she going to be okay?"

He stepped back, nodding. "I think so," he told her. "I hope so."

This was good. Libbie could see the guilt etched onto his features now. He felt bad about doubting her, about judging her. He couldn't believe anything bad about someone who stood here before him like this, clearly so full of sympathy and empathy.

Libbie had always been good at faking those.

"I was out at yoga," she told him. "When I got back, there were cops all over the place. I thought there had been some kind of massacre."

More guilt on his features. Had he forgotten about Walter? The dead body in his garden?

"They kept me away from my apartment for a few hours. I thought of coming straight here, but I figured you guys would need time to yourself. I didn't realize..." She nodded toward Alice. "I thought Alice would be... awake."

"It's kind of you to come. It must have been awful for you to find all that when you got home."

It was lovely that he felt so guilty for how this might have affected her! He really did take the polite option to extremes, particularly when only the night before he'd been telling his wife how awful Libbie was.

"She's going to be okay, though?"

He nodded, a little more confidently this time. "Yes. Yes, everyone says so. It's the most horrible thing, going through this with someone you love. The thought of losing them."

Libbie gave him her best sympathy look. She put a

hand on his arm and he didn't flinch. Every move she made was a test.

"You're not going to lose her," she said. "You're pulling through this. *Alice* is. And if you need anything, well, I'm here for you."

He even smiled at that. He really did struggle to think badly of Libbie in her presence.

"Listen, Tom. You must have been here for hours. I bet you haven't left Alice's side, have you? Why don't you take a break now? Get some fresh air. Make any calls you should be making. Get yourself something to eat. I know you might not feel like that now, but you have to look after yourself too. Alice would want it. And you have to be well if you're going to look after her."

Still he hesitated.

"Go on. You know it makes sense. Look, I'll stay here so she's not alone. I've got my phone. The moment she stirs, I promise I'll call."

Even before he'd left the room, Libbie had moved to take his place in the chair at Alice's bedside.

And as she'd moved, she'd been assessing everything.

The view from the doorway.

The heart monitor. It was switched to silent, but the trace across the small screen showed that it was connected and working. The moment it started to flatline, alarms would be triggered at the nearest nursing station.

Alice herself had not moved, other than the rise and fall of her chest. Her eyes were closed, her head tipped slightly to one side.

An IV line ran from the back of one wrist up to a bag of saline suspended from a support by the bed.

Was that old thing about air bubbles in an IV line being fatal an old wives' tale? She didn't think so, but didn't know how fast—or painful—it would be.

A knife, run quickly across the throat to sever jugular, windpipe, and carotid would be the surest thing. But messy.

She remembered the flood flowing from Walter's head wound earlier.

Felt that thrill all over again.

She shouldn't get carried away. Not when she'd reached this far!

She stood, paused to check the doorway again to make sure she was alone with Alice and not likely to be disturbed.

Then she reached for a spare pillow that lay on another chair by the bed.

Simple was nearly always best.

"Alice?" she said, as she stood poised, the pillow raised. "Alice are you awake?"

She didn't expect anything. It was worth a try, though.

And then, all of Libbie's Christmases came at once, as Alice's eyes fluttered, opened, briefly found focus.

"Oh, Alice," said Libbie.

She smiled, leaned closer, and even in that instant, Alice drifted out of consciousness again. She lowered the pillow toward Alice, and—

She heard a scuff of feet. In a single flowing movement, she kept going, reaching for Alice's head to raise it as she tucked the pillow beneath.

Ignoring the presence in the doorway, she straightened, smiled, and said, "There you are, dear Alice. That should make you a little more comfortable."

She turned, and saw a man in a scruffy suit standing there, studying her closely. What had he seen?

She smiled. Said, "Doctor…?"

The guy shook his head and came into the room. "Not Doc," he said. "Detective. Malwitz. And you must be…?"

"Libbie Burchett," she said. The guy was hard to read. Dark eyes that never stayed still. "Can I help you?"

"I came to see Mrs. Granger," he said. "Or Mister."

"Tom's just stepped out. He's exhausted. I'm their friend. Their tenant, too. I live in the basement apartment."

"I know." For a moment she wondered just how much he knew, then he smiled, and went on, "I've just come from their place. We're looking into the death of a Mr. Walter Jones there earlier."

"He's dead? Your officer wouldn't say. How awful."

"Afraid so, ma'am. We just need to do things properly. Ask a few questions."

"What happened? I know you can't say, but, well, I live there. If there's some lunatic out there…"

"It's okay. I don't think we have a serial killer on the loose, ma'am. If there was any real suggestion of anything worse than a tragic accident they'd have sent out someone far more senior than me."

He was trying to make a joke, trying to reassure her. The guy really had no idea just how much more reassured she felt now! He had pretty much just told her they wanted to close this.

"We just need to establish a timeline, make sure we're not missing anything. We just have to make sure all the dots join up and there's nothing suspicious. You mind I ask a few questions now? Would that be okay?"

So they hadn't completely dismissed the possibility of foul play, after all. Libbie reminded herself she needed to tread carefully.

"Fine, Detective," she said. "But I'm not sure how much I can tell you."

"Do you have any idea why the deceased would be at your address earlier today?"

Time for a little misdirection, perhaps.

"Who was it?" she asked. "You said it was Walter Jones? How sad. He worked with Alice. They were close friends, I know. I haven't seen him at the house before. But, well, I had the feeling he might have a thing for Alice, from the way she talked about him. Is that silly?"

"A thing? How do you mean, a thing?"

"Oh, all from his side, I can assure you of that. Alice and Tom are so sweet together. But, well, she kind of attracts it. There's Walter, and there's Rusty…"

The officer's demeanor changed immediately. A new alertness, a narrowing of the eyes.

"Rusty?"

"The neighborhood kid. Used to do odd jobs at the house until Tom told him to stay away."

"Now why would Mr. Granger do something like that?"

"Well, Rusty had a thing for Alice. You know what boys are like. He was kind of intense, though. I don't know quite what happened between Rusty and Tom, but the boy stopped coming around after that. I could see how Rusty might not like Walter calling around, though…"

She looked away, then looked back up to meet Malwitz's eyes. "Oh, Detective. You don't think…? Please don't do anything on what I've said. I'd hate to think I'd gotten the boy into trouble. He's a sweet kid. Always means well."

"Rusty. Do you have a surname for the kid? An address?"

She did, but she wasn't going to give it up straight away. She was going to keep Detective Malwitz talking just a bit more before she gave up the information he wanted. She was enjoying this too much to make it *that* easy for him.

CHAPTER 32

This time when Alice woke, it was the real thing. As if her body had decided now was the time to do it properly, rather than drifting in and out of consciousness and all states between.

Tom was there, in one of the room's two chairs. He was slumped sideways in what must be a horribly uncomfortable position.

They were in a hospital room, that much was clear. She heard machine sounds from beyond the room, the low hum of a generator, perhaps, and random electronic beeps and whines. Occasional voices. The air smelled of antiseptics that were supposed to be aromatic, but only reminded her of chemicals.

At first, she'd thought it must be the middle of the night. The room was about as dark as a hospital room ever gets, after all. The main lights turned off, and the room only lit by the glow from monitors and the light coming in through the doorway.

She realized it must be earlier though. The voices. The sounds of activity.

How long had she been here?

She had no idea.

Much of the time since she'd left the house for Whitetail Lane was a blur, or completely absent.

She remembered arguing with Franco Vialli.

She remembered all the signs of the impending hypoglycemic shock. The ones you dismiss, thinking *No, it's not going to happen this time.* As if willpower alone was a substitute for medicine.

That must be what had happened. Why she was here.

She remembered…

Tom was watching her, his expression unreadable.

And at last she knew why.

"Walter?" she managed to say.

The slight shake of her husband's head answered more fully than any words could have done.

Walter.

She hadn't noticed him move, but now Tom leaned over her, delicately balancing himself on the bed so as not to disturb her. His cheek was cold against hers and the stubble scratched.

"Oh, Tom."

"Sweetie."

They pressed cheeks together and she felt the reassuring presence of his body over her, only a few points of delicate contact, as if she were a flower that might be crushed.

"You had a hypo," he told her, straightening, moving to pull his chair closer and sit. He took her hand in both of his. "For some reason your shot of glucagon didn't work fast enough to keep you afloat."

She didn't care. She should, she knew, but...

"Walter?"

"The police think it was an accident. A fall. He hit his head."

"I found him."

"I know. You called 911. And... well, it was obvious you'd tried to save him."

The blood. She knew he must've been referring to Walter's blood on her hands and clothes.

There were so many unanswered questions, not the least of which was what Walter might have been doing at the house. She closed her eyes again. It was all too much.

She opened them again. "Tom?" She waited until he was looking. "I think Libbie tried to kill me. Here. Earlier."

She saw his whole body tense. His mouth opened, then closed again. No words.

"I woke earlier. Kind of. I wasn't properly conscious, but I could see. I understood enough to know I was in a hospital room. And she was there."

"She *was* here. She came visiting."

"She had a pillow. She was standing right over me. And just for a second I *knew* she was going to press it down over my face. I so desperately wanted to move, but my body wouldn't respond. I tried to call for help, but I couldn't make my voice work. It was like the worst kind of nightmare."

"But she didn't…"

"Someone came."

The silence stretched out.

"You don't think maybe it was a dream, sweetie? It sounds like the classic dream of powerlessness: something awful about to happen and you can't move, can't speak, can't do any of the things that might make a difference."

Tom's suggestion was convincing, even if he didn't sound convinced himself.

"She did come to visit," he said again. "It was the weirdest thing. Right up until that point I was convinced she was the devil incarnate. I had five minutes with Jason Grande this morning, and we went over the eviction process. As soon as I said she seemed to be using a fake identity he was onto it, said that would invalidate any lease. Talking to Jason seemed to make everything real: she's a fake, she stirs things up, she might be guilty of just about anything, or so I believed."

He shrugged. "But then when she came by the hospital, well, as soon as you're in her presence none of that seems credible somehow. She has that eager puppy-dog charm thing going on. She'd do anything to help you. She just… *disarms* you."

Tom was floundering. Struggling to explain what it was that Libbie Burchett did to people.

"It's impossible to dislike her, isn't it?" Alice said.

He smiled. She'd found the words he'd been struggling to put together himself. "That's exactly it. When she came here earlier and she was so upset to see you like this, I felt like such a bad person."

"And yet…"

He smiled, but it was a bitter smile. "When she's not here to charm and distract you, it's far easier to remember exactly why we want her out of our lives, uh?"

"It is."

Her throat hurt and, as if he'd read her mind, Tom moved closer with a glass of water and a straw.

"Thank you."

He kissed her forehead tenderly before sitting again.

"Poor Walter. I tried so hard to save him. But I was so close to blacking out. I nearly didn't make it back into the house."

"There was nothing you could do."

"He fell?"

"That's what they think."

He'd said that before. *Think.*

"But?"

"The lawn rake was there," he told her. "But I know I left that by the tool shed. I remember. I was so angry… angry with the goddamn leaves, would you believe? That time I tried to rake them up but the wind kept blowing them around. So how did the rake get there, on the path, so anyone could trip on it?"

She didn't know what he was getting at. That someone had moved the rake to booby-trap the path? That was beyond belief. Unless someone had put it there *afterward…*

"Are the police confident it was an accident?"

Tom shrugged. "They're asking a lot of questions. That might just be procedure."

"Or?"

"I keep asking myself why Walter was at the house? We both know he's not the unannounced house call kind of guy, right?" He paused as if to correct himself, but didn't. *Was* not *is*...

Alice was studying her husband closely. Surprised that, even in the thick of all that was going on, she should feel a hint of relief that Tom hadn't leaped to a paranoid, jealous explanation for Walter's presence.

Had he turned a corner? Finally moved on from that damaging behavior pattern?

She squeezed his hand where it lay on top of hers. Gave him a weak smile.

"Sorry," he said. "Is this too much? You must be exhausted. You should be resting, having some of that delicious sugar-free Jell-O."

She squeezed again, ignoring his attempt at humor. "No, we need to talk. About all this. I need to understand."

"Well when you do, if you could just share it with me?" A smile, a wink. The old Tom, even in the middle of all this. It was good to see.

"I'm glad you saw Jason." She had known he was going to call, but to actually have a discussion so quickly was good. He was a busy man. "Is he putting things in motion?"

"I have a follow-up arranged with him next week. We'll go through all we know about the situation and draw up some options."

"That's good. We need her out of our lives. I don't care if that puppy-dog charm is entirely the real thing and there's nothing at all wrong with her. She gives me the creeps. She has to go."

"Totally. She creeps me out, too. I'm working on it."

He moved in with the water again and Alice took several long sips. She knew she had to hydrate before they'd take the drip out of her wrist. The hospital routine was familiar.

She couldn't believe she'd let herself get so ill again. She really had gotten either complacent or forgetful about keeping her supplies of meds and candies replenished. It could so easily have been much worse.

"Is my phone there? I think they'll have put my purse in the cabinet." They always put belongings in the cabinet. Hospital routine.

Tom was giving her a look.

"What?"

"You're not checking your work emails, sweetie. Mapleview can wait for once."

She didn't remind him that she'd been taken off Mapleview. And at least part of the reason for that was that he was right. Michael Tuckett might have taken her off it, but she still hoped to prove him wrong, and she couldn't do that if she took her eye off the ball.

He always got like this when she fell ill. The protective thing.

He knew she wasn't up to much right now. Hell, she

could barely even see straight.

"I just… would *you* check for me? I'll let you be the judge of whether I should know."

She couldn't put her finger on it. Most of the time she was the epitome of the rational modern professional. Methodical, logical. But sometimes… sometimes there was something indefinable. An instinct thing. A hunch.

And when she felt that, it was nearly always for good reason.

Tom looked as if he was going to keep arguing, but maybe he sensed it as well. Or maybe he sensed what a hard time she'd give him before he finally gave in to the inevitable.

He reached for the cabinet, found Alice's purse, and moments later was thumbing the passcode into her cellphone.

Impatient now, Alice waited as Tom scrolled through messages. What was he taking so long to check? Email? Text messages? Messenger? Freaking baseball scores?

Finally, she cracked. "Well? Anything I should know about?"

"Oh, sorry. Mostly junk and office noise. I'd forgotten how much junk circulates at Pierson Newport. Lots of messages from folks wishing you well. CeeCee Jonson, Jilly Tuckett, Emma Cheng. A few from neighbors. You want me to read them out?"

"No, thanks, it's fine. Anything from Walter?" She'd finally put her finger on the source of her unease. Something Tom had said. That Walter wasn't the kind of guy to call around unannounced. He'd have messaged her first to say he was on his way, at least.

"No, nothing."

That was strange.

"Email or text," she said. That was how he preferred to contact people. Messages he could think about as he composed them. Messages he could edit before sending.

Tom was shaking his head. Then: "Ah… there's a voicemail. Sorry, your phone layout's different to mine. I didn't spot the icons."

"Not different. *Organized.*"

Tom pressed something on the screen, and suddenly Walter's voice emerged from the speaker, mid-sentence.

Alice felt sick hearing his voice like that. A voice she'd never hear again.

And after she'd heard the message she felt sick for an altogether different reason.

"—found some interesting things about her. Like her real name isn't Burchett, it's Cottrill. Elizabeth Cottrill. And once you have the right name, well, let's just say she's a woman with history. *Violent* history. Like…"

His voice stopped then and Alice thought the connection might have been cut. But then, after a long pause, Walter resumed.

"Now's not the time. Not on voicemail. Listen, Alice, I'm heading over. We need to talk. Urgently. You really need to know what I've found out."

Then the line did cut and Alice was left staring at Tom.

"What did he mean? *Violent history?*"

"I don't know, but..." Did Libbie know Walter was onto her? Had she somehow found out? And if so...

Had she been responsible for his accident? Had she killed him to silence him? From the look on Tom's ashen face he was clearly thinking along the same lines.

Had they been sharing their house with a murderer?

CHAPTER 33

Alice looked so frail and weak. It broke Tom's heart to see her this way.

Sitting there as she clawed her way back to consciousness, he was reminded of his earlier resolve. Get a job. Put himself out there in the world. Get a goddamn *grip*.

He had to tackle this. Had to put things right so that Alice could focus on her recovery. He'd wavered again when Libbie had come to the hospital, but no more.

She had to go.

He'd already decided that much even before listening to Walter's message. Walter had sounded desperate. A man on a mission. He wished the guy had told them more in his message. Hadn't felt the need to do it in person.

So Libbie's real name was Cottrill. Tom struggled to see the implications, other than it being something they could use to build the case of fake identity Jason Grande had told him would invalidate the lease.

But he'd hinted at so much more.

Let's just say she's a woman with history. Violent history.

What had he meant by that?

At first, Tom had dismissed Alice's claim that Libbie had tried to smother her with a pillow. She'd admitted she was delirious at the time, drifting in and out of consciousness.

Even now, with the accumulating evidence that Libbie was up to something, he found it hard to believe that of her.

But Walter's message changed all that.

A woman with a violent history.

"I'm going to take care of this," he'd told Alice. "I'm going to get to the bottom of it all."

"Tom?"

"It's fine, sweetie. You're safe here."

He wished he believed it. As he left, he spoke to one of the nurses. "She's suffering anxiety," he told the young man. "She often does after an episode like this. Would you keep a close eye on her? I know you would anyway, of course, but just…?"

The nurse had smiled, nodded and reassured him, and Tom had gone on his way.

Now, he paused at the wide glass double doors of the Pierson Newport main office. He took the keycard he'd taken from Alice's purse and swiped it through the reader. The doors gave that familiar muffled click and opened when he pushed.

It was early evening now and he hoped no one would still be here.

Inside, he followed a once-familiar route across the lobby and through to the open-plan area. He'd had his first desk space here, years ago, before he'd graduated to a separate office. Lights were on in the big corner office.

He stopped, considering his options, but it was too late. Michael Tuckett had seen him.

Now, the big man emerged from his office and stood, filling the doorway.

"Tom," he said.

"Michael."

"How's Alice?"

Tom found himself unable to answer. All he could see was that weak form in the big hospital bed.

He shrugged and finally managed to say, "She's pulling through."

"Good. That's good to hear. And how are you holding up?"

Tom had always been a favorite of Michael's. His protégé.

"I'm okay. Back on track."

"Good."

Things had never been so stilted between them before.

"I'm sorry about Walter," Tom said. Tuckett had never really liked Walter, but still.

Tuckett nodded, but said nothing.

"I just came to get some things for Alice. I won't be long."

"How did you get in, Tom? You had your keycard taken off you after…"

After last time. The time when Tom had hit rock bottom, lost his grip on the world. The time he'd punched Michael Tuckett right on that rolling, jowly jaw.

"Get her things and go, Tom. She shouldn't have given you her card. She'd be in a lot of trouble for a transgression like that if she wasn't…"

Again, Tuckett let his words trail away mid-sentence.

Wasn't *what?*

Tuckett straightened. "Well, I know now isn't a good time, Tom. You need to focus on getting Alice better. But you must know it's over here. Alice screwed up big-time on Mapleview. If her window-dressing on that early draft of the pitch documents had gotten through, we'd have been exposed to lawsuits that would have destroyed the company."

Tom seethed with the injustice. He knew how hard Alice had worked on the pitch and he knew she would never normally make those kinds of mistakes. But for Tuckett to imply those mistakes might have been something more, a deliberate attempt to manipulate the pitch, well… Even now he'd have hoped for better from the man.

"Can you hold off until she's better?" he begged.

Now wasn't the time to confront Tuckett and his accusations. It certainly wasn't the time to punch him again, no matter how tempting that was. The man had, effectively, fired Alice while she lay in a hospital bed.

Tuckett sighed, as if making a massive concession.

"Just a few more days," Tom urged. "Maybe then you'll have a different view."

If he could prove what unfair pressures Alice had been subjected to, if the truth of whatever Libbie was up to emerged, maybe Tuckett would change his mind.

Tuckett turned away, dismissing him.

Tom went across to Alice's office, turned the light on, and then sidestepped two doors down and slipped into Walter's much smaller office.

Easing himself into the desk chair, he checked the line of sight. Just as he remembered, unless Tuckett came out of his office again, he wouldn't be able to see where Tom was. Even if he emerged, the light in Alice's office might be enough to convince him that was where Tom was.

He tapped at the keyboard's space bar, bringing the two wide monitors to life in a startling burst of light in the darkened room.

He peered out of the office again, but there was no sign of Tuckett.

The computer was prompting him to log in. It had remembered the last log-in as *wdjones*, which was good, and now Tom keyed in the password Alice had given him before he left the hospital: t3RR!FF1C.

He was immediately granted access.

It was weird, the relationship between Walter and Alice, but Tom had gotten past the jealousy. The two were friends. Sympaticos. He was sure there had been more on Walter's side, but he didn't doubt Alice.

Had been...

It was easy to drift through, forgetting the gravity of this situation. Someone had *died*. Walter.

The fact the cops were sniffing around meant that this was a suspicious death of some sort.

This was serious.

Walter's computer desktop was neat and orderly. But even so, where to start looking?

Tom knew what he was looking for, just not where to find it. Walter had been investigating Libbie, had found something. This was an office machine, so he wouldn't have left anything obvious. Sure enough, the desktop shortcuts all pointed to work-related software and folders. If he had files on here, they could be buried just about anywhere.

Walter knew this stuff, and he knew how to cover his tracks.

Walter had left Chrome running and Tom clicked on it to bring the browser window back up. There were only three tabs open, one for the Pierson Newport intranet, one for his email, and one for CNN.

Tom's laptop had about twenty browser tabs open at any one time. Walter sure was methodical. Or he'd tidied up after himself before leaving the office.

The first two tabs were probably permanent, for mail and work, so Tom guessed the third tab was the one Walter had most recently used for non-work browsing. He clicked the Back button a couple of times, backtracking through news stories.

Then he came to more random things: a Google Map of Manhattan, another of upstate New York, a couple more news websites, the official web page of some kind of hospital, a couple of gaming communities, a bunch of pages from the NYU website.

STEVE RICHER AND NICHOLAS GIFFORD

Tom couldn't see an obvious connection between any of these.

He called up the full browser history and saw more of the same eclectic mix.

Walter had clearly had a reason to look at all this stuff, but without knowing that reason they just appeared random.

In reality, they were pretty random: he wouldn't only have been looking for things relating to Libbie. Most of these pages in his history probably had nothing at all to do with what Tom was looking for.

He sat back in the chair, frustrated.

Then he remembered his own advice to Alice when she'd had computer problems and thought she'd lost a bunch of work files. It was advice right up there with *Have you tried turning it off and on again?*

He slid the mouse pointer bottom-left, and clicked through to Recent Files. Walter had found something out and he'd called Alice, then gone straight to the house.

In that case, if he'd kept any records, then whatever he'd found would be in his list of most recent files!

He found them immediately, opening each document as he went. Again, Walter had been methodical. All in a folder called *Perfect Tenant*, there was a spreadsheet called *timeline.xslx*, a text document called *perfecttenant.docx*, and a subfolder called *libbie images*.

The spreadsheet consisted of a single sheet, little more than a list with a column for date and one for details. Automatically, Tom's eyes jumped to the bottom of the list to find the most recent items.

312

Entries for the last few days included *Rusty*, *Photo shoot*, and *Pierson Newport misc anomalies*. Had Alice given him these details, or had he found them himself?

Before then, there were entries for when Libbie had moved into the apartment, and when she'd first visited to inspect the property.

And before that: *Release date.*

Release?

Had she been in jail? Above that, dated ninety days before, he found an entry for Libbie's admission to a secure mental health facility in upstate New York. He switched windows to the web browser and flicked through the history to find that Google map: sure enough, it centered on that medical facility.

He returned to the spreadsheet, but it was frustrating, a summary with no detail. She'd been in a secure facility before coming here, there had been some kind of hearing, but for what?

He switched to the document Walter had called *perfecttenant.docx*. It consisted of a number of sub-sections, each with a title that corresponded with entries in the timeline: *Hearing, Hospital, Rental.*

Again, he glanced at the more recent entries first. Under *Rental*, Walter had outlined incidents involving Rusty, Marissa, and Pierson Newport.

Marissa: being used to drive a wedge? How? Why?

Rusty: photo montage? Accomplice or patsy?

Pierson Newport: document manipulation? Hacking? Sabotage?

But what really interested him was earlier, before she'd entered their lives. If Walter's notes were to be believed, Libbie had been committed to a secure hospital after accusations she'd beaten a dog to death with a baseball bat.

Tom sat there actually shaking his head in disbelief.

Surely, that must be another person?

She'd been put on trial for the incident, but the trial had been suspended on health grounds and the judge had committed her for a minimum of ninety days at the hospital.

Again, Walter's notes were minimal, but he'd included links in the document.

Tom clicked on the first link and found an official record of the aborted trial from the County Court.

He skimmed through it, feeling sick. The account of the violence meted out on the poor dog, barely more than a puppy, was both heartbreaking and described in cold, graphic detail.

The judge's comments as he committed Libbie for treatment were understated in the way only an official statement can be. ...*cause for grave concern ... public welfare grounds ... obsessive personality disorder ... anger management ... risk of escalation...*

Obsessive personality disorder. Escalation. He had to get all this to Jason Grande. They really had to get Libbie out of their lives!

Walter had found a whole bunch of official records about the trial and the hospital, most of it densely worded legalese. Tom skimmed until he could take no more.

If Libbie Burchett—or whatever her name was—was not a full-blown psychopath, she was well on her way to becoming one!

One of the documents had implied this, while avoiding coming right out and saying it. *Sociopathy* was mentioned in one of the files.

Tom tried to remember the difference between a psychopath and a sociopath. Neither had the ability to empathize with other people and both were cold, manipulative, selfish and cruel. He thought the distinction came down to psychopaths being born that way, while sociopaths became that way because something damaged them. Maybe? He wasn't sure.

He wondered what had made Libbie the way she was.

He paused to check at the office doorway. No sign of Tuckett. He didn't believe he'd left yet: he wouldn't leave Tom alone in the building. But at least he was giving him some space.

He went back to Walter's desk and sat.

Walter had been thorough, but he hadn't picked up on all the strange things that had been happening since Libbie turned up.

In particular, there was that mascot. It had been one of the first things she'd given them, an unexpected act of generosity that both played on his hobby and touched on the long-standing joke about his support for the Brewers.

But it was a summer camp mascot, one that reached back into Tom's youth.

That had to mean something.

He opened a new browser tab and typed in *Long Valley*

Summer Camp, and then added *Libbie Cottrill*, using the real surname Walter had found for her.

The search came up with a random set of results. Long, valley, summer and camp were all common words, after all. He put that search term in quotes to force the results to be more specific and then decided to change Libbie to Elizabeth, the full version of her name that had been used in the court proceedings.

Elizabeth Cottrill.

It was like seeing an approaching car's headlights over the horizon before actually seeing what was coming.

He could sense his brain playing catch-up.

He found a set of results from an old Flickr account. A bunch of images of kids by a lake that was set deep in a forest. Long Valley camp.

The kids were all wearing orange t-shirts, the same shade as the painted-over jersey on the summer camp mascot figurine Libbie had given him.

One by one, he clicked on the right arrow, working through the old photographs.

Until he found it.

Another group of kids, standing with arms around each other's shoulders, grinning and waving for the camera.

One of the kids was a twelve-year-old Tom, his features rounded by baby-fat and his then-golden hair longer than he recalled. It was unmistakably him. He was standing on the right-hand side of the group with Tony Capaldi, Simon Woodforde, and Andy Krabbe, all under the watchful eye of one of the camp assistants.

And there, standing at the front of the group photo, equally unmistakable with that shock of chestnut hair and the defiant tilt of the head, was Libbie Burchett, known then as Elizabeth Cottrill.

CHAPTER 34

Alice tried to sleep after Tom left.

She couldn't, though. The hospital was too noisy and her body was in a strangely agitated state. She couldn't recall if this was a normal response, as her physiology adjusted itself back to normal blood sugar levels again.

She didn't care.

All she knew was that she was unsettled, agitated.

It didn't help that the hot nurse had kept checking on her. He kept coming in and disturbing her peace until finally she demanded to know why he was being so solicitous. He confessed that Tom had asked him to keep a close check on her.

"He said you were suffering anxiety."

"Anxiety? I am now. Look, I just want to settle down. I could do that so much better without this thing."

She raised an arm to indicate the drip, and the cannula taped in position on the back of her wrist. He checked her charts, and finally agreed she didn't need the drip any more.

It still didn't help her settle, though.

She'd be going home in the morning. She just wished she could go now. All the noise here. All the sounds of activity, the people rushing past her door, the...

Someone was standing in the doorway, a big, angular figure that almost had to duck to get under the frame.

"Rusty? What are you doing here? Is everything okay?"

"Mrs. Granger." He seemed out of breath.

"What is it, Rusty?"

Even at the worst of times, she hadn't been easy with the way Tom had acted against the boy. She still couldn't bring herself to believe he was any kind of threat.

"It's Mr. Granger," he said. He wouldn't step into the room, as if some invisible boundary existed to stop him. "He sent me here. Said that it's urgent."

Alice glanced across at her purse. If Tom had called, she hadn't seen or heard anything. But then he'd made a show of putting her phone out of reach in her purse before he left. Told her she needed to concentrate on getting better and not on catching up with her work emails, which they both knew she wanted to do.

He must have found out something. She knew he'd gone to see if there was anything on Walter's computer.

"What is it, Rusty? Why did Tom send you?"

"He... I didn't quite understand, Mrs. Granger. He said he'd discovered something terrible and you're in danger here at the hospital. He gave me an address where I'm to drop you, where you'll be safe. What's going on, Mrs. Granger? It just doesn't make sense that he'd want you to bail from the hospital like that."

The boy was out of his depth. Maybe they all were, but it was written clear across his pock-marked face. He was a boy who liked routine, who liked certainties in his life, and struggled with anything that deviated from that.

"It's okay, Rusty. You did well. Thank you."

She pushed herself upright and swung her legs clear of the bedding, turning to sit on the edge of the mattress.

Rusty's eyes flashed down at the exposed flesh of her legs, and then away, his cheeks flushing a deep crimson.

"What're you doing, Mrs. Granger?"

"I'm about to get dressed, Rusty. So I think you should give me that address and leave before you see something you shouldn't, all right?"

He'd already taken a couple of steps backward, his gaze still averted.

"I can't leave you, Mrs. Granger. I'm to take you there. That's what he said."

"No, Rusty. You've done enough. But thank you."

She remembered Libbie's warnings about Rusty, but when she looked at him she just saw a scared, confused kid, not some deranged psychopath. There was only one person who met that description in all this, and Alice wanted Rusty safely away from it all.

"Go home, Rusty."

She reached for the fastening of her hospital gown. Cruel to play him with his own shyness, but Tom wouldn't have sent this warning if he didn't mean it. She had to move.

"I'll wait out in the hallway."

"No, Rusty. Just go. You're a real kind-hearted gentleman for wanting to stay, but I've got this." Then she played her final, almost childish, trump card. "If you like me, Rusty, go home now, knowing you've done the right thing."

He stared at her, clearly torn. It was a riddle he couldn't solve. He liked her—of course he did!—so he should go, but then if he liked her so much he had to stay and make sure she was okay.

His need for order triumphed. She'd given him a clear instruction, and he always did what Mrs. Granger asked. That was the way of his world.

"I guess, if you're *sure*...?"

"I'm sure."

Without further argument, Rusty turned and left.

When Alice went over to the door to check, there was no sign of him in the hallway.

She pushed the door closed and turned.

She only had a few things here. The clothes she'd been wearing had been taken away by the police; they had Walter's blood on them from when she'd found him. But Tom had brought some fresh ones in for when she got out tomorrow.

She pulled on underwear, jogging pants, bra, t-shirt, sweatshirt and sneakers. It was a random combo, and not things she normally wore, but it would do.

"And what do you think you're doing?"

She turned. The hot nurse stood in the doorway, tall and muscular. Shaking his shaved head. "You look as if you're going for a run."

She looked down at herself. The sweatshirt, the jogging pants, the sneakers.

"I… I needed some fresh air."

"You need some rest." He came into the room. "Listen, I know you just want to get out of here, but you need to rest for the time being. You can get all the fresh air you need tomorrow, you hear me?"

"I guess. I just…"

"I know. But if you think you're going out for a nature walk on my watch, you're badly mistaken."

She reached for her top and paused, eyebrows raised.

The nurse laughed. "I seen it all before, believe me, sister," he said. Then he raised his hands in defeat and moved toward the door. "But I'll give you your privacy, just so long as you get back into that bed."

When he came back a few minutes later, she was lying under the covers, her eyes closed.

She waited, listening to the sounds he made moving about the room, and then to the silence that followed. When she was sure he'd left, she climbed back out of bed, still fully clothed.

She was fine now. She didn't need to be here.

And if Tom's warning was to be believed, here was the worst place for her to remain.

She went out into the hallway. No sign of the nurse. A different nurse rushed past, barely giving her a glance.

Alice straightened, took a deep breath. Unless she

bumped into anyone who knew her, she'd be fine. Just another person wandering through the hospital. A visitor, or an off-duty member of staff.

She moved along the hallway, anxious to get away from her room at least, before pausing to try to find her bearings.

She'd been unconscious when they brought her here, but she'd spent enough time in this hospital to have at least a rough idea of the layout. She started to walk again. Found a sign pointing to the main exit and kept on going.

She expected to be stopped at any moment.

She didn't know what her rights were. Could a person just walk out of hospital? She'd seen TV programs and movies where patients checked themselves out against their doctors' advice, but did that mean there was some kind of official process to follow?

Then again, what were they going to do, arrest her and charge her with walking out of a public building? Still, the best process she could think of right now was not being spotted.

She came to the hospital's main reception area and hesitated. Surely, someone would stop her now? She pulled the sleeve of her sweatshirt down, covering up her patient ID wristband.

Then she took a deep breath and walked out boldly from the hallway where she'd been loitering.

A receptionist looked up, and then away. Patients and other visitors sat in the waiting area, even at this hour.

The security guard smiled at her as she passed him.

She entered the rotating door, let it spin a half turn as

she followed it around, and finally stepped out into the cold night air.

She moved away from the brightest lighting.

When she took her cellphone from her purse and checked, there was nothing from Tom. He'd known she had her phone on silent, and it was out of reach from her hospital bed. That must be why he'd sent Rusty.

She found him in Favorites and was just about to press dial when she heard voices from inside the reception area.

At first, she thought it was nothing, just some kind of random altercation. A tall black man in jeans and a hoodie was gesturing, shouting at the receptionist, the security guy.

Then she recognized him. Hot nurse, changed out of his scrubs. His shift must have ended and he was on his way home and... he'd spotted Alice, standing outside.

Shit.

She turned away, assessing her options.

Just turning quickly like that was enough to make her dizzy. Maybe she wasn't as fully recovered as she'd believed.

She couldn't just run. She wouldn't stand a chance.

That was when she spotted the taxi stand, saw a cab sitting there, its engine running even though the driver stood outside, his hefty butt resting against the driver-side door, a cigarette hanging from the corner of his mouth.

"You give me a ride?" she said, hurrying over.

"Sure thing, lady. Where you want to go?"

"Anywhere," she said, already tugging on the door. "Just away from here. Fast."

CHAPTER 35

Walter's research had exposed a part of Tom's life he'd long since buried away. A time when he'd been unhappy, when he'd struggled with all kinds of things.

This thing with Libbie… it was all his fault.

Was this karma? Karma dressed up in the form of Libbie Cottrill, come to hunt him down and wreak her revenge.

It was all his fault.

But that didn't make it right.

And that wasn't going to bring poor Walter Jones back to life again.

He had to put a stop to this. One way or another, this thing was going to end tonight.

As he drove away from the hospital, it all went round and round in his head. How had he not worked it out sooner? How had he failed to recognize her?

That summer when he was twelve. His first summer camp. The first time he'd been away anywhere without his parents, apart from a couple of long weekends with his grandparents.

He remembered watching their car drive away. In his

memory, he was a little kid in short pants, standing with a heap of luggage at the roadside, a heavy teardrop making its way down his face. In reality, though, he knew they'd already put his case in the cabin, and it was his mom who was crying as she waved out of the passenger window. Tom had just been impatient to get on with things. He wanted to explore. Wanted to make new friends.

As soon as the car was out of sight, he'd turned and run to the lakeside. He'd never seen such a huge expanse of water and there were kids out there already in kayaks and on a huge raft made from lashed together barrels and planks of wood.

Tony Capaldi, Simon Woodforde, and Andy Krabbe were, by chance, the first kids he'd approached. A couple of years older than Tom, they were sitting at the end of a narrow wooden jetty, their feet dangling over the water. Tank tops, shorts, baseball caps turned backwards, the latest Nikes on the dock behind them, where they'd taken them off.

The three had a roll-up cigarette they were passing between them. They clearly weren't scared of anything, or anyone. They *owned* this place.

Tom wanted to be like them. He wanted to *be* them.

He realized he was loitering, rocking from foot to foot like a toddler who needs to pee. "Yo," he said. "What's up?"

Why had he said that? He didn't talk like that.

The one he later came to know as Tony turned his head slowly, eyed him up.

All of a sudden, Tom had never felt so small.

After a pause long enough to drown in, Tony Capaldi said to his friends, "Hey, guys. Look what we got here. We got ourselves a new bitch to play with."

They laughed and, after a short hesitation, Tom laughed too. He didn't know what he was laughing at, just that the cool guys were laughing so he should laugh. And now he wanted to be like them more than anything.

Following the exchange, they ignored him. He went to sit on a different part of the pier, feet dangling. The water was cold. He didn't know if he should leave or go and join them. It was weird, the need to belong. He'd never felt like that before.

Then Tony called along to him. "Hey, bitch. We need some Cokes."

He got them Cokes. Paid for it himself, happy to have been noticed, to have been included in some way.

That night, in his bunk, Tom found himself crying for no reason. He didn't think he was homesick, although he'd woken to the image of his mother leaving in the car, crying. He didn't understand his feelings.

He'd made new friends, even if they did call him *bitch*. He had four whole weeks of this ahead of him. So why was he crying?

He didn't know. Just knew he most certainly was not homesick.

Next day, Tony, Simon and Andy started calling him crybaby instead of bitch. It was not an improvement.

We need sodas, crybaby.

What're you doing down there, crybaby? And when he asked them down where, one of them would push him hard in

328

the chest so he ended up sprawling in the dirt. *Down there.*

He couldn't remember how long it had taken him to work out that they weren't *including* him by treating him like this. They were doing anything *but* including him.

It felt like weeks, but was probably only a matter of days. Long enough for him to come to understand that he had an entire summer of this to get through. Long enough to realize that they were already escalating, pushing him harder, hitting him harder, and if it was this bad already then what would they be doing to him by the end of summer?

Long enough for him to work out that his only escape was if he could somehow redirect their attention.

Find another target.

Someone more vulnerable than him.

Someone like that chestnut-haired girl who never quite seemed to fit in. The one who stood aloof when everyone else was throwing themselves into the summer camp's activities. The one who made it perfectly clear she regarded herself as something a whole lot better than everyone else here at Long Valley.

Little snot-nosed Elizabeth Cottrill.

He remembered the exact moment when Tony Capaldi had him by the collar and for once he'd met the bully's look and said, "Yeah, but at least I don't shit my pants like Lizzie Cottrill."

He'd made that up. Just words he'd grabbed out of the thin air, a claim that might at least briefly distract Tony.

He didn't think they'd leap on it and turn on her like they did. It was Simon Woodforde who was the first to do the chocolate thing. Made Elizabeth sit on a whole block of the stuff until it melted and then they told everyone she'd messed herself, and she ran away into the forest to hide her shame.

Tom felt sick even now when he recalled the flood of relief he'd felt when the three bullies turned their attention on someone else. The sense of belonging he'd felt when they included him in their games, when they made *him* the one who told her someone had spat in her food. Even now, he didn't know if they actually spat in her food or just told her they had so she'd never know what she was eating.

In therapy after his breakdown last year, he'd even gone over this, exploring the guilt he'd stored up for all these years.

"Sometimes we have to accept we're powerless over certain things," the therapist had told him at the end of one of their sessions. "You were twelve. You were the victim of bullying. You couldn't have stopped them. All it does now is continue to harm you, unless you can learn how to file it away and move on."

He'd tried to stop them. Even tried to make them turn on *him* again, but it hadn't worked.

They were bullies and they'd found a much softer target. One that kept them entertained that entire summer and even into the next, until Elizabeth had suddenly left camp, never to return. Understandably so.

And now she was here. He couldn't blame her for hating him. For blaming him. He would, in her position.

Earlier, he'd had every intention of confronting her, telling her the game was up, kicking her out.

Right now, after seeing what Walter had discovered, he just wanted to beg her forgiveness.

His therapist may have been right about the need to file away his guilt, but that didn't mean the guilt vanished. Ever.

~ ~ ~ ~

If summer camp had given him the worst times of his life, it had also given him some of the best.

The following summer he'd shown up a couple of weeks late, his arm in a sling after a mountain bike accident. One consequence of this was that Tony, Simon, and Andy had already picked their targets for the summer and they barely seemed to even notice he'd arrived.

Another was that he couldn't take part in most of the activities, so he ended up an outsider, looking on while everyone else had all the fun.

Everyone apart from the golden-haired girl with the sad eyes that lit up and completely transformed her face whenever one of his corny jokes managed to make her smile.

In the beginning, he didn't understand why she was acting like an outsider too, and he thought maybe she had some kind of mystery illness that meant she couldn't join in. Later, he found out there had been some kind of boating accident out on the lake at the start of the summer, and she'd been indirectly involved. After that she hadn't been able to go near the water.

At the time, though, none of that mattered to him. She was a kid his age, she was an outcast like him, and the two

STEVE RICHER AND NICHOLAS GIFFORD

developed a bond that got them both through the summer. Even better, he found out that she was from his own hometown, although she attended a different school.

They called themselves the Misfits, although her actual name was Alice.

~ ~ ~ ~

Tom pulled over at the side of the road.

Since leaving the Pierson Newport offices, he'd been driving around, taking an ever-more circuitous route home.

What was he going to say to Libbie? Was he really going to ask her to forgive him?

She was insane. What was it? A sociopath, with an obsessive personality disorder.

She might even somehow be responsible for what had happened to Walter, even if it was some kind of tragic accident.

And he knew now that he was the target of all this.

He wasn't scared of her, though. He was confident he could handle her.

But... He didn't want her to hurt any more. She must have obsessed about what had happened at summer camp for years. She needed careful handling, and him wading in alone was not going to help her.

But that's what she needed. Help. Treatment. Support.

He dug his phone out of a pocket and dialed a number he'd been given earlier.

"Detective Malwitz?" It was raining now, the wind rocking the car as he sat there. He had to raise his voice to be heard. "Yes, Tom Granger here. Listen, I think I've worked a few things out. I don't know what it adds up to, but I think it might help you."

"I just love it when someone else does my job for me, Mr. Granger. No, no, I wasn't being glib. I mean it. So what have you worked out?"

He told him about the files on Walter's computer, about Libbie Burchett, or Elizabeth Cottrill, as she had been then.

He told him about summer camp. About the bullying, and his part in it. He didn't hold back. In a bizarre way, it felt good to talk about it again, to lay out his guilt to the world.

"And now you think she's coming after you?"

"I don't know what she's doing." But yes, now that he'd said it all out loud, he knew she was after some kind of revenge.

"Well, that's all very helpful, Mr. Granger. We'll definitely take a closer look at Ms. Burchett, or Cottrill, or whatever she's called. I'm searching the databases for anything we have on her right here on the screen in front of me as we speak."

"So what happens next?"

"Next, Mr. Granger, is you trying not to get involved, you hear? You've done some detective work and that's great, but you do any more than you have and you're interfering with an investigation."

"But..."

STEVE RICHER AND NICHOLAS GIFFORD

"I know that sounds harsh, but we're the professionals. This is what we do. If she's dangerous then we're the guys to deal with it. And if she just needs some kind of medical or psychological help then we're the ones who will make the right calls. You understand? Just stay away for tonight and leave us to do some investigating."

"But she lives in the basement apartment of my house. What am I supposed to do tonight?"

"I'd advise you to stay away and not inflame the situation. Is there some place you can go for tonight? Some place safe. Maybe make sure your wife's safe at the hospital and then find yourself somewhere near there for the night?"

"I'll work something out."

He would.

But first he would swing by the house to pick up a few things.

And if Libbie was there? He genuinely didn't know what he would do. Tell her to pack her things and go. Beg her forgiveness. Or simply let her wreak whatever revenge she was after.

It might be any of those. But somehow, this thing had to come to an end tonight, and it was clear Detective Malwitz was on a different, far slower, timetable.

CHAPTER 36

When he got home, the place was dark, both upstairs and down in the basement apartment.

That was probably the best thing.

He still didn't know what he'd have said to Libbie if she'd been here.

He hadn't even known quite what he expected to find. When he'd come back this afternoon to pick up a few things for Alice, the cops had still been here. They'd taped off the path around the side of the house like a crime scene, which he'd supposed it was. A potential one, at least.

But now there was nothing. No cops. Not even any tape marking off the scene.

Was that an indication of their thinking? No suggestion of foul play, just a tragic freak accident.

Earlier that day, Detective Malwitz had implied as much. His questioning of Tom had been perfunctory and he'd said more than once that they were just following procedure.

Now, he wondered how seriously Malwitz had taken his call about Libbie's past. The detective said he was searching their databases for anything they had on her, but would his investigations go any further than that?

Thinking about it, he hadn't really given the detective much to go on. Plenty that pointed to Libbie having some kind of vendetta against *him*, but nothing that suggested involvement in anything criminal.

Malwitz had been humoring him, no more than that.

He pulled up on the gravel in front of the house.

Climbing out, he pulled his jacket tighter around himself. The rain had eased now, but the wind was cold.

He went to the corner of the building. Odd to think that this was where Walter had met his end. The place would be changed forever. There would not be a single time either he or Alice walked past this spot and didn't think of Walter.

The basement apartment was in complete darkness.

She might be asleep in there, of course. It was late enough now that someone might reasonably have gone to bed. There was no sign of her Toyota, though.

He turned away, went back around to the porch, and let himself into the house.

Malwitz had said they should stay away from home tonight while he did some digging. Right now, that suited Tom. He didn't want to be here alone.

He went upstairs and filled an overnight bag. A change of clothes, some toiletries. Some meds for Alice in case the hospital discharged her early tomorrow and they still had to stay away.

He worried about her, alone at the hospital. He'd asked that nurse to check up on her, but still. Would she be safe there tonight, if he assumed the worst about Libbie? The cop had advised him to stay safe tonight, after all, so that must apply to Alice too.

With that notion in his head, he felt a hint of panic.

He was being paranoid, he knew.

But now that the thought had struck, he knew he'd have to make sure she was safe, too. He went back down, the bag over his shoulder. Outside, it was raining again. He dropped the bag in the trunk.

He had to make sure they were going to be safe. And the best way to do that was to know what they were up against.

And so he pulled his jacket tighter around himself again and went around the corner of the house.

Stepping carefully around the place where Walter had fallen, he came to stand before the basement apartment door.

Still no lights, no sounds from within.

He peered through a window, but saw nothing in the gloom.

He took his keys from his pocket and searched through them for the one for the apartment. He slid it home, turned, and before he had time to change his mind he stepped inside.

Cautiously, he moved from room to room, checking to make sure that the place really was as empty as it seemed.

Nobody was here.

Rather than flip any of the lights on, he used the flashlight on his phone to look around. He didn't know what he hoped to find.

What had he expected? Some kind of psychopath's wall planner with details of all her scheming and manipulations? This was stupid.

He should leave now, while he could. Do exactly as Detective Malwitz had said and find somewhere safe for the night. Leave it to the cops. And just in case, he should go to Jason Grande tomorrow with all the new information he had and get the eviction process in motion.

He still felt that guilt, that sense of responsibility, but right now, standing here and holding his breath, he just wanted resolution.

He moved to a cabinet, pulled a drawer and riffled through the contents. Tape, scissors, screwdrivers, and other household tools. The next door held papers and bills, letters. He checked through them but they were mundane, nothing obviously incriminating in any way.

That voice in the back of his mind kept telling him that he should go. In the bedroom, he just felt creepy. He shouldn't be going through her clothes like this. It was wrong on so many levels.

He was about to leave the room, but then hesitated. He reached for one last drawer and pulled it open. Scrapbooks. Three of them. He put them on the bed, side by side, still convinced he was wasting his time.

The first he opened did nothing to convince him he was wrong. Pictures cut from magazines of shoes and purses and items of clothing on tall, angularly skinny models. Labels in neat handwriting accompanied the pictures, identifying the items' designers. Christian

Louboutin, Jimmy Choo, Vera Wang, Stella McCartney, and lots more names he'd never heard of. It was like some teenager's high school project.

He almost didn't bother looking in the next scrapbook.

He was a completer-finisher, though. Alice always teased him about that, the way once he'd started something he had to see it through to the end. So he flipped the cover over, and when he saw the first picture he almost dropped his phone.

A wedding photograph. *His* wedding photograph.

One of the ones where he stood with his arms looped around Alice's waist, and they gazed into each other's eyes.

Except in this picture there were no eyes, just holes in the print, gouged by something sharp. And scrawled across the photograph in black marker pen were the words *DIE TORTURER DIE!!*

He had to force himself to turn the next page, then the next, and then it became an automatic thing, the flip, flip, flip of the pages.

Photographs. Newspaper cuttings from the rare occasions he or Alice had made the local press for something at work, or a charitable event they'd been involved with. Pages from old school yearbooks. Pictures printed from Facebook and other online sources.

Tom and Alice, together or individually.

Damn, there were even recent photos, ones Libbie must have taken herself.

Tom in the house upstairs, photographed through a

STEVE RICHER AND NICHOLAS GIFFORD

window. Alice at Pierson Newport, or out and about in town.

And all of them disfigured. Vandalized. Eyes and faces gouged out. Words scrawled: *BITCH… TRAITOR… DIE!*

She was sick. Twisted. A sociopath with an obsessive personality disorder, just as the judge had said.

She'd gone to that secure hospital for treatment, but it clearly hadn't worked.

He almost didn't dare open the third scrapbook. But it couldn't be any worse than this, could it?

The first page held a photo of a group of kids by a lake. It was similar to the one he'd found online from when he'd been at Long Valley Summer Camp—it must have been taken around the same time.

Even though the group of kids was larger in this picture, it was easy to spot Tom and the others.

Tom, Tony Capaldi, Simon Woodforde, Andy Krabbe.

They were the ones with their faces scraped away.

He flipped the page and saw a picture of Tony, a few years older, hair slicked down, sporting a neatly tailored tux and a doe-eyed girl on his arm. A page from his high school yearbook followed. Tony was a natural born leader, apparently, and heading off to college on a football scholarship. With his face scraped off.

Another flip of a page and the faceless Tony's college career was over. Football injuries and arrests for barroom brawls and supplying drugs to minors, and his bright future had been shot down in tatters.

More flips of the page mapped his decline until Tom came to a short news story and a single paragraph obituary.

Tony Capaldi, a young man who had shown great promise, had died at the age of twenty-seven, clubbed to death in the street. Blood tests had shown that he'd indulged in a cocktail of alcohol and a variety of illegal substances before he'd met his end.

Tony had been the ringleader when Tom had known him, the one who always pushed them further. A fiery teenager with a troubled family background and a deeply-seated cruel streak.

He'd made Tom's time at summer camp miserable for a time.

But still…

It was awful to see the story of a life gone so tragically wrong.

He flipped the page again. Simon Woodforde.

Simon had found more success in life. He'd married, had kids, done well professionally—as a dental surgeon, of all things. He seemed happy, as far as you could tell from the faceless photographs.

He'd died three years ago, according to the glowing obituaries included in the scrapbook.

Drugs. Alcohol. Bludgeoned with a blunt weapon, most probably a baseball bat.

The pattern was obvious. The similarities.

He couldn't bring himself to believe it, though. Couldn't imagine Libbie being responsible for the deaths of these two grown men.

Tony had been a football player, after all. He was big and strong. But his life had spiraled downward, and if he'd been incapacitated by booze and drugs first of all, he might have been unable to fight back...

And Libbie had been sent to a secure hospital after being arrested for bludgeoning a dog to death... with a baseball bat.

He turned the page again. Andy Krabbe.

Andy with his face scratched away and his successful career as an apparently popular high school teacher. Andy who tragically died in a mountain fall a few weeks before his first child was due. Found a day after the fall, his head caved in from impact.

Andy had died—been killed?—only this spring. A short time before Libbie had been sent away for the incident with the dog.

The conclusion was obvious.

Libbie had been involved in all three deaths. Either directly, or somehow tormenting the men until drink, drugs, and frustration had put them at risk.

And now she was here, living in the basement of Tom's own home.

It was obvious that he was next.

He gathered up the scrapbooks. He'd take them to Malwitz, lay them out before him and challenge the cop to actually do something this time.

He knew he shouldn't be here, even though it was his property. Would that make the scrapbooks inadmissible as evidence? He didn't know. But he couldn't leave them here for Libbie to dispose of. He needed them if he was to convince Malwitz of the seriousness of all this.

"Did you enjoy reading those?"

He hadn't heard her enter. Hadn't heard her come to stand in the bedroom doorway.

How long had she been watching him?

She had a strange look on her face. Cold. Measuring. Was that the last look Tony, Simon, and Andy had seen?

"This has gone too far, Libbie," he said, keeping his voice even.

The other three had been weak. Weak as teenagers, as most bullies were. Weak as men, he was sure.

Tom was made of different stuff. He wasn't going to let her win.

"It hasn't gone far enough."

She was smiling. She was enjoying this.

And she was blocking the doorway.

"I'm taking these," he told her, gesturing with the books. "You can do what you like. Get into that car of yours and run. But they'll find you. They'll track you down and find you."

She stayed silent, still smiling.

"I felt sorry for you," he said. "Truly sorry. Sorry for what happened back then. I always have been. That kind of guilt, it eats away at you. It really does. But this has to end here."

"Sorry for me? You had a crush on me, Tom. You

always did."

She gave a little wiggle of the hips as she spoke, finishing with a sharp smack on her own ass.

"You want a piece of this now, Tom? You know you do."

He moved to go past her, using the scrapbooks as a shield between them.

She moved quickly, reached for the books and grabbed them, ripping them from his grip so they fell to the floor.

He reacted fast, grabbing her by the wrists, stopping her clawed hands from scraping at his eyes. Her arms trembled in his grip, straining to get at him.

"You killed them, didn't you? Tony, Simon, Andy."

She managed a slight shrug. Said, "So what? They deserved it. They ruined me. Destroyed my life before it had even begun." She gave a short laugh then. "And to think that all I got put away for was that damn dog!"

"It'll catch up with you. It's *caught* up with you. Detective Malwitz's on your tail right now."

As he held her, he struggled to work out his next move. How could he secure her? Keep her here until the cops arrived? It wasn't physically possible. But he could hardly just step back and let her go.

"That dog was annoying. It kept barking. Yap, yap, yap! It had to be stopped. I did people a favor. They should've given me a medal."

She was certifiably insane. He didn't know how to deal with it.

"And talking of dogs…" She paused, that smile back on her face. "Now it's time to take down the worst of them all."

What did she mean? Did she mean him? He could see why she might: while Tony had been the ringleader, it was Tom who'd done all he could to redirect the bullies' attentions away from himself and onto a softer target… onto Libbie. Had she somehow worked that out?

But how did she think she had the upper hand here?

What did she know that he didn't?

He tried to be ready for whatever move she might try, but even so he wasn't prepared for the move she *did* make.

She smiled even more widely, then said, "But before we resolve the issues between *us*, Tom, don't you think you'd better go save your darling wife?"

He stared.

What…?

Then she winked, smiled again, and said, "Go on, Tom. Go save her, *sweetie*."

CHAPTER 37

"You sure you want to be dropped off here, lady?"

The cab driver was reluctant to let Alice go. He leaned across his passenger seat now, eying his passenger up and down as she stood on the Whitetail Lane sidewalk.

She was only wearing those joggers and sweatshirt, and the night was blowing up a storm. She hugged herself as the wind and rain whipped around her, willing the cab to leave.

Eventually, the guy shook his head, still muttering, and pulled away.

Soon she was alone in the street, gazing into the darkness for Tom.

She was shivering with the cold. Already cursing her husband for dragging her out here to the income property. He must have his reasons, but still... Surely there was a better place than this. What was wrong with a nice, cozy room at the Holiday Inn?

The property was deserted. She picked her way along the path through the overgrown front yard, lighting the way with her phone. They'd need to get someone to clear this lot, if they could afford it. Maybe Rusty, now that he appeared to be back in favor with Tom.

That wind was sharp! The kind of Arctic wind that cut through your clothing and right on through to the bone.

She wished she had a coat. Gloves. Anything.

She wished she'd never left that noisy, uncomfortable—but warm!—hospital room.

Just then, as if to reinforce her sense that this was all wrong, she heard a terrible flapping sound coming from somewhere above. She looked up sharply. The light from her phone was inadequate, but there was nevertheless enough illumination for her to see a big, dark sheet lifting and flapping in the gale.

The temporary fix on the hole in the roof hadn't even lasted a day in these conditions.

"Hello?"

She'd paused in the doorway.

It wasn't the house that spooked her, but the possibility of what it might contain. Abandoned construction sites like this were an easy haven for junkies, drunks, kids. She didn't know what she might be walking into.

Except Tom had told her to meet him here, she reminded herself.

"Hello? Tom?"

It was hard to hear anything. The flapping, roaring sounds of the torn roof covering echoed around inside the empty building, swamping any other sounds.

She pushed inside.

Franco Vialli and his crew had wasted no time clearing the site—the botched fix on the roof a clear indication of their haste to leave. All their tools were gone, and lots of the materials she remembered being stored here, too. Did they have the right to take all that? She'd have to check the invoices later, to see he hadn't taken anything they'd already paid for.

The whole business was such a mess. She'd *liked* Franco Vialli. Trusted him. She felt so let down by his attitude.

She moved across the lobby, but then was brought up short by an impact on her foot, a sharp bolt of pain.

"Ah!"

She'd stubbed her toe on what the cellphone's light revealed to be a brick, one of the few things Vialli *hadn't* removed from the site.

The pain made her eyes water. She hoped she hadn't broken a toe. How embarrassing would that be? A return trip to the hospital for a broken bone so soon after a narrow escape?

"Tom? Sweetheart?"

This was getting too much. She felt weak already. She knew a lot of that was psychological, but she'd been in the hospital for a reason. And here she was, without meds again and no idea how her blood sugar levels were. She clearly hadn't learned a thing from recent events.

The inside lobby had several doors opening off it, as well a flight of stairs that led up to the next floor.

She swept the light of her phone around. There really was no sign Tom had been here at all. For a moment, she wondered if Rusty had been playing a cruel joke. Revenge for the way he'd been treated, perhaps. It made sense, right? It was plausible.

But no. She'd never doubted he was a good kid at heart. And far too straightforward a person to play games like this.

As she lowered her phone again, she spotted something. She'd almost missed it: a note, stuck to a nail protruding from the top of the post at the foot of the stairs.

Odd that there was a nail in the new woodwork, but maybe Vialli or one of his guys had done it for some reason.

The note consisted of an arrow pointing up the stairs, a winky face— ;-) —and one word: *SWEETIE*.

As far as she could see in this dim light, it looked like Tom's writing. She couldn't remember ever having seen him use emoticons in his messages, but she got it. The wink and smile, the *sweetie…* that was so *Tom*.

"Tom?" She called louder now, confident there was nobody malicious lurking in the shadows, trying to be heard over the roar and flap of the damaged roofing.

She shone her light up the stairs. The wood was new, put in early in the work to allow easy access for the workers fitting out upstairs. It was covered in sheets of plastic for protection, so that each footstep crunched.

"Tom, are you there?"

Halfway up, she paused. Surely, he'd have heard her by now if he was here? Maybe he was on his way. Maybe he'd been delayed.

She kept going. Another step. Another.

When she put her weight on the next step something was different. The wood shifted a little under her weight. There was a creak, a snapping sound, and then, as if in slow motion, the wood sagged and then buckled under her weight.

She lurched forward, arms flailing.

Her phone clattered off down the stairs, the light casting manic, tumbling shadows before cutting out altogether.

Briefly, she thought she'd managed to catch herself against the handrail. But then she heard a dull cracking sound that came simultaneously with a shaft of pain rushing up from her lower leg.

Blackness swept over her, then. Nothing.

Just black.

~ ~ ~ ~

Pain.

Her right leg, low down. Her back, just above the pelvis.

She was scared to move, even though her position, half-sprawled across the stairs, was both uncomfortable in itself and also made the pain worse.

She tried to calm herself. Tried to figure it out.

She tried to straighten herself, find a slightly less painful position. Moving, in itself, was reassuring: the pain in her back was not an indication of a serious injury. She wasn't paralyzed.

She didn't understand why the stairs had given way. They were new! Had Vialli fitted them wrong?

She felt around the hole. Either side of her leg, the edges of the hole were straight, as if cut by a saw.

She reached down into the hole, feeling her leg and wincing at the pain.

Wet heat. Blood.

She caught her hand on something sharp.

Nails. Hammered through the riser from the outside so the points jutted out into the gap. Put there deliberately to shred the leg of anyone whose foot landed in this trap.

Booby-trapped.

How many other traps were there? Removed floorboards. Tripwires. She didn't know. All she knew was she'd found *this* one.

Rusty? Had he known about this? Of course not...

He'd passed on the message to her to come here, but he'd never said how Tom had given him the message. She'd assumed face to face, but it could easily have been a text message, something anonymous. Something that could have come from just about anyone.

And that note at the foot of the stairs: it could have been written by anyone too. The use of a hand-drawn arrow and a winky face to minimize the amount of actual identifiable writing. The use of upper-case letters in the *SWEETIE*, to make the writing harder to recognize.

She didn't believe Tom had left that note.

She felt around to the front of her shin. The pain was

excruciating. She found more blood, more shredded clothing. Felt a jagged ridge across the bone, a disjoint. She'd broken her leg. That dull crack she'd heard before blacking out had been bone snapping.

Briefly, she felt as if she might black out again.

She clamped her jaw tight, forced herself to breathe deep. She had to ride out the shock and pain. Had to *deal* with this.

That was when she heard a sound above the roar of the storm and the flapping of the roof.

The slam of a car door, and then moments later the rattle of a door opening before slamming closed.

Someone was here. In the house with her.

And she couldn't move.

~ ~ ~ ~

He drove hard, despite the treacherous conditions.

Don't you think you'd better go save your darling wife? Go on, Tom. Go save her, sweetie.

The look in her eye…

She knew she had him.

All thoughts of somehow detaining Libbie Cottrill for the cops were abandoned.

All thoughts of salvaging those scrapbooks as some kind of evidence: gone.

All he knew was that Libbie had done something to Alice and he had to get to her.

Libbie, a woman he now knew for certain was capable of murder.

Tony Capaldi. Simon Woodforde. Andy Krabbe.

Walter's blood, still fresh on their path.

"Where?" he'd demanded, gripping her wrists tighter, twisting them. Trying not to feel too repelled by the rush of satisfaction he felt when he saw pain flash across the woman's evil features.

He twisted harder and she gasped.

He could hurt her. Disable her until the cops arrived.

"Whitetail Lane," she said through gritted teeth. "But you'd better hurry."

He let her go. That last comment was enough to remove any thoughts of anything but rushing across town to the investment property to find Alice.

He pushed her away from him, letting go of her wrists at the last minute so she stumbled and fell, sprawling face down on the apartment floor. And when he'd glanced back before leaving, he saw her lying there, rubbing her wrists and smiling. Winking.

"Run, Tom. You don't have any time to spare."

Now, he pulled up at the curb. Rain flooded down the windshield and he could hear the wind whistling and howling.

He didn't hesitate, almost tumbling out onto the sidewalk in his haste.

The rain was cold, the wind colder.

He ran through the front yard to the house, wet

vegetation lashing at his legs.

He stumbled against the door and it flew open, banging against the wall.

He saw her straight away, his surge of relief tempered as he registered the pain and fear etched onto her features.

And the awkward way she stood on the stairs. It took a moment to work out the geometry, then he saw that her right leg had plunged through a gap in the steps. Her torso was twisted as she clung to the handrail for support.

He rushed to her, stopping with his knees resting on the step below her. He took her in his arms to support some of her weight as her body slumped against him.

"Oh, Alice!"

She was crying now. Great sobs of relief and pain intermingled.

"What happened, Alice? What's wrong?"

"My… my leg. I think it's broken. She sabotaged the house, Tom. Be careful, there could be more traps."

He took his phone and aimed the light. It was easy to see where the wood of the step had been cut. He saw the blood, too, dark on Alice's shredded jogging pants.

"There are nails in there. I don't know what else."

He reached down, exploring the cavity by touch.

"This is going to hurt," he said, and he sensed her nodding more than saw it.

Cradling her leg in his hand as well as he could, he started to ease it free. Alice's body tensed and he stopped.

"I'm sorry, sweetie, but I have to get you out of here."

He pulled gently again. He felt her tensing from the agony, but this time kept going until she managed to half-sit on the stairs. Her damaged leg stretched out before her.

"I'm going to carry you, sweetie, all right?"

"Okay."

"Just like when we were newlyweds, carrying you over the threshold." She forced a smile. "Put your arms around my neck and I'll support you as best I can, but it's going to hurt again. I have the car outside. Okay? On the count of three. One. Two—"

"How sweet. You really think she can count that high? You *know* how good she is with figures."

He turned his head. Libbie was silhouetted in the open doorway.

And she was aiming a handgun right at them.

CHAPTER 38

"Get out of here, Libbie. Don't make things any worse."

Tom's voice sounded surprisingly steady to Alice. Had he always had this strength? Maybe. It just seemed to have deserted him in the last year or so.

He had his arm around Alice and she pressed against him, finding comfort and also hoping she was returning some of that comfort to him. She was very aware of how he was taking every second Libbie gave them to edge himself ever farther in front of her, offering himself as a human shield.

She felt powerless. Hell, she couldn't even move! Her leg was throbbing heavily after the pain of extracting it from the sabotaged stairs.

"The only way I could make things worse at this moment would be if I let you two get out of here alive."

Strange. It was Libbie's familiar voice, but the perky eagerness was gone. It was replaced by something far darker. A certainty that was chilling.

"Why?" Tom asked. Alice knew he was playing for time and Libbie must've known that too. "Why bring us *here?*"

"Why not?" Libbie was actually enjoying this! "It's as good a place as any. And it's an easy story for those dumbass cops to swallow. Owners killed by drug addicts using their renovation project as a drug den. Don't worry. I've already planted a few needles and other paraphernalia about the place. I am, as the reality crime shows on TV say, a forensically-aware murderer."

Alice felt as if she was going to black out again. Blood sugar, pain, fear… absolute shock to hear another human being talking this way.

"Let Alice go. This is just between you and me, Libbie."

No! How could Tom even think she could live on in the knowledge he'd traded her life for his?

And what did he mean, *between him and Libbie*? What part of all this had Alice missed?

He turned half toward her now, as if he'd realized she didn't understand.

"It's all about summer camp. Long Valley. Libbie was there too. She was bullied. By a bunch of us."

Us? Was Tom saying he'd been a bully? How could that be true?

"Me. Tony Capaldi. Simon Woodforde. Andy Krabbe. I tried to stop them, but they were older. I hated myself for going along with it all."

Alice vaguely recognized the names from her own time at Long Valley.

"She killed them. All three of them. Tony, Simon, Andy. That's why she's here now. She's going for the complete set."

The words made sense as sentences, but bore no relation to Alice's experience of the world. Of people.

She'd killed them. Murdered them.

And now she was here for Tom...

And she was standing there, still aiming the gun, and *smiling*.

"Oh no, Tom, darling," Libbie said with amusement. "You're right in some of the details, but so terribly, *terribly* wrong on the most important part."

She paused, drawing the moment out.

Ultimately, she continued. "Yes, I killed them. And I made sure they understood exactly why they were dying before I finally let them go."

Again she paused, briefly even closing her eyes as if savoring the recollection.

Alice felt Tom tensing, as if about to make a move, but then Libbie's eyes snapped open and she twitched the gun at him, as if to remind him who was in control.

"But you, Tom? You flatter yourself. You were just the puny little kid who tagged along for the attention. A weakling. I always knew those three were the real bullies, and Capaldi was the ringleader. I gave *him* special attention, believe me. He knew why he was dying, and in the end he was begging for it."

Alice was still struggling to keep up. She understood about the summer camp. They'd said enough to tie in with her already bad memories of the place for it to all make sense.

But now Libbie was saying she didn't care about Tom.

So why was she doing this?

"Those three were just a trial run, though," said Libbie. "I was saving the best to last."

Now, with chilling intensity, her eyes focused on Alice.

"You don't remember, do you, Alice? You don't remember me. You don't remember what you did."

Alice stared.

"It's you, Alice. You're the one I've come for. You're the reason for all of this."

And as she spoke, the muzzle of the gun shifted, coming to point directly at Alice.

"You, Alice. The time has finally come."

~ ~ ~ ~

"Does my name mean nothing to you? Are you that cold?"

Her name. Libbie Burchett. Libbie Cottrill.

It didn't.

"Long Valley Summer Camp. The boat."

Alice stared. Her memories of Long Valley were always cast in shadow. In tragedy. But she didn't understand how that connected to Libbie.

"The accident," said Tom. "But I don't understand..."

"June Cottrill. She was my mother."

"I... I never knew that was her name. I never knew who she was. My parents... the folks at the camp. They

359

tried to shield me from all that."

That summer, the summer when—later—she'd met Tom.

The reason she was the loner kid, the one who wouldn't get involved in anything, and in particular any of the water-based activities. The boat.

The accident.

She'd been kayaking out in the middle of the lake, chasing some of the other kids. It had been a wild, high-spirited thing. They'd all gotten carried away.

Two of the boats had collided and Alice's had flipped. They all knew how to get out of a turned boat, of course, but Alice had gotten her legs tangled and couldn't get out.

She remembered it all so vividly, even now. The desperation. The deep ache in her lungs as she desperately held onto what breath hadn't been knocked out of her.

The panic.

But she'd managed. She'd righted the boat by herself.

She'd felt such a sense of achievement.

And then she'd wondered why everyone was shouting, pointing, screaming.

"I was out there too," said Libbie. "Out in a boat with my mom. She'd only come visiting because I was having such a bad time with the bullying. She was the only one who'd ever cared about me."

Alice understood now and it made her forget the pain in her leg. "Libbie…"

"My mother saw what had happened to you and she

didn't hesitate. She jumped in, but she didn't realize how uneven the lake was at that point, rocks just below the surface. She hit her head. She drowned, Alice. Right in front of me. Just like Tony, Simon, and Andy hit their heads. Just like Walter did. I've discovered I *like* hitting heads. Bringing things full circle."

Tom and Alice didn't dare glance at each other, although they didn't need to. Everything was becoming clear.

Libbie shrugged. "They had to die. The three of them. Not because they bullied me, but because the only reason Mom was there that day was because of what they did. They brought her there. And you stopped her from leaving. Do you understand that, Alice? It's important you do, before you die. You need to see you brought this on yourself."

"It was a tragedy," Alice said. "An awful tragedy. But it was nobody's fault. Can't you see that? She saw me in distress and her first instinct was to help, because she was the kind of person who cared, just as she went to visit you because she cared. She was a good person. What would she think of what you're doing, Libbie? How sad would she be?"

For a moment, she thought her plea to Libbie's conscience—or at least to her attachment to her mother—might work. But then Libbie shrugged, gave that evil, cold smile again, and said, "We'll never know, will we? She's dead. And all because of you."

As she'd spoken she'd allowed the gun to sag a little in her hands, but now she straightened her aim. Alice knew it was all over.

Tom jumped.

He threw himself forward, straight at Libbie.

Alice saw his hands reaching for the gun, swinging to knock it clear. And then there was a flash, the deafening explosion of the gunshot ringing in her ears.

She heard a man's cry, a grunt.

She felt the look of shock on her husband's face.

Saw him clutching at his midriff, and only then saw the blood as he tumbled to the ground on top of Libbie.

CHAPTER 39

Everything froze.

Tom lay there, not moving. It was hard to see in the building's low light, but that dark patch on the floor was spreading, and it was his blood.

She'd killed him. He'd tried to save Alice and Libbie had shot him.

"No!" Alice cried.

Libbie lay there too, but she was moving, her chest heaving for air.

And inches from her hand sat the dark shape of the handgun.

Alice hurled herself forward, putting her weight on her left leg and trying to ignore the pain from her right.

She fell full stretch, reaching for the gun.

She couldn't get a grip, but she managed to push at it, flipping it away into the shadows.

And then Libbie closed on her, rising and twisting, swinging down on the back of Alice's head with a two-fisted blow.

Alice's skull rang and her face mashed against the floor. She twisted in the dirt, trying to find purchase.

Libbie came down on top of her again, fists and elbows landing simultaneously in her torso. Bolts of pain stabbed through her body from impacts on belly and breasts.

She tried to get a hold and pushed, muscle-memory from those long-ago college self-defense classes kicking in.

Libbie went sprawling away into the shadows.

Alice tried to stand, but couldn't. Tried to crawl, dragging her ruined leg.

She thought she'd made it. She was almost at the front door.

Then she felt hands close around her trailing ankle, and suddenly the full weight of Libbie's body hauling her back by her broken leg.

"Not so fast, bitch."

Alice screamed. She felt bones shifting and crunching. Dislocating. Death was beginning to look like an acceptable prospect. She tried to turn so she could at least face her foe, but the pain was too intense.

She braced herself, preparing to fight with all she had left.

But it never came.

She saw Libbie, a dark shape poised over her, ready to strike.

And then…

Another shape. A swift movement. A thud of impact and a female grunt and cry.

Libbie fell sideways, as if she'd just melted into a heap on the floor.

And the other big shape stopped, spinning toward Alice, and said, "Mrs. Granger? Are you okay, Mrs. Granger?"

Rusty!

She'd never been so pleased to see someone as she was to see Rusty now.

He reached down for her, but she snatched her hand away.

"No. No, Rusty, don't try to help me up. I think my leg's broken."

Think. She knew. She would remember the grinding of broken bones as Libbie had pulled on that leg for the rest of her life.

Then reality sank in just a little more.

"Tom," she gasped. "She shot him."

Rusty turned, trying to locate Tom's fallen form.

She watched him move, merge with the shadows.

Then…

"Mr. Granger? Are you okay, Mr. Granger?"

And another voice. Tom. A grunt, and then, "No. I don't know. I think…"

"Tom?"

"I'm okay, sweetie. Just a nick."

It was more than just a nick. She knew that. But he was alive. He was talking. He was trying to make one of his stupid jokes.

He was alive!

"I know you said not to come with you, Mrs. Granger." Rusty sounded hesitant, as if even now he feared he was going to get in trouble for disobeying her instructions. "I know you said that if I liked you, I should do what you say and let you go on your own. But I figured I liked you enough that sometimes it's right not to have to do exactly what you say."

"We have to get out of here. Check her, Rusty. Check Libbie. Make sure she's safe... that we're safe."

She'd heard the thud from whatever Rusty had used to hit Libbie with. She didn't think Libbie would be doing anything for the time being. Alice levered herself into a sitting position.

She was getting used to dealing with the pain. Numbed to it. She hoped that wasn't a bad sign, loss of feeling as a result of what Libbie had done when she'd pulled on the broken limb.

She turned, putting her weight on both hands and her good knee.

Rusty would have his hands full getting Tom out and she knew they had to move. They couldn't just wait here.

She sensed movement around her. Rusty.

Then she heard him say, "Ms. Burchett? I..."

And then he fell silent as another dark figure rose from the shadows, moved to one side, and Alice saw the muzzle of that gun pointing right at her once again.

She looked up and saw Libbie's cold snarl one more

time. Her teeth were white against a face painted dark with blood from the wound Rusty had inflicted.

Then Rusty threw himself in between them just as another gunshot exploded in the small space.

Rusty fell clutching at his chest.

Libbie remained standing.

Alice stared up at her, agape. Then she recognized the hard shape pressed up against her knuckles. She shifted her weight to free the hand, coming to rest painfully on the knee of her shattered leg.

She closed her hands around the shape and pushed forward like a sprinter launching herself off the blocks. Her fingers closed around the blunt object. It was the brick she'd tripped on earlier.

In a flash, she swung her arm as she flew through the air, swinging the hard brick.

Bringing it down hard.

The feel and sound of brick on skull, of bone and meat breaking under the impact, was unlike anything Alice had experienced before. It wasn't something she ever wanted to experience again.

Libbie collapsed, Alice on top of her, her hand still closed around the brick, even though it was embedded deep in the other woman's skull.

They hit the ground together and at long last Alice relinquished her grip. She managed to roll away from Libbie's unmoving form.

She managed to reach out a hand across the floor, finding Tom's face. She relaxed only when she felt the flutter of his breath on her hand.

"Oh, baby," she said softly to him. "Please tell me you have your phone. Because there's no way I'm moving again under my own steam tonight."

CHAPTER 40

Franco Vialli and his crew had put up Christmas decorations at the Whitetail Lane place. Tinsel around the front door, even a small tree in the foyer.

The place would be finished in time for Christmas.

After the storm damage to the roof and the damage Libbie Cottrill had done to the place, the insurance payout had been enough to cover the rest of the work. Franco was happy because he got to finish the work the best way, not just the cheapest way, and he'd been fully paid up in advance of completion.

Tom was happy because they'd agreed to put the place on the market after New Year's.

And Alice was secretly happy, because she'd come around to Tom's view. She wanted to sell the property, too. The place held too many sad memories, after all that had happened here.

Something changes about a place when you've seen someone die there.

They'd just completed the final inspection. All that remained was a snagging list of minor details they'd spotted for Franco to deal with, and then the place would be finished.

It still felt strange to Alice, walking through that foyer. She could never be here and not relive that awful moment when Tom had taken a bullet in the stomach.

When Rusty had stepped in front of her and taken a shot full in the chest for her.

Or the moment when that brick had come down on Libbie's skull, killing her as she'd killed four men before her.

They stepped out onto the porch.

Even the yard was looking good now. The overgrown vegetation had been trimmed back. The bushes pruned into shape. The flowerbeds cleared for spring.

"Hey there, Mrs. Granger. Mr. Granger."

Rusty came around the building, rubbing his muddy hands on his jeans in just the way his mother had probably told him a hundred times not to do.

"I hope you're taking it easy, Rusty," said Tom. "Not many people take a bullet in the chest and get back to work so quickly afterward, you know."

Rusty grinned. He knew Tom was joking. He'd finally worked out how to tell.

"I'm fine," he said. "I just wanted to ask if you'd mind me finishing here a little early?"

"Oh?"

Alice smiled. Tom was playing it innocent, but she knew Marissa Sigley had asked him to help her with the Christmas decorations earlier. He'd said he couldn't, but maybe she should ask Rusty. The girl had been surprised. She didn't think Rusty even knew she existed, she told them. And Alice had seen the look in Marissa's eye, the smile when they assured her Rusty had noticed her all right.

"Scrub up a bit, Rusty, okay? Treat Marissa well. You want to make the right impression."

"And if all else fails, show her your war wound," said Tom. "Chicks dig wounds."

Rusty laughed again, this time to cover his blushing.

~ ~ ~ ~

Tom glanced across at Alice as they headed home in her Ford Focus. Her leg was mending well, but she wasn't up to driving yet. He didn't mind. He was happy to drive. They were a team. Always had been, always would be.

They were good.

"Has Michael Tuckett told you when you're going to be VP yet?" he asked her.

"I'm too busy right now," she said with a laugh. "Now that we've landed Mapleview, it's all hands to the deck. Maybe when things ease off a bit."

"Yeah, right. And less of that *we* stuff, okay? *You're* the one who landed Mapleview."

"I'd never have done it without Walter."

They fell silent for a time, as they drove across town.

Before making his fateful rush to the house to warn Alice, Walter had sent a quick email to Michael Tuckett. He'd advised him to hold fire on Alice, and that information about why she'd been under so much pressure would emerge soon.

It had been unusual enough for the normally unassuming Walter to be so direct with his boss that Tuckett had taken it seriously. So when details had emerged about how Libbie had interfered with so much of Alice's activities, he'd looked again at her work.

"I'm not putting you back on this out of misplaced sympathy or anything like that," Tuckett had told her. "I'm doing it because your work was good, and almost complete. We're running with your pitch, with the full backing of the company." He'd paused before adding, "And it would be great if you could give your presentation to Mapleview with your leg still in a cast. Let's milk that sympathy vote for all it's worth, uh?"

The extra money from Alice's bonus and impending promotion would make a huge difference. Enough for Tom to carry on just as he had done for the past year with his contracting work.

But he needed more.

"Sweetie?" he said. "I've been thinking."

"As long as it's not about cheerleaders, I'm good with that."

They laughed.

"I've been thinking about going back to work. Getting a job again. Not just hiding in the house and freelancing."

"I know."

He stared.

"Of course I know. You've been hinting and hesitating for weeks. You don't hide things well, you know. I didn't want to push, though."

Alice had always been able to read him well. That's one of the reasons he had over-reacted when she tried to gently point out to him that he was tipping over the mental precipice again earlier in the fall. The truth hurts sometimes.

"You're okay with that, sweetie?"

"Of course I am. I'm glad the time is right. But I have one condition."

"What's that?"

"That you don't come and try to take *my* job."

~ ~ ~ ~

Today had been a day of significant developments.

The final inspection at Whitetail Lane.

The talk of jobs and careers and their future.

Setting Rusty up with Marissa Sigley at last.

And now, as they pulled up in their drive, Tom saw an unfamiliar car parked at the curb, a flashy, low-slung Audi. A guy climbed out, as if he'd been waiting for them.

He looked to be in his late thirties, but that mop of wild chestnut hair gave him a still-youthful look.

"Mr. and Mrs. Granger?"

He *had* been waiting. They'd had their share of reporters and cranks coming here over the past couple of months, but this guy looked like neither.

Instinctively, Tom moved slightly in front of Alice, as

if ready to take a bullet for her again. It was an automatic thing, and one they often laughed about now. Alice always insisted that it wasn't fair: it was *her* turn to take the next one.

The man had his hands up, palms toward them, as if he expected a hostile response.

"I'm sorry for intruding, after all you guys have been through. But if you'd just give me a minute of your time?"

Tom and Alice stood and waited for him to go on. There was something about the guy that was strangely familiar. Strangely disturbing, too.

"My name's Jonathan Cottrill, and I—"

"We don't want any trouble," said Alice, moving up beside Tom as if she really was ready to take the next bullet.

"I know. Believe me, I know." The poor guy had raised his hands even higher now, as if he was trying to surrender. "I just want to have a word with you about my sister."

Tom put a hand on Alice's arm, calming her. They'd both been seeing therapists. Post-traumatic shock. He knew how close a panic reaction was when he saw it. He knew how to read Alice almost as well as she could read him.

"I just wanted to... I don't know. You can't apologize for anything like this, can you? You can't make amends. But sometimes seeing a face, seeing the real people involved. It helps me, and I hope it might help you to know that nobody holds a grudge against you. Only sympathy. And sorrow."

"You want to come inside?" That was Alice, the panic response quickly replaced by her familiar empathy.

A few minutes later, the three sat at the kitchen table, coffee brewing in the background.

"I feel somehow responsible," Tom said. "Your sister had an awful time at summer camp and I know I was at least partly responsible."

"I've read all the reports," Jonathan Cottrill assured them. "I know you weren't to blame for anything more than things a million kids do day in and day out. You didn't make my little sister what she was."

"But…"

The visitor shook his head. "She was always that way. That's why she was sent to summer camp and I didn't have to go. That's why Mom went to see her that time: she thought Lizzie was starting to have another episode."

He hesitated for a moment before going on. "And that was why, when Mom passed, I went to live with family but Lizzie went into the system. Nobody could handle her. Nobody *wanted* to handle her. As I said, she always had problems. I'm just so sorry things escalated this way. She should never have been let out of that secure institution. I told them that at the time, but her doctor insisted she should be given a chance to start over."

"Well, I hope you've found some kind of peace," Alice told him. "It was tragic. It was awful. But everyone here has come through it, and we're moving on."

Tom saw the look that flashed across his wife's face as she said that. Not everyone had pulled through. Not poor Walter.

Jonathan Cottrill nodded. "You're very kind," he said. "I don't know what I hoped for by coming here, but I guess I couldn't have asked for anything more than that." He wavered before speaking again. "But there's a little more. You see, my family has done well. My folks were hard-working. They had a good business and when my father died my mother kept it going. Until, *she* passed."

He paused to lick his lips, before continuing. "What I'm saying is, Lizzie had quite a lot of money behind her. She had an up-market apartment in Manhattan. A trust fund. Some good investments. Listen, I don't want you guys to be offended or anything, and I don't know how you're fixed, but I'd like that money to do some good, rather than just sitting there doing nothing. I'd like to give you some of it. Hell, *all* of it."

Tom glanced at Alice and he knew instantly her mind was in the same place as his.

Things were good. She really was going to make VP one day soon and she'd already promised him at least one trip business-class. The Whitetail Lane property was near completion, and when they sold it the only problem they had was what to do with the proceeds.

It was a generous offer, but…

"That's very kind," said Tom. "But no. Do something else with your sister's money. Do some good with it."

"I just knew you'd say that, but I really want to do something specific. Something that at least feels like it's fixing something she broke."

Again, Tom and Alice exchanged a look.

"Well…" Tom said, and before he could continue Alice moved in to complete the thought.

"There's a boy we know," she said. "Young and eager. Would do anything for anybody."

"Like taking a bullet…"

"And he's spent the last two years working his butt off for his college fund."

"He sure could do with some help."

"And he's missed a few weeks of work this fall because of… Well, because he was busy saving others—"

"Taking that bullet."

Jonathan Cottrill knew exactly who they meant. He was smiling. They all were.

"Just give me a ballpark figure," he told them. "And I'll double it. Triple it. Whatever. Just tell me how I can make a payment into this fine young man's college fund."

~ ~ ~ ~

Finally, they sat alone. Just Tom and Alice.

It felt like it had been such a long day. But a good one. A day where so many things had moved on in very positive ways.

"You good, sweetie?"

"I am."

This was pretty damned near perfect.

It was hard to think, as December drew to a close, that such an awful year could end up in a place as good as this.

Just as Tom was about to try to put some of this into words, the house phone rang. He went across to get it, and listened for a moment.

"What is it, sweetheart?"

He listened a bit more, then said, "It's someone who's seen an ad. They said they know it's an old ad, but just wondered if we were still looking to rent out our basement apartment. They have references. They say they'd be the perfect tenant."

He paused then.

Smiled. Winked.

And said, "What do you think, sweetie? You think we should give it a try? I mean, what's the worst that could happen?"

THE END

ABOUT THE AUTHORS

Steve Richer is the international bestselling author of *Stranger Danger*, *The President Killed His Wife*, and *The Pope's Suicide*. He went to law school and film school before considering becoming a sherpa, though he abandoned the idea upon discovering what a sherpa really was. Now he spends his days writing books.

He specializes in fun, over the top thrillers that read like action movies. He splits his time between Montreal and Miami.

You can Like Steve on Facebook for all the latest news.

facebook.com/OfficialSteveRicher

Sign up for the newsletter now and receive a free novel and exclusive short story!

SteveRicherBooks.com

Nick Gifford is the bestselling author of *Piggies*, *Flesh and Blood*, *Like Father* and *Erased*, and he has been described by the Sunday Express as "The king of children's horror". He writes crime and suspense fiction for adults under his grown-up name, Nicholas Gifford.

His work has been optioned for film by major movie companies, and has featured on various bestseller lists, at one time out-ranking JK Rowling's Harry Potter books.

Find out more about him at

NickGifford.co.uk/Nicholas

or on Facebook at

facebook.com/TheNickGifford

ALSO BY STEVE RICHER

The President Killed His Wife (Rogan Bricks 1)

Counterblow (Rogan Bricks 2)

Murder Island (Rogan Bricks 3)

The Pope's Suicide

Stranger Danger

Critical Salvage

Terror Bounty

Park Avenue Blackmail

The Kennedy Secret

The Gilded Treachery

Never Bloodless

The Atomic Eagle

Sigma Division

38041016R00233

Made in the USA
Lexington, KY
02 May 2019